Janet Thomas has lived in Cornwall all her life and has a deep-rooted affection for the area and people. An avid reader from an early age, Janet spent her working life in the county library service, where she met and married her librarian husband. After raising three daughters, Janet gained an arts degree and is now a full-time author.

ROUGH HERITAGE

Rose Vidney and Joss Pencarrow form an unlikely childhood friendship. Rose is the daughter of a poor miner, whilst Joss is the local squire's son in the nineteenth-century mining heartland where they grow up. Meeting again as adults, their friendship is rekindled and it seems they are to be inextricably entwined forever. Destiny has marked Rose as Joss's nemesis, and he hers. Soon their stormy and forbidden love affair will tear both their lives apart. As tragic events are played out against the timeless Cornish coast, can Rose and Joss achieve true happiness against all the odds?

Books *by Janet Thomas*
Published *by The House of Ulverscroft:*

THE TIDES OF TIME
SUMMER SOJOURN
THE DANCING MAIDENS

JANET THOMAS

ROUGH HERITAGE

Complete and Unabridged

ULVERSCROFT
Leicester

First published in Great Britain in 2005 by
Robert Hale Limited
London

First Large Print Edition
published 2005
by arrangement with
Robert Hale Limited
London

British Library CIP Data

Thomas, Janet, *1936* Oct. 24
   Rough heritage.—Large print ed.—
Ulverscroft large print series: romance
1. Cornwall (England)—Fiction
2. Love stories 3. Large type books
I. Title
823.9′2 [F]

ISBN 1–84617–099–0

Published by
F. A. Thorpe (Publishing)
Anstey, Leicestershire

Set by Words & Graphics Ltd.
Anstey, Leicestershire
Printed and bound in Great Britain by
T. J. International Ltd., Padstow, Cornwall

This book is printed on acid-free paper

1

'Say 'please',' the bully sneered as his huge bulk loomed over the little girl. 'Say 'please Reuben' and I'll leave you go.'

An excruciating pain shot through Rose's skull as Reuben Clemo, ringleader of the gang and her own cousin, seized a handful of her hair in his great fist and yanked her round to face him. But Rose clenched her teeth and stared back defiantly at him. Never! To beg for mercy was just not in her nature. Her fingernails bit into her palms as she willed herself not to scream.

The other children had linked hands and were dancing around them now. They were singing as usual, the jingle they had made up to the tune of 'Bobby Shafto', which they loved to torment her with. Rose clapped her hands over her ears. It seemed to go on for ever.

'Little Rosie Vidney's ma,
She weren't married to her pa,
Rosie is a little b —
Bonnie Rosie Vidney.'

Rose stifled a sob. Why can't they just shut up. It's not my fault. Why pick on me? The injustice of it made her burn with smothered fury. But Cornish mining folk were tough and hardy. So were their children. Rose kicked out hard with one bare and dirty foot at the shins of the boy who held her fast. He could hardly have felt the blow, but it was enough to divert his attention for a second. A second was enough. Rose wriggled free and slipped through the circle.

Like a frightened rabbit she was off. Through the stunted gorse and heather that grew by the tin-stream, its murky water bright red with mineral remains. Over the plank bridge and the clutter of tin-washing machinery — the water-wheels, the buddles, the dressing-sheds. Up the far bank and the slope of the hill beyond.

Her heart was thudding as much with fright as from exertion, and panic spurred her relentlessly on in spite of her rasping breath and the dryness of her throat. She could hear the clump of her pursuer's boots, and he was gaining on her.

Rose crashed her way through stands of waist-high bracken which sent out clutching branches to snare her. Brambles and gorse drew blood from her tiring legs. She stumbled heedlessly over the sharp stones beneath her feet, but when she caught a toe in a trailing root of heather, it was her undoing. She stumbled and fell winded to the ground.

Immediately she struggled to get up, but a beefy hand was forcing her to the ground and she was powerless. Gasping for breath with painful, ragged sobs Rose licked dry lips and tried to scream, but the filthy hand was clamped firmly over her mouth and she could only mumble: 'Let — me — go!' An attempt to bite his thumb brought her a stinging cuff on the ear.

'Shut up you, or I'll tell yer pa you showed me yer drawers.'

Liar, liar! Rose silently fumed as she wriggled and squirmed in vain beneath his strength. A blast of Reuben Clemo's bad breath filled her nostrils and her stomach heaved. For four of her ten years he had been after her, tormenting her in sly, underhand ways which could never be found out. Instinctively Rose knew that violence was the only way he could express himself and knew too, why her cousin hated her so. She wriggled again. Again the fist descended.

'That's one for my ma — you killed her, you little sod! As good as, anyroad. She never had no time fer me no more after she was landed with you.' Reuben's small, black boot-button eyes burned in his fleshy face,

3

consumed with hate and jealousy.

Again Rose wailed inwardly — but it's not *my* fault, not any of it! Not *my* fault my mother died when I was born. Not my fault that she and Pa weren't wed, not *my* fault that your ma was my pa's sister. And not *my* fault either that you and she came to live with us.

Rose gasped in sudden agony as a sharp stone dug into her back and jerked her head long enough to utter one piercing scream of anguish. It was like a red rag to a bull. Enraged, Reuben Clemo lifted her by the shoulders and thumped her backwards with a crash that made her head swim as it cracked against a boulder.

Rose tried to curl herself into a protective ball, but her tormentor was now panting with exertion — or something. Horrified, Rose felt him wrenching her flimsy shift above her waist. He was tugging at his braces now — and she was powerless. He stank of stale sweat and of another nauseous smell which terrified her even more.

Rose had spent her life in a community where drink was the only escape from poverty, and where privacy was unknown. She had long ago learned all about the ways of a man with a woman. For Joe, her weak and feckless father, after Aunt Winnie's death

4

from consumption — that had been when she was six and Reuben ten — had married the slatternly Ellie. Ellie's father kept the kiddley-wink, the beer-shop where Joe spent so much of his time. They had since produced three sons and a baby daughter and Rose had been minding them all ever since. Oh yes, Rose knew full well what her cousin was about and knew that it spelt terror.

He was grunting now like the pig he so much resembled. Rose, through a haze of pain and fright saw his little black eyes glittering as he pressed himself the full length of her body. Every small bone was being crushed by his weight. Now she could feel his disgusting slimy 'thing' against her leg. It was pulsating with a life of its own. Sick-making. Feebly Rose tried to draw in a breath to scream once more. But movement was impossible, the scream came out as a whisper and everything was hazy now. Perhaps she was going to die.

★ ★ ★

The boy was whistling blithely as he nudged his chestnut mare up the tortuous track which led to the summit of Carn Brea. It was a bright and cloudless day in August and the sun was warm on his back in spite of the

5

breeze which was blowing in from the coast and cooling the boulder-strewn hill-top.

He dismounted, tethered the horse to a tough bush of heather and clambered to the top of the granite outcrop where he sprawled on his stomach, his chin in his hands, and looked seawards. On this clear day, both coasts were visible from this height and his gaze travelled from the distinctive outline of St Michael's Mount in the south to the panorama of St Ives and Hayle towards the north. From this distance the sprawl of mine engine-houses and chimney-stacks between the carn and the sea looked like toy models, and the huddle of cottages reduced to doll's-houses. With its squalor softened by remoteness, the scene was even picturesque.

Gradually Joss became aware of a commotion of some sort to his left and far below him. He raised his head but could see nothing. Then a piercing scream tore through the lazy afternoon and brought him to his feet. He scrambled down the sheer side of the great granite rock-pile, slipping and sliding in his haste, and came out on to a flat platform a few feet from the ground. Now he could see what was going on. Taking in the situation at a glance, he hurled himself down on top of Reuben Clemo's spread-eagled form. No match for the bully in size or physical strength, the boy had however the advantage of surprise, and was able to heave Reuben to his feet and deliver a punch to his jaw which sent him reeling.

'What the devil . . . do you think . . . you're doing to that child! You . . . you *monster*! You filthy . . . *pig*!' He rained punches and kicks as with his breeches round his ankles the bully roared and swiped back in a futile effort to defend himself.

Rose slowly opened her eyes. She could breathe again! How good the fresh air tasted as she dragged great gulps of it into her cramped lungs. She was free! Then she heard the sounds of the fight. She painfully hoisted herself into a sitting position, but by then it was all over, and she could not resist a smile.

Reuben Clemo was running down the hill as fast as he could, clutching his breeches in one hand and holding the other to his bleeding nose. The stranger, who had chased him to the brow, was pelting him with stones and clods of earth. When one of these found its mark on the back of his head he turned round and yelled over his shoulder:

'I'll get you both for this one day, jest see if I don't, I'll get me own back on the both of you.'

Rose trembled at the venom in his voice. She knew he meant it. Reuben never forgot a slight, let alone a full-scale beating like this.

'He will too,' she groaned, one hand clapped to her mouth in alarm. 'Oh, what'll he do next? What am I going to do?'

'I say, are you all right?' came an anxious voice at her elbow. 'Did he . . . you know . . . Did he hurt you?'

Rose jumped up and whirled around, clutching her ribs as a sudden stab of pain sliced through her. She was ready with a sharp retort, but at the sight of the boy who stood there her mouth dropped open.

For this was no village lad. His face was clean, he wore a neat dove-grey jacket and his eyes, which were a deep violet-blue, looked kind and gentle. About sixteen she guessed, unable to take her eyes off this elegant stranger.

'I said, are you all right?' The boy sat down on a grassy hummock and wiped his knuckles in a snowy handkerchief. To Rose it looked as big as a bed-sheet. She was still goggling at him. Never in her life had anyone asked, or cared how she felt.

'How, what do you want to know for?' she demanded suspiciously, a frown wrinkling her small dirty face. It was her rescuer's turn to look at a loss.

'I only meant, did he . . . you know?' He reddened slightly.

'Aw.' Rose understood. 'No, he never *done* it. Only nearly. He would have — but you come just in time.' She gathered the shreds of her tattered garment around her with unselfconscious dignity and lifted her chin to look more closely at him.

'I'm Joss,' he volunteered. 'Short for Joscelyn, which I hate. What's your name?'

'Rose.'

'Right, Rose, come on, I'll take you home. Or should you be in school?'

'School? Look at me! Do it look as if I do go to *school*!' She spat scornfully. Anger filled her, blazing up like a living flame. What could he know of the life she led? He with his white shirt and shiny boots. 'Look at this here frilly white pinafore, and me black stockings and button-boots. See the ribbons in me hair!' she minced and mocked.

Joss looked uncomfortable.

'Rose, I'm sorry. I was stupid not to realize.' He did not add that this was his first personal contact with a child from the mining community. He had imagined until now that all children went to school as a matter of course. But he realized now, school cost money. And looking at the stick-thin urchin beside him had made Joss begin to think for himself for the first time in his life.

Until now the heir to Great Place, son of

9

the local squire and mineral lord of the area, who was the chief employer of the local work-force, had taken the family money and privileges for granted and not thought very deeply about either.

'Cor, I wish I did,' Rose blurted. For to go to school, to learn to read and write and find answers to all the questions that teemed in her brain, was the impossible dream she carried deep within herself always.

The pathos in her voice, at odds with her former spirit, struck some chord of sympathy in the boy standing before her. Joss surveyed the little figure thoughtfully. Cleaned up she would be quite a pretty child. Her russet hair was exactly the shade of the winter bracken which lingered beneath the clumps of this year's leaves and her eyes were bright, intelligent and as green as emeralds.

'I wonder . . . ' he muttered to himself.

'What? What you said?'

He ignored her, deep in thought still. Joss was back in the walled garden of Great Place with his father, recalling their conversation of a few weeks ago. They had been sitting on a stone bench basking in the sun, outside the greenhouse where a huge vine loaded with ripening fruit twined above them. All round the red-brick walls of the vegetable-garden were espaliered apple and pear trees. Robert

Pencarrow stared unseeingly at the serried rows of carrots and cabbages and thumped his cane on the ground for emphasis.

'I've said it before and I'll say it again boy, it's nature not nurture that counts. Blood will always out.'

They had wandered into a debate then about social class. 'You're saying that a working man — or woman — cannot be taught the social graces and learn how to mix and move in society,' Joss had said, 'even if they haven't been born to it? If they come into money, I mean.'

'Breeding boy, breeding and wealth that goes back through the generations, that's the only thing that counts. Money made from trade,' he spat out the word with contempt, 'is not the same thing at all. Neither is a self-made man, I tell you. Hurrumph.'

'See enough, can you?' jeered Joss's companion and he was jerked back to the present. 'What you staring at me for? Haven't you never seen no girls afore?'

'I was just wondering,' Joss began. For here was a challenge. He would put his father's theory to the test. This could be just what he needed to pass the long vacation before he went up to Oxford in October. With studies over and time hanging on his hands, he would see what he could make of this little

11

scrap of humanity who was now glowering at him from under lowered brows, her eyes shooting green sparks of defiance.

'Rose,' he said hesitantly, wondering what the reaction would be from this unpredictable sprite, 'how would it be — I mean — would you like me to give you some lessons? Teach you a bit of reading and writing . . . ? Would you like that?'

Like it? Rose's face lit up like sunshine and her answering grin banished all Joss's nervousness. For here was the answer to her wishes. To read! And write! Never in her wildest dreams had she thought there would ever be a way.

'Cor — *yes!*' she said, nodding emphatically, and her eyes blazed like stars in her small pale face.

'Right, we'll do it,' Joss went on, gratified. 'Can you meet me here again tomorrow? I'll look out some books and things and we can make a start.'

Rose nodded again. However difficult it would be to get away, whatever problems she would have to face, this would be worth it. She lifted a beaming face to the older boy and Joss, sensing her thoughts, felt a stirring of something like affection and a fierce protectiveness for this small determined mite.

★　★　★

Her happy dreams carried Rose through the rest of the day. Back at the cob-and-thatch cottage that was her home, she tackled the household chores with a lighter heart. Even when she found the earthenware water-pitchers were empty yet again, she went willingly down the road to the pump. The cumbersome jugs were heavy even when empty. Now with a gallon of water in each, Rose wished as she staggered back with them that her road lay downhill and not up.

Much later, having done the family wash, she rinsed out the last of the baby napkins and dried her hands, swollen and red from their long immersion. Rose carried the heavy pail out to the back yard where a line was strung between two posts and where a few scrawny chickens scratched and pecked in the dirt. The smell from the earth closet near the back door was seeming stronger than usual in the summer heat. Normally it was something they all took for granted, but coupled with the stench from the rubbish heap across the yard, today it made Rose wrinkle her nose in disgust. Thomas, Sammy and Dan, her half-brothers aged seven, five and three were squabbling over something, their shrill voices grating on Rose's nerves.

'Shut up, you lot,' she shouted, 'you'll wake the baby.' Tiny Sarah was lying in a wooden box in the shade of the hedge.

Suddenly Sammy broke away from the group and came racing towards the house scattering screeching chickens in all directions. Venting his temper on the nearest thing, the boy aimed a kick at the bucket, knocking it over and spilling its contents in the dirt. A sly grin crossed his peaky face as he saw Rose's dismay and he poked his tongue out at her. Rose took a swipe at the flying figure and Sammy tripped and landed heavily, skinning one knee. With a howl ten times louder than necessary he hobbled into the house, and Rose's heart sank as she heard her father's voice soothing and petting the child. He *would* have to come in at just that moment. She could guess what was coming.

With a sigh Rose bent to gather up the scattered washing. At least most of it had already been on the line. She shook the worst of the dust from the others and pegged them out as well. She would *not* rinse them out again.

She was bending to pick up the empty bucket when the blow caught her on the side of the head and sent her sprawling. She had known it would come but had been caught unawares even so.

'Thass fer hitting them what's smaller'n you,' came Joe Vidney's voice, slurred again from drinking. 'Great maid like you — ought to be 'shamed of yerself.' He stumbled off and Rose looked after him in disgust, holding a hand to her burning ear.

She crossed the yard to sit in the shade of the hedge near where the baby lay. Still asleep, thank goodness, Rose thought, peeping in at her. She knew her father drank because of the hopelessness of their lives, but if he didn't drink the money away they could live a little better. It was a vicious circle. Rose curled her arms around her knees. Usually from here she could hear all the noise from the mines which surrounded the village — the steady hiss and thud of the great beam-engines which pumped out water and raised the ore; the clatter of the stamping-mills and rising above it all the sweet singing of the balmaidens as they worked.

But in this year of 1843 tin-mining was in a bad way. There were rumours rife in the district that Wheal Fancy where Joe and Ellie both worked, might have to close. Rose shuddered to think what a plight the family would be in then.

Conversely, copper prices were still up and those mines large enough and wealthy enough to dig deeper, were finding copper which frequently underlay the worked-out tin levels. Rose's thoughts drifted back to Joss, and her stomach did a flip of excitement. She would begin her lessons tomorrow!

While Rose was day-dreaming, inside the cottage Joe Vidney was recovering from his drunken state to face again the cold reality of his life. He gave a vast yawn which split his weasly face, exposing stumps of rotten teeth, and ran a hand through his sparse sandy hair.

As the shrill voices of his children drifted in through the window he felt a slight twinge of guilt as he recalled the clout he had given Rose. He shouldn't really have done it, it was only the drink that made him take out his temper on the girl. Poor little toad didn't deserve it really — but there she always was, like a thorn in the flesh, reminding him of happier times when the house was clean and comfortable and there was a meal waiting for him when he came off core. That had been when Hester was alive . . . and the child was so like her. All that springy hair, and the eyes — oh those eyes! Dammit, was he never to be allowed to forget!

Joe glanced around at the shambles of the room and spat disgustedly on the flagged floor. At that moment Ellie his wife burst into the room and banged the door behind her. Joe jumped guiltily and ground out the evidence with the toe of his boot.

Fat and blowsy, Ellie stopped to draw breath, then took one look at her husband.

'What you sitting there for you lazy sod,' she yelled. 'Get up off yer backside or you'll be late fer core! Next thing you'll be laid off — you do knaw how bad things are up there, same as I do.'

Joe growled but rose to his feet. Times were indeed getting harder and the prospect of being thrown out of work loomed large unless there was a sudden rise in the price of tin ore. As a surface labourer, Joe knew that he would be one of the first to go. With less stuff being raised there would be fewer men needed to shift it.

'Aw, shut yer mouth woman, always nag, nag, nag. Late or no, you'll be out of a job yerself afore long, same as me. Won't be no balmaidens needed neither if there isn't no ore fer breaking up.'

With this parting sally he sidled out of the house and turned up the lane towards the mine. However, rumour had become reality and Joe arrived just in time to join the grim-faced crowd which had gathered on a flat area of reddened waste ground to hear what their employers had to say.

On an elevated vantage-point on the 'burrows' or spoil-tips, stood the mine captain and some of the frock-coated, top-hatted shareholders straight from their meeting at the nearby count-house. Prominent among them was Sir Robert Pencarrow.

Rank upon rank in rust-streaked working-clothes, some still wearing their hard hats with a stub of candle attached, the miners were joined by the balmaidens in their white bonnets and aprons, all knowing what was to come but hoping for an eleventh-hour reprieve just the same.

Sir Robert stepped forward into a silence so profound that the skitter of pebbles under his boots was audible even to those at the back of the crowd. His florid complexion was a shade brighter than usual as he cleared his throat and stroked his goatee beard before beginning.

'I am sorry to have to announce that from today it has been decided to close down Wheal Fancy. I'm sure this will come as no surprise to those of you who are aware of the present slump in the price of tin ore.'

He broke off as the rumblings of the men below him grew louder.

'What's he expect us to live on — fresh air?'

'If he paid decent wages in the first place,' shouted one of the surface workers, 'we could have put a bit by . . . '

'He'll have to whistle fer his bleddy rent money, this rate.'

'Listen will you, he's still talking.'

'Let me assure you this is none of our choosing. Among several reasons for the closure is the recent discovery of a rich copper lode at Kapunda in Australia. And so many of our skilled workers have emigrated that we cannot carry on without them . . . '

'Thass right too,' came a mutter. 'Jim Pengelly and Henry Bray went off awnly last week. Knaw them did you?'

'Shut yer mouth and listen to the man, Bert. Might learn something if you keep yer tongue quiet fer five minutes . . . '

'And this along with the slump in prices has led to such a decline in the profits that regrettably there is no alternative . . . '

'Profits me eye — can't see the likes of they going short of their dividends, can you? 'Tes we what are left to carry the can, boy, you and me what got families to feed and clothe and rent-money ter find.'

'Ess, we shall all be on the parish this rate, Tom. There idden no work nowhere. Couple of us went down to Wheal Vor last week — walked all the way there and back — and traipsed from mine to mine till me boots wore through, all fer nothing. Chased off by the copper men we was — had stones thrown at us and all. 'Tes some thing, I tell you.'

But the top-hats were dispersing, the meeting was over, the carriages bowling away.

★ ★ ★

Rose was up very early the next day and bustling through the household chores which must be done before she could set off to meet Joss. She skimmed through the absolutely necessary things like fetching in the water and left the rest. Pa had gone off somewhere to look for work and Ma was walking into Redruth to see if there was a cleaning job to be had in any of the big houses there. Although without much hope, because for every one that came up these days, hundreds were waiting. It was a time of great privation for the mining families now that Wheal Fancy had closed.

'Come us on, you three,' Rose called to her charges. 'Get this down you.' She placed their breakfast bowls of skimmed milk with a few bits of bread broken into it, on the table.

'Aw, Rosie, I don't like it,' Dan wailed, his bottom lip pouting mutinously. Rose gritted her teeth in exasperation. Please God they wouldn't start playing up today of all days.

'I want bread and butter,' chimed in Sammy, banging his spoon on the table in tune with the chant. Soon they had all joined in and the noise was deafening.

'*Quiet!*' Rose yelled above the hubbub. 'We haven't got no butter. It's 'sky-blue and sinkers' or nothing. Tell you what,' she added before a full-scale mutiny broke out, 'first one to finish gets a sugar-bag to suck. Right?'

It worked like magic. Silence fell apart from the slurping noises which followed. Rose went to the scullery and tore a bit of flour-bag into three strips, put a few grains of precious sugar in each and tied the ends in a knot. It is a reckless waste of sugar, she told herself, for goodness knows where the next lot will come from, but I *will* get off, and if this is the only way . . . There, one for each of them and that should keep the peace.

She had decided that she would leave the two youngest boys with Tommy, but there was no way out of taking the baby with her. Tommy would delight in telling tales and he really was too young to look after her too. The last thing Rose wanted to do was draw attention to her comings and goings.

'Tom, I got to go to the shop,' Rose lied, shooing them outside, all three happily sucking on their sticky treats. 'Stay in the yard and look after they two. Don't you go nowhere near that tin-stream, mind!' She hoisted the baby into a makeshift sling over

21

her hip and started off.

Sarah was a happy, placid little girl and would be no trouble apart from her weight, Rose thought as she started on her uphill journey. She loved her dearly — at ten months she was not yet old enough to torment Rose like her brothers did. She gurgled happily and sucked a thumb as Rose made for the carn. She looked back once. Tommy was swinging on the rickety gate and stuck his tongue out at Rose before running round the side of the house and disappearing. Good, he hadn't seen which way Rose was heading.

By the time she reached the summit after several rests along the way, Rose's legs were aching and she was breathing heavily. She untied the sling and thankfully set the baby down on the grass beside her while she lay on her stomach and fanned her hot face with a frond of bracken. It was another glorious day. On the horizon the distant rim of azure water was shimmering in the heat haze.

Joss was late. Rose doubted whether he would come at all. He might well have changed his mind by now about the promise he had made on the spur of the moment. Well, why should he bother with her when he could do as he pleased with his holiday? Rose steeled herself against probable disappointment. She sat up and shielded her eyes from the sun to peer down the empty track, and her shoulders slumped.

Then a sudden noise behind her made her start. There he was! Coming the other way. His horse had kicked against a loose stone. Joss was here!

'Sorry I'm late, Rose.' Astonishment was written all over his face as he noticed the baby. Sarah gave a chortle and made to crawl towards the horse as Joss slid from its back.

'I thought you'd changed yer mind. I was just going. Can't hang around here all day,' Rose retorted with her chin in the air. She grabbed Sarah by her little gown and restrained her. Joss was unfastening a leather pouch from his saddle.

'Look, I found a copy-book, a slate and chalk and this picture book with the words underneath. They were up in the attic, that's why I took so long. But you must have known I'd come,' he added indignantly. 'I promised.'

For in his world a gentleman's word was his bond. In Rose's you never told the truth if a lie was more expedient. The two were poles apart.

Little Sarah had turned her attention from the horse to the things Joss had placed on the grass, and immediately made a grab for the piece of chalk which was heading straight for her mouth. Rose took it gently from her as Joss's eyes widened.

'I say — a baby! Do you have to look after it?'

Rose nodded and hugged the child.

'There's three boys younger'n me at home. I do look out fer they too.' Her face fell as she wondered what they were up to at that moment.

Joss saw the anxiety in her eyes.

'Rose, how old are you?' he asked.

'Ten, nearly eleven. How?'

'Don't you ever go out and play with your friends?'

'Haven't got no friends. Don't want none anyhow. They do only tease me, see.' Rose hung her head but Joss had seen the quiver of her lips and the way her mouth turned down at the corners.

'Why do they tease you so?'

' 'Cos — 'cos my pa and ma weren't married when they had me. She were married already. She ran off and left her husband, then she died having me.'

'Were they teasing you yesterday? Was that what happened when the bully chased you?'

Rose nodded.

'He's my cousin,' she said bitterly. 'He's always like that. He used to live with we but

24

now he's on a farm out Tregajorran. He've got it in fer me, always have had.' She nibbled at her bottom lip. 'I never done nothing. My Aunty Winnie was his mother and because she were a widow she come to look after we after Ma died. And Reuben was jealous.' Rose made another grab for Sarah who had seized the picture-book with glee. 'Then Aunty Winnie got ill with the consumption and died of it. He have blamed me ever since. I was six then, he's four years older.'

The wistful look on her expressive face as she delivered this catalogue of horrors touched Joss in a way he had never experienced before.

'But that's preposterous!' He was at a loss for words to describe the indignation he felt, and his sympathy for this poor little waif who seemed to accept so stoically all that life had thrown at her.

Rose raised her head and stared at him.

'Where do you live to?' she asked.

'Oh, er, over there. Beyond the village. Illogan way.' Joss waved a dismissive hand. If he told her he came from Great Place she would probably run away and never come back.

'Your hands are some smooth,' observed his small companion. 'Don't you do no work?'

'Oh well, I go to school still, you see.'

'What's your second name?'

Joss, busy with slate and chalk replied automatically:

'Pencarrow, what's yours?' and could have bitten off his tongue.

'*Pencarrow?* Cor, you're *gentry* then! I never spoke to no gentry afore.' Most of the locals paid deference to the Pencarrow family — they depended on the squire for their livelihood.

Joss's eyes softened at the awestruck look on her face.

'Look Rose, I'm Joss your friend and that's all that matters,' he replied seriously. 'When we're up here we shall be just Rose and Joss and our different backgrounds don't count for anything. Right? And you still haven't told me your second name.'

'Vidney,' said Rose absently. 'We-ell, all right, I suppose,' she added, obviously unconvinced.

'Well, smile, Rose Vidney, and let's get some work done or we shall have wasted the morning.'

★   ★   ★

By trial and error they stumbled over the first steps in Rose's education. Their meeting-place was always the same, among the piled

26

boulders on the summit of Carn Brea. The great granite formations, eroded by years of exposure to the elements, had been given names to match. One of Rose's exercises had been to write them on her slate and spell them to her 'tutor'. The Giant's Head, the Tortoise, the Elephant, and one known as Cups and Saucers because of the circular depressions in its flat surface.

'You're doing really well, Rose,' Joss remarked one day after hearing her read, 'for a beginner.' Rose's vivid face lit up and she pushed a strand of bright hair out of her eyes. He was surprised himself at how quickly she was learning. 'And you've never had lessons before?'

Rose nibbled her bottom lip.

'Aunty Winnie used to send me to Sunday School sometimes when she was alive, and we did a bit of drawing and stuff. The older ones did reading but I never went long enough to learn nothing.'

'Well, I'll see you again tomorrow.' Joss was packing up the books and slate. The holiday was flying now that he had become so immersed in this experiment. He was almost reluctant to take up his own studies again.

As for Rose, her heart sang as she practised letters on the slate and spelt out the words of the dog-eared old primer. She snatched as much time as she could without arousing suspicion at home. What no one knew about they could not take from her. Joss was her hero, her knight in shining armour, and she would have died for him.

* * *

'Have you told your father that you're learning to read, Rose?' asked Joss one day, watching his pupil's lips move over the words she could now read silently to herself, only occasionally asking him for help.

Her eyebrows rose to her hairline in a look of astonishment.

'Cor, tell Pa? Not likely! Give me a belting he would, fer wasting me time. And he'd stop me coming up here. What he don't know can't hurt.'

'Say 'doesn't' Rose, instead of 'don't',' Joss instructed her. 'You may as well learn to speak correctly as well. You should say 'doesn't'.'

'Aw. All right.'

'When you read proper books you'll see that's right.' Joss leaned back against a warm boulder and placed his hands behind his head. Sarah had crawled over to him and with a wail suddenly went sprawling over Joss's outstretched knees. Awkwardly the boy picked her up. He had never held a baby before and the feel of the warm, squirming little body against his chest was satisfying. Then his expression changed.

'Oh Rose — she's hurt herself! Look at that great red mark on her head. Quick — you take her.' He passed over the crying baby.

'Aw, she idden hurt,' Rose replied matter-of-factly. She bounced the child up and down and the crying stopped. The calm maturity displayed in one so young amazed Joss.

'What's her name?' he asked, fascinated by the baby, who was now trying to stuff the hem of her dress into her mouth.

Rose snorted in derision and indicated the dress as she disengaged it.

'Can't you read, neither?' she chortled, 'Look.' Daintily embroidered on the little yoke was the name 'Sarah', enclosed in a wreath of tiny forget-me-knots in faded blue silk. 'Ma had a bundle of hand-me-downs gived her and this here was in it. Funny, weren't it. Oh!' Rose clapped a hand to her mouth as she saw Joss frown. ' 'Tis some hard to speak proper,' she wailed. 'I shall forget all you said as soon as I do get home.'

'I know it is, but you must keep trying. You'll soon get the hang of it. Listen to the way I speak and copy me.'

Rose was watching him, birdlike with her

head cocked to one side. 'That's all very well so long as I got you to copy,' she retorted. 'When I get home I shall forget. Anyway, they'll laugh at me even more if I suddenly start talking proper.'

Joss felt a pang of conscience. Was he asking too much of Rose? What would she do with her 'education', sketchy as it was? Was he just making her dissatisfied with her place in life, or was he encouraging her to rise above it? Maybe it was just as well that the holidays were nearly over after all.

'I got to go,' Rose announced, glancing at the sinking sun, and she scrambled to her feet. As she scooped up the baby her skinny frame staggered under the weight. Sarah was getting too heavy now to carry easily up the steep hill.

'You got any brothers or sisters, have you?' she asked as she tied the old shawl into a sling again.

'I've got twin brothers younger than me,' Joss replied.

'Cor, your ma do have nearly as much washing as we then, with three boys in the house,' said Rose with feeling. 'I bet all they white shirts do take some rubbing!'

'Um, yes.' Joss almost laughed out loud at the thought of Jennifer, his elegant mother, bent over a dolly tub scrubbing shirt collars.

Struggling to keep a straight face he said: 'Not 'do take', Rose. What did I say?'

'Oh lor!' the girl wailed and clapped a hand over her mouth. 'I fergot again.' She heaved the baby higher and sighed. 'We're going to have to meet somewhere else,' she said. 'I can't carry she up here no more — any more I mean,' as Joss frowned again. 'I'll see you down by the tin-stream instead. It do fair wear me out, carting she around.'

'All right,' agreed Joss, gathering up the books. 'I'll be in that clearing by the bridge you always come over, by the ruined wall. Bye.'

Rose noticed that little Sarah had fallen asleep just as she reached the bridge which crossed the tin-stream on the way home. Hot and out of breath, she laid the baby gently down on the bank and sank down beside her. Although it was only a few steps to her home, Rose needed a rest.

She could see the cottage perched on the opposite bank, and her brothers playing in the yard. As she watched, she saw her father's familiar figure rolling up the lane and realized with a sinking heart that he was drunk again. Then as he rounded the corner of the house and disappeared, the sound of upraised voices came floating on the still air. Used as she was to her father and stepmother's constant bickering, this sounded far and away more serious to Rose's ears. Something had happened.

Rose glanced down at the baby. She was sleeping soundly and would be all right for a minute. Rose was going to creep up to the house and see what was going on. She sped over the bridge, up the bank and approached the cottage from the rear.

So Joe had come home roaring drunk yet again. Rose cast her mind back to that morning when she had seen Ellie dole out a few precious pennies to him as he had left to walk to a farm a few miles away where they had heard that hands were being taken on for the harvesting, and guessed the rest.

She risked a peep around the corner of the cottage. Ellie was standing on the doorstep with arms akimbo while Joe, his shifty eyes cast down, was kicking a hole in the fraying doormat.

'You've drunk it haven't you? You lazy, good-fer-nothing sod! What about that job? What are us going to eat termorrer?'

'Shut yer mouth woman, I'm a miner, not a bleddy farm labourer.' His feeble attempt at assertiveness crumbled to nothing as he lurched and clutched at the door-frame for support.

'Yer bleddy useless, Joe Vidney, that's all

you are,' screeched his wife, shaking a fist under his nose. 'Well, have I got news fer you!' She paused for effect as he goggled at her and waited. 'I'm leaving,' stated Ellie baldly. Rose's eyes widened.

So did Joe's.

'Leaving?' The slack mouth dropped further open. 'What yer mean, *leaving*? Where going to?' he slurred. 'Can't leave — yer me wife.'

'Not no more I aren't. I've had enough of you. I'm taking the childer and I'm going to me widowed sister down St Ives. She been asking me fer ages, ever since I told her what you was like. Got plenty of room she have, and there's work in the fish-gutting down there. So I'm going. Cart's coming fer we on Saturday. Your maid can stop here with you. Idden no room fer she.'

Rose clapped a hand to her mouth and clutched at the wall for support as the implications of all this sank in.

'Ah, gus on then, get out,' Joe growled with drunken bravado. 'Sick of yer bleddy nagging anyhow.' He turned, gave the door an almighty kick and turned back down the lane, probably to the haven of the Miners' Arms from which he must have just come.

Rose stood rooted to the spot for a few minutes, her legs trembling with shock and her head reeling as she struggled to take in what she had just learnt. Then she remembered the baby and forced herself to move, retracing her steps to the riverbank where she had laid down the small bundle.

The blanket was lying exactly where she had left it. Only now it was empty and of baby Sarah there was no sign.

Rose's stomach gave a lurch and both hands flew to her face. Sarah must have woken up and crawled away somewhere. That was it. But she couldn't have gone very far, Rose had only been gone for a couple of minutes.

'Sarah! Sarah! Where are you? Come to Rose, come on . . . ' She began to search the undergrowth on the bank of the stream. The stream. Rose looked down at the swiftly flowing water. Red with the iron tailings from the mines. Deep. And as red as blood. Her stomach heaved again and she felt sick. 'Sar-ah!' she called desperately, flailing at the brambles with her bare hands. To and fro she floundered in circles, and still there was no sign of the child.

Then, 'Ma! Ma!' Rose shrieked, tearing across the bridge and up the slope. 'Oh Ma, come quickly . . . '

Ellie's round, pink face appeared at the door, her straight mousy hair on end.

34

'What's the matter, maid, house afire is it or what?'

Rose's breath rasped in her throat.

'Sarah — she's gone.' Her voice was little more than a whisper.

'What yer mean, *gone*? Gone where to?'

'I don't know. She's gone — disappeared,' Rose gasped. 'One minute she was there, on the bank, in her blanket.' Her shoulders heaved. 'Then when I went back, she was gone. Ma, I can't find her nowhere — you got to come!' Rose burst into tears.

At last the urgency of the situation penetrated Ellie's brain.

'You mean ter say you *left* her, my dearest cheeld — on the bank of the river and went *off*!' She seized the collar of Rose's dress and shook her like a dog with a rat.

'It was only for a minute, I swear it — she was sleeping — and I was back in no time — stop it, Ma, you're hurting me!' Rose felt her face reddening as Ellie twisted the collar tighter until she could hardly breathe.

'Thass nothing to what I'll do if you don't get back there double-quick and find that babe. You — Tom,' she called over her shoulder to the eldest of the three boys who were standing open-mouthed and for once deathly silent, behind her. 'Run and get yer pa, quick, and make sure that he do come.

35

You,' she gave Rose a poke in the ribs, 'come us on — show me where she was to.' And they began to run down towards the stream.

A couple of farm hands were hoeing turnips in a nearby field as they passed and jumped the hedge to join in the search as Ellie yelled for help.

'I'll come with you missus,' said one. 'Bill, you go and round up more men. Fetch billhooks to cut through the bushes and send someone downstream as far as the sluice-gate.'

A vision of her baby sister's little body caught up in the detritus that gathered beside the filthy sluice was too much for Rose. She turned aside and threw up the contents of her stomach into the bracken. White as a sheet and trembling with shock and fear, she staggered impotently behind the others.

Half the village turned out to help in the search, beating the undergrowth to a far greater distance than a baby of that age could possibly have crawled. They searched along in the river too, and with more success, for caught up in the rubbish at the gate of the sluice like a broken doll, was the tiny drowned body.

★ ★ ★

There were many hands outstretched in comfort and consolation after the tragedy. But not to Rose. She crept about the house like a small white ghost and, as if sensing the awfulness of what had happened, her three brothers grew closer and united in their misery, and gave her the only comfort she received.

Ellie was half out of her mind with grief and rage, sitting in the kitchen for hour after hour with her apron over her face, rocking to and fro and would not be comforted.

Joe had crumpled like a pricked balloon and spent all his waking hours in the Miners' Arms where he would beg drinks from anyone who felt sorry enough for him to oblige. He had given Rose a thrashing whose scars would stay with her for months, but she hardly felt it. She curled herself into a ball like a small wild creature and wished she were dead too.

But life had to go on. The funeral came and went. Rose was too deep in trauma for it to make any impression. The only thing that penetrated her numbed brain was the fact that Saturday was drawing near and Ellie and her family were leaving for St Ives on Saturday — for good.

Rose would be left alone with her father. The thought appalled her. When he was drunk he beat her, and these days he was scarcely ever sober. There was no one to protect her from his rages and Rose decided after many sleepless nights that her only course of action was to run away. But the burning question that kept her tossing and turning all night was, where could she go?

2

Joss arrived at the place where Rose had arranged they should meet and was surprised that she had not yet arrived. Usually she was there before him, her small face glowing with eagerness to get started. He continued to be amazed at the way she soaked up all he taught her, and remembered everything. Her reading had now reached the stage where he could teach her little more, and her writing was improving in leaps and bounds. Today he had brought plenty of work to leave with her, to soften the blow of having to tell her that this was to be her last lesson. Joss's summer recess had come to an end and he was due to leave for university in a couple of days.

Joss stretched out on a patch of rough, sun-warmed grass beside the tin-stream and tossed a twig into the murky water, watching as the red mouth snapped it up and swallowed it like an animal digesting a meal. Where on earth was Rose? Joss shifted restlessly and looked all around. Maybe she'd gone up the carn after all, forgetting they were meeting here. But it had been her suggestion — because of the baby's weight.

She was hardly likely to forget. He sighed and rose to his feet, whistling to the pony. He'd better go up the hill just to make sure.

From that vantage point he scanned the surrounding countryside. But there was no sign of a small figure pushing her way through the bracken, no sign of a head of chestnut curls emerging from behind one of the giant boulders, no pair of laughing eyes lying in wait to jump out at him for a surprise.

Joss felt a keen sense of disappointment. Then, as the minutes ticked by, one of anger. Drat the child! Surely she could have sent a message somehow? Then, more realistically, he recalled what he knew of Rose's home life and withdrew the unspoken remark. But obviously she wasn't coming.

Grim-faced, Joss seized the horse's reins. He descended the narrow, stony track faster than was advisable and arrived at the bottom in a cloud of dust. A couple of youths were leaning on the parapet of the bridge when he got there, idly throwing stones into the water. Joss reined in and hailed them.

'Do you know where Rose Vidney lives?' he asked without preamble.

They both looked up startled, and one touched his cap in deference to Joss's superior status.

'Yes sir,' he replied pointing a finger. 'Up there.' Then the other boy added: 'But she've gone.'

'Gone?' Joss frowned. 'Gone where?'

The youth shrugged skinny shoulders beneath an outgrown tweed jacket.

'Dunnaw. The baby drowned, see, and her feyther gived her a hiding and she ran off.'

Joss's jaw dropped as he struggled to take in this staggering information.

'*Drowned?* B-but . . . ' Realizing that the two youths were staring at him in surprise, obviously wondering why a member of the gentry should be so concerned about the feckless Vidney family, he gave a curt nod, tossed them a sixpence and rode away.

Concerned as he was, there was nothing he could do, and no way he could trace Rose's whereabouts without making a fool of himself. Poor little Rose. Presumably she'd run to some other relations to stay with while she came to terms with the tragedy. And there was absolutely nothing he could do about it.

* * *

Joss enjoyed his time at university. A good all-rounder, not brilliant at any one subject, he managed to acquit himself well enough in exams and was generally well-liked by his

41

peers. With his tall, lean frame and arresting violet eyes he found that he had no shortage of girlfriends in the town if he wanted them. Sometimes he took what was willingly offered, but for the most part Joss was his own man and planned to stay that way. At odd moments during the next few years he would recall the odd little urchin he had befriended one summer, and wondered idly what had become of Rose. He would have liked to know how she eventually turned out.

Dick Hamilton had become Joss's closest friend. A Yorkshire man, Dick was bluff and outspoken, with an impish grin and easy charm, the opposite of Joss's more reticent nature. They were foils for one another and had soon taken to spending their free time together.

It was a Sunday afternoon and they had been out for a tramp through the country-side, over softly rolling hills and into a small wood. There they had thrown themselves down on a carpet of pine needles, Joss with his back to a fallen log, Dick flat on his stomach in a beam of sunshine. The post-finals round of hectic celebrations was over and in the hiatus before 'going down' they had fallen into a serious mood.

'So, Dick,' said Joss, 'what are you going to do with yourself now that finals are over?'

His friend chewed lazily on a grass stalk.

'Same as you I suppose,' he replied. 'Take up the running of the estate eventually. I'm the eldest son too, you know.' Dick's father had made a fortune in the woollen mills and had an estate in the Yorkshire dales of similar size to Great Place. 'That *is* what you're going to do, I suppose?'

'I don't know,' Joss murmured. Dick's eyes widened and he looked at his friend in surprise. Joss was gazing at the distant hills with an unreadable expression on his face. 'I feel . . . ' he hesitated, 'you'll think this sounds daft, but I think that I should do something to . . . well, kind of *earn* it first. All that life of luxury and privilege. Do you know what I mean? Not just fall into it and take it for granted because I happen to be born to it. Do you understand?' He turned enquiringly to look Dick in the face.

'Oh.' Dick rolled over and sat up, clasping his hands around his knees. 'Sure I see what you mean, of course I do.' He paused. 'But the way I feel is, that if there weren't families like ours to — well, to look after if you like, the working-class people, then those people would be even worse off. I mean, my pater employs hundreds of workers on the estate and in the mills who wouldn't have a job or a home otherwise. And he looks after them

43

when they're old and sick too. And I *don't* feel bad about it, I can't honestly say I do. Pa says we're born to our responsibility for the people in our employ and that's our role in life. And you don't agree with that?'

Joss chewed a thumbnail.

'I see what you're getting at, but it's not quite the same in Cornwall. Yes, we've got the estate and the tenants and we treat them like you do. But it's the miners I was really thinking about.'

'The miners?' Dick looked at him blankly.

'Yes. You see, Papa owns the land which is being mined for tin and copper and he's got the mineral rights because of that, which is part of his income. As well as what he makes on mining shares, plus all sorts of side benefits too. But the men who actually dig out the ore are completely dependent on the rise and fall of tin prices. They get a percentage of what they raise. Right?'

'Right.' Dick nodded.

'Well, for the last few years there's been a decline in tin mining, and coinciding with it have been a couple of poor harvests as well. Some of the mining families even reached starvation level and started rioting. Breaking open warehouses to help themselves to flour.' He drew his brows together in a frown. 'Now my father, I know, isn't *really* concerned. He just pooh-poohs it and refuses to acknowledge that there is genuine need. He says that they can always find money for drink and that a spell in prison will bring them to their senses.'

'I see,' said Dick thoughtfully at this outburst. 'And what do you think you can do about it, Joss? Not much, surely?'

Joss sighed. 'I don't really know. But it can't be right Dick, can it. That some should have so much and others so little?'

'Well, ' 'twas ever thus', you know. To quote — well, somebody or other.'

'But that's no reason why it always should be, is it?' Joss snapped, momentarily needled by his friend's banter.

'Sorry, I know you're being serious.'

'What really got to me was this. When I was down last summer there was this frightful accident in one of my father's mines. Two men were killed in a blasting operation which went wrong and two others had limbs torn off. I was out for a ride and I saw them being brought up. I've never been able to forget it, Dick. The blood — and the women screaming. Three of the men were a father and two sons. I went behind a bush and threw up.' Joss rose to his feet and began to pace back and forth. 'I want to do something to improve mining conditions, Dick. It's what

45

I really care about. And before I can do that, I have to know more about the job.' He came to a halt and sat down abruptly beside Dick. 'I want to study mining engineering. I might even get some practical experience down a mine myself.'

Dick whistled in surprise.

Now that Joss had given voice to his ideals it was as if a dam had burst and he couldn't stop talking. 'And it would just show my old man a thing or two as well,' he went on. 'All my life he's been trying to turn me into an image of himself. He wants nothing more than for things to go on in the same old way. It doesn't enter his head that I might want anything different.' His face was grim. 'He doesn't even know the real me. We never have a meaningful conversation.'

'Well,' Dick broke in, 'if that's what you've decided to do, it strikes me the sooner you start the better.'

'I wish it were that simple,' Joss muttered. 'I'm just dreading telling my parents. It's this class thing, you know? A Pencarrow wanting to get a job. Earning his own living! I can imagine the old man's face when I tell him. But why the deuce shouldn't I?' He glowered.

'Why not indeed?' Dick shrugged. 'I say, Joss, I've had an idea. Why not *write* to your father? Send him a letter explaining how you feel, and break the news gently. That way he'll have time to think about it before he sees you.'

'Brilliant! That's a marvellous idea.' Joss clapped Dick on the shoulder, sending him toppling backwards.

'Think nothing of it, I get them all the time,' Dick joked, picking himself up.

Joss pulled out his pocket-watch and looked at it.

'Time we were getting back, we've been up here for ages.'

'We have, but if Uncle Dick has helped you sort out your life, it's all been worth while.'

'Idiot. But thanks, Dick.'

'Hope it all works out for you.' He gave Joss a nudge in the ribs with an elbow. 'Race you down that slope!'

And they arrived together in a panting heap at the bottom of the hill.

★ ★ ★

The confrontation with his father was quite as bad as anything Joss had anticipated. The letter had made little difference. It burst upon him one evening after dinner. As Joss was passing the study, Sir Robert suddenly appeared in the doorway. With a jerk of his head he motioned his son to enter, and firmly closed the door.

The room was snug and warm, with walls of panelled wood and hangings of heavy red chenille keeping out the first nip of autumn. The air was pungent with cigar smoke, and a decanter of whisky stood on a side table. Joss was not, however, invited to sit down or share a drink. His father strode across the room to his large walnut desk and drew forth a letter from one of the pigeon-holes. Joss recognized it.

Sir Robert tossed it across the desk top towards him.

'Now, I want an explanation of this piece of nonsense,' he barked. Still standing, he leaned both hands on the leather blotter in front of him and fixed Joss with a steely glare. Just like a schoolmaster, Joss thought. He'll whisk out a cane in a minute and tell me to bend over.

'That *is* the explanation, Papa. I've nothing to add to what I've written.' Joss knew his legs were trembling, and hated himself for this sign of weakness. He leaned on the back of a chair to steady himself and tried to appear calm.

Sir Robert's naturally florid complexion turned a shade darker. Even his sandy moustache seemed to bristle with anger, and his jowls shook as he exploded:

'You a Pencarrow, a member of one of the most respected families in the county, want to toss away your birthright as if it's of no consequence — to become a common *miner*? I cannot believe I'm hearing this correctly. Have you really taken leave of your senses?'

He paused for breath and thumped on the desk with a fist. The silver inkstand shuddered. Joss took a long, appraising look at his father. Being away from home had distanced them, and he realized now that he had never really liked him very much. Pompous, selfish, obsessed with keeping up appearances, ruthless and narrow-minded were a few of the adjectives that crossed his mind.

'You had better believe it Papa, because I'm quite serious,' replied Joss, speaking more calmly than he felt. 'Far from rejecting my birthright, I intend to prepare myself for it by gaining first-hand knowledge of how the money we live on is earned for us. And I shan't do that by sitting behind a desk like this.' He gestured with an open palm.

'So you've developed a social conscience while you've been away. Been mixing with a bunch of bloody radicals, have you?' Robert snarled. 'That Hamilton fellow's ideas rubbing off on you, are they? I could tell what he was the first time he came down here. His

49

family are no more than jumped-up hill farmers not three generations old, for all their pretensions.'

'You leave Dick out of this,' Joss retorted, seeing red. 'He had nothing to do with it. Credit me with enough intelligence to know my own mind, will you.'

Robert glowered. Joss, possessed of the same stubborn streak as his father, glared back. All his nervousness had vanished now and he was perfectly calm.

'And my mind is made up. I shall go to Dolcoath. As you know, it's the biggest of the mines and has been able to survive the slump by turning to copper. I'm willing to do anything to start with — even the lowest labouring job if I have to. In my spare time I shall study mining engineering and work my way up.'

'You stupid young pup!' his father hissed. Flecks of spittle sprayed over his lapel and Joss eyed him with distaste. 'You haven't the faintest idea what you're letting yourself in for. A Pencarrow sweating it out at the bottom of a mine — heaving rocks around like a common labourer!' His voice quietened to icy fury and he began to pace up and down the Turkey carpet, hands clasped behind his back.

'Well, I'll tell you one thing here and now.

Don't think for one minute you can come crawling back here when the going gets tough.' He turned on his heel and stabbed a forefinger at his son. 'I'm warning you, if you leave this house, you leave for good. And you won't get a penny out of me. Not now, not ever.'

Joss had expected this but refused to be blackmailed. He had a small sum inherited from his grandmother which he intended to use as a buffer to get him started.

'Quite so. I wouldn't touch a penny of your precious money if you begged me. That's the whole point of the thing.' He took a deep breath and squared his shoulders. 'So, I won't embarrass you by staying under your roof any longer.' Joss held his head high and looked the older man firmly in the eye. 'And I can only pity you for your narrow-mindedness,' he added, before turning on his heel and leaving the room.

★   ★   ★

Joss left home the following day, despite his mother's protestations. Jennifer had fluttered between the two of them, trying to pacify her husband and persuade her son to change his mind, with signal lack of success on both fronts.

So Joss took his leave of his tearful mother and subdued brothers and departed for Camborne, where he would put up at Matthews' Hotel until his new life should begin. He had already sent a letter to the manager of Dolcoath mine, explaining his unusual circumstances, and had received a polite reply requesting him to call at the mine office.

It was a chilly day for September when Joss guided his mount through the tortuous mine workings. Spread over a wide area, the scene was one of frantic activity and the din was deafening. Smoke belched from countless engine-house chimneys around the many shaft-heads. These steam-engines worked the pumps, hauled the ore to the surface and powered the stamping mills which crushed it to fragments.

Joss dismounted. Leading the frightened horse, he came upon a pit-head just as a group of men were coming up from underground. They were dripping with sweat and streaked with the iron-red colour which was everywhere, on machines, on their boots, in the soil beneath their feet.

'Which way to the captain's office?' Joss asked a youngster, not forgetting to give the manager his courtesy title. Although the child was not much more than ten years old he was as dirt-streaked as the rest, and pointed a skinny arm.

'Over there mister,' he replied. Surprised, Joss thanked him. What did a lad of that age do underground, for goodness sake?

Joss hitched his horse to a post and knocked on the office door. With a flip of excitement he realized that for the first time in his life he was going to be considered on merit alone and not for his family connections.

He stepped over the threshold to a gruff 'Come in', and found himself face to face with a burly figure in a white drill coat and wearing a bowler-hat. A full flowing beard covered his chest and a pair of keen and penetrating hazel eyes looked Joss closely up and down.

'Mr Pencarrow. My name's Thomas.' A large hand shot out and grasped Joss's own. 'Sit down boy, sit down.' He seated himself behind his desk, removed the hat and indicated a hard-backed chair nearby. The desk was piled high with a clutter of leather-cornered account books with marbled covers, maps, wire hooks holding bills and receipts and an array of pens, ink-bottles and stubs of sealing-wax. An oil-lamp suspended on chains hung low and was already lighted.

'So you're the young gentleman who wants

to come and play at being a miner,' said Captain Thomas as he proceeded to light up a foul-smelling pipe. He blew the smoke towards the blackened beams of the ceiling.

Needled, Joss straightened up.

'I've no intention of playing. Sir,' he added as an afterthought, remembering his position. But his eyes flashed with anger and his voice was indignant as he added: 'I didn't decide on the spur of the moment to do this. In fact I had an almighty row with my father over it and we parted on bad terms.'

Unperturbed, the mine captain leaned back and crossed one leg over the other.

'So why are you here, then?'

Joss launched into an explanation of his disagreement with his father's complacent attitude.

'So you're doing this just to spite your father, to prove you know better than he does.' The other man quirked an eyebrow and drew deeply on his pipe.

'No!' Joss's indignation blazed on his face. 'It's not like that at all. I want to improve conditions for the miners whom my father is responsible for. He doesn't see them as people at all. He has no idea how they live and doesn't want to know. And the only way I can learn is by joining them.'

'And what do you think you know about

miners' lives that has turned you into such a do-gooder?' enquired the older man with a touch of sarcasm.

He doesn't think I'm serious either, Joss fumed, and he leaned closer to the desk. Forgetting he was beholden to this man if he was to get any further forward, he said angrily:

'When I was about sixteen, Mr Thomas, I came across a child. A little girl. She was only ten years old, she was ragged, barefoot and covered in bruises where she had been beaten by her drunken father. She told me she did most of the work about the house and she had sole charge of a baby because both her parents were at work. She also had three younger brothers and kept an eye on them all. She would have loved to go to school, she said, but it was impossible, both because of the lack of money and because she was needed to do all the chores at home.'

Joss paused for breath then rose to his feet and paced restlessly round the room.

'A few years after that I happened to see something which made a profound impression on me and one which I've never forgotten. There had been a blasting accident and they were bringing up the dead and injured from down below. One woman there had lost her entire working family — her husband and two sons. She had a baby in her arms and three small children clinging to her skirts. How was she to survive after that? Living presumably in a rented cottage, she would have lost her home as well.' He returned to look the mine captain in the eye. 'And that, Mr Thomas, is why I'm here today.'

The mine captain steadily returned his gaze, then held out a rough and horny hand. Joss grasped it with his smooth one and wondered if his own would ever feel like that.

'All right boy, you'll do. I'll give you a try. Report here six o'clock next Wednesday.'

'Thank you sir,' said his new employee.

★   ★   ★

Guided by a card stuck in the corner of a shop window, Joss found lodgings in Camborne with a family called Blewett. The wife, Nell had agreed to cook and wash for him as she did for the two other single men who shared the cottage with her and her husband Martin, and their four children.

Martin Blewett was a miner at Wheal Hope, one of the Pencarrow mines which was perched on the cliffs about three miles away at Porthtowan. Joss found that he got on well with the older man and when their time off

56

coincided he spent hours chatting to him and learning about mining.

'And you were only ten, Martin, did you say, when you went underground for the first time?' The two of them were sitting on a tall settle in front of the Cornish range in Nell's kitchen. It was loaded with drying washing, more of which hung on a rack above them which was worked by a pulley. Saucepans and a kettle bubbled on the hob. The black lead shone and the brass knobs and fittings gleamed brightly. A neglected range, known locally as a 'slab', was a sign of a slatternly housewife and Nell was far from that.

'Yes, went down with my father. My first job was to work the fan down one of the ends. Some boring it were too, sitting down there in the dark — couldn't waste good candle, see, when I could manage without. Frightening too, to begin with, with all sorts of strange noises, but I felt some important I tell you. Thirty years ago now that were, but I still remember it like it were yesterday.'

He drew in a wheezy breath and started to cough. At first Joss had been alarmed by the coughing fits from which Martin never seemed to be free, until Nell explained one day that he, like countless other miners, was suffering from years of exposure to the bad air and dust-laden atmosphere underground.

Instinctively Joss had understood then why she took in lodgers — as insurance against the time when Martin could no longer work.

'And how are you liking it over to Dolcoath, boy?' Martin asked when he had recovered his breath.

'Well, it's early days yet,' said Joss guardedly. 'Everything's still very strange. I've only been there a few months. The most tiring thing I find is climbing back up those endless iron ladders after a shift. Hundreds of feet — you think you're never going to get to 'grass'.' Privately he was thinking as well how torn and bleeding his hands had been at first, and how they were now as tough and calloused as the rest. He remembered with a smile the first time he had shaken hands with the mine captain and wondered if his own would ever be like that.

'Think yourself lucky you're at Dolcoath, boy. At least it's a safe mine. Safe as any can be. Captain Thomas do care about the men and in a big concern like that they got the money for maintenance. Smaller mines can't do it, see.' He rasped a hand across his bearded chin.

'Down Wheal Hope now,' he went on, taking a pipe out of his pocket and tamping tobacco into it, 'they do tell us that they haven't got no money even for shoring timber. And being so near the sea a lot of they levels do run right out under the water. ''Tis a bit scary when you can hear the waves roaring over your head and you know there's only a bit of undermined rock holding the roof up. And that's shored with rotting timber.'

Joss shuddered to think of it. It sounded like a nightmare place to work. Obviously Pencarrow Consols had a lot to answer for. He thought of his father's complacent face with fury.

'We're some worried about it,' Martin went on. 'Captain Trenerry and all the old-timers like me who do see what's going on. That mine is a death-trap, boy.' He drew on the comfort of his pipe and started coughing again.

'It sounds like it,' Joss replied with feeling.

'For years, and I mean years, Captain Jack have been trying and trying to get through to your father and his company to do something about the maintenance.' Martin and Nell were two people who knew Joss's real identity, simply because Nell had recognized him, having once been a housemaid at Great Place.

Joss had told no one apart from Captain Thomas who he really was. When asked his name he slurred it to something like

'Ncarrow'. Nancarrow was a common local name and so far he had got away with it. Obviously he could not disguise the fact that he had never been down a mine before, but the captain and he had agreed that to all intents and purposes he was someone with local roots but who had been born 'upcountry', come back to live, and wanted to learn the job. This would also account for his lack of the working men's Cornish accent.

'As far as safety goes, I mean, things is going from bad to worse,' Martin went on, 'but they do say that money's so tight they can't afford this and they can't afford that.'

'Why are you telling *me* all this, Martin? I can't do anything about it, can I?'

Martin turned and looked Joss in the eye.

'You might be able to. I was wondering whether you'd be willing to come down yourself and see we aren't just making a fuss about nothing. I figured that with you being a miner yourself now, like, the powers that be might listen to you.'

Joss glowed at the compliment, but his face was serious as he replied:

'I'd be glad to, Martin, but if you think I'm likely to have any influence over my father, I shall have to disappoint you. He would take less notice of me than of anybody. But yes, I'll come down with you, certainly. How about tomorrow morning?'

'Thanks boy, that'll be fine. I'll meet you over there.'

★　★　★

Joss was looking forward to seeing Wheal Hope and felt he knew enough by now about how a good mine was run, from his own experience at Dolcoath. He rode the three or four miles to Porthtowan through narrow lanes where the hedges were thick with wild spring flowers. Primroses lay like clotted cream in sheltered places. Bright pink campions rubbed shoulders with nodding bluebells, while stitchwort and Queen Anne's lace frothed in the ditches. Then the lanes fell away and the road began to rise steeply towards the coast, where Wheal Hope balanced precariously close to the rugged edge of the cliff.

Once down the mine, Joss was appalled at what he saw. The first thing he noticed was the rickety condition of the ladders, the men's lifeline. Several rungs were broken or rusted and in some places a large gap showed where some were completely missing. For a tired man, already exhausted from an eight-hour shift, it would only take one step on to a rung that wasn't there to send him hurtling to his death.

The walls of the shaft were very damp and became increasingly wetter as they descended. The sound of dripping water was all around them and where the roof was shored up with props the timbers were green and slimy. Even in the dim light of the candles they were wearing on their hats, Joss could see that portions of them were obviously rotten.

When they stepped off the ladders at the lowest level, sixty fathoms down, Joss started as a hollow, roaring noise boomed all around them. It was like nothing he had ever heard before. It filled the cavern, growling like an angry beast kept in check for now but threatening to break free at any moment.

'The sea,' said Martin simply. 'We're under the sea here. Look.' He pointed to the beads of moisture on the lowering black roof. 'Seepage, that is. Taste it, boy.'

Joss took a drop on his finger and carried it to his lips.

'It's salt,' he said with concern.

Martin nodded solemnly. 'That's what I do mean, see?' They began to walk up the passage one behind the other, their boots splashing through more surface water. The sounds of men at work became louder. 'We're following a lode along here, looks like a good one, that's why we do take the risk. All this here water should have been shifted,' Martin added as they waded thigh-deep through a pool, 'but the bleddy old pump can't cope.'

Joss nodded.

'I can mind the time,' Martin went on, 'when this bal was one of the best. And it could be again,' he turned and stabbed the air for emphasis, 'with a bit of money spent on it. Ore's still here, plenty of it. Tin's beginning to pick up again — 'tes a crying shame. Well, what do you think boy, now you've seen it for yourself?'

'I'm convinced,' he said shortly. Privately Joss had been appalled at the state of the mine, but they had begun the long climb back, which put paid to conversation for a while.

By the time they emerged at 'grass' Martin was gasping for breath. He collapsed on to an upturned wheelbarrow while his whole body was racked by a coughing spasm. At a shout from the direction of the counthouse Joss turned to see Jack Trenerry, the mine captain, striding towards them, a stocky figure in the white drill coat and bowler-hat which Joss now knew indicated his position.

'Ah, Joss, glad I caught you — been wanting a word. All right, Blewett?' he asked with concern in his eyes. Martin nodded and wiped a handkerchief across his face as the cough abated.

'Martin's been showing me over the mine,' said Joss, grim-faced. 'Things are quite as bad as he was telling me, aren't they?'

'That's what I wanted to see you about. I know Martin's already told you this, but we're at our wit's end. Somebody have got to go before Sir Robert and the board and make them understand. We need action, not words. And I reckon you're the one to do it.'

This put Joss squarely on the spot. Here was a chance to put his ideals to the test. The whole reason why he had gone into mining at all was to try to help the men by his first-hand knowledge of their problems. Now they were looking to him to do just that. Could he do it? It would mean meeting his father face to face . . . Joss had not spoken to him since the day he left home, and was not looking forward to doing so now.

'What I thought was this, see. It's the end of the month and there's a counthouse dinner and meeting of the adventurers coming up.' 'Adventurers' were the shareholders, as Joss knew. 'It might be a good time to bring up the subject again. I reckon with you to speak up for us, Joss, it might make a bigger impression.'

'I doubt it,' said Joss bitterly, 'but if you and Martin come with me and back me up, I'll do the best I can. But knowing my father, I can't really see him changing his mind.'

Jack Trenerry tipped his hat and ran a hand through his thinning grey hair. 'I shall have to go to the dinner myself, but I'm sure Martin will. I'll see you there.'

He replaced the bowler and gave it a decisive tap, before firmly shaking the younger man's hand to seal the bargain. 'Thanks boy, I appreciate it.' He clapped Joss on the shoulder. 'I'll let you know the exact date and time when I've confirmed it myself.' He raised a hand and disappeared round the corner of the gunpowder store.

★　★　★

The day of the meeting came round and Joss turned up against his inclinations to meet Martin Blewett at Wheal Hope. What he did not expect, however, was to see the entire group of men who had just come off core drawn up in silence outside the counthouse instead of going home in the usual way.

'Every man just come up have stayed on to back us up,' said Martin tersely as they climbed the steps and entered the count-house.

The meeting was over, the board had considered the balance sheets and had enjoyed a satisfactory four-course meal. They were savouring their port and cigars when Joss and Martin came in. The air was thick with a haze of tobacco and the lingering aroma of roast beef. At the top table sat Sir Robert and the committee, along with Jack Trenerry, the mine captain, grim-faced and silent. The rest of the long room was filled with tables where sat the many adventurers, investors who had a stake in Wheal Hope, large or small. The smallest investments had long ago been nicknamed 'knife and fork' shares, as it was said that their owners only bought them for the free dinners.

Martin removed his hat and with hob-nailed boots clumping on the wooden floor, he and Joss approached the top table. Robert Pencarrow's face was a picture of astonishment as he saw his son.

'You!' he thundered.

'Sir,' Martin intervened, 'we are here as a deputation from the men of Wheal Hope.'

'Well, what is it, man?' came the testy reply. 'It had better be important to warrant this intrusion.'

'Oh, it is sir. Conditions are so very bad down the mine there is likely to be an accident there any time. So with respect, sir, while these gentlemen are all assembled here, we are come to ask you to give some attention to repairs and maintenance. Mr Joss is here to back me up and all the men off last core are outside waiting for your answer — they're that worried, see. With Wheal Fancy and the other bals closing, they can't get work nowhere else, but they'm frightened for their lives down Wheal Hope.' Martin had spoken firmly and clearly, but Sir Robert's eyes were fixed on his son and his face was scarlet.

'Just what the hell you think *you're* doing here I can't possibly imagine. Poking your nose into our affairs! Wheal Hope is absolutely nothing to do with you.'

Jack Trenerry spoke then.

'I asked your son here today, sir,' he said quietly. 'I was hoping you would give him the chance of backing up what we've been saying for so long.'

'On the contrary, Father, I was invited to see Wheal Hope and the conditions are quite frankly appalling. As a working miner myself — '

'Pooh,' said his father in derision.

Unperturbed, Joss went on: 'I consider it my duty to do anything I can to help my fellows fight for basic safeguards — essentials which should be theirs by right and not having to be begged for.'

'Enough!' his father roared, jumping to his feet and thumping the table. 'You come here preaching to me of rights. No one has rights at Wheal Hope — they're damned lucky to have a job at all — as you pointed out yourself, work is scarce. Production is down, tin prices are down, but costs continue to rise. What about *my* rights, eh? How can I carry out these improvements when the money's not there, tell me.'

'It's a matter of grave urgency sir,' Martin persisted stubbornly. Joss was looking around in disgust at the remains of the vast meal and cast a contemptuous eye over the empty decanters and glasses, and at the many gold watch-chains straining over their owners' ample waistcoats. His father saw the pointed look.

'Hurrumph,' he snorted. 'However, it's well known that I put safety measures before profit margins.' Joss's eyes widened. 'Well, man,' Sir Robert said to Martin, 'I'll have the captain and the mine carpenter between them draw up a list of the basic essentials you say are needed. Just the basics, I repeat. Not that I can promise anything with the price of timber what it is. I see Harvey's over at Hayle have put their prices up yet again. But we'll take a vote on it at the next meeting and see.'

'But sir . . . '

'The next meeting? . . . '

'Father, you can't . . . '

Martin, Joss and Jack protested simultaneously.

'As for you,' Joss's father towered over him from the platform on which the table stood, his eyes bulging. 'Get out of here before I do something I shall regret!'

Joss coolly stared him down.

'Don't forget the ladders as well, Father, or you will be faced with something you really will regret.'

He turned on his heel and left the room. Furious with his father for his pig-headed obstinacy and with himself for not having gained more for the men, he strode down the steps to a chorus of shouts and yells from those outside. Jack Trenerry had already slipped out of a side door and broken the news to them.

'Bleddy old skinflints,' came a bellow, echoed by an angry roar from many throats. 'Take a vote will they? Next meeting? That's another bleddy month! We shall all be blawed to kingdom come by then, shouldn't wonder!'

Joss, watching in alarm, saw the furious men swarming under the windows of the counthouse with fists raised, hurling abuse at their employer. There was a steady stream of diners leaving by the back entrance as inconspicuously as possible as the uproar became steadily louder. Carriages were bowling in convoy down the rutted road and away.

'Better fit they put the money they just ate down the mine,' one voiced yelled after them. 'Won't be no mine left soon, then where they going to get their free dinners to!'

A handful of gravel suddenly hit a window with a rattle like hail-stones. Another shout went up and soon a hail of missiles was hurtling through the air. Joss leapt down the steps and tried in vain to restore some kind of order. But it was impossible to make himself heard.

'Rabble-rousers! Scum!' Joss could see his father standing at the top of the steps, brandishing his cane in fury. 'I'll see you all hauled up before the bench for this!'

Joss sprinted up the steps and took hold of his father's arm.

'Get back inside. It's not safe out here — you're making yourself a target,' he urged.

'Take your hands off me, you young pup,' Robert hissed, glowering at his son.

Joss grasped his elbow in a grip of steel and glared back.

'You send just one of those men to jail,' he said between clenched teeth, 'and I shall go with him. You'll find that very embarrassing when I tell the press as I shall, just why I'm there. So think about it,' he added coolly as his father seemed about to explode.

Joss had dropped the grip on his father's arm when he had been distracted by the sight of one burly miner hefting a huge stone he had picked up from the top of a nearby wall. He was aiming it at the nearest window just as Robert had turned to leave and was passing beneath it on the way to his waiting carriage.

'Look out!' Joss yelled as the man's arm swung back. Joss dived for his father and with a flying leap felled him to the ground to roll safely out of harm's way.

But the rock never reached the window. Joss caught the full force of it on one shoulder and crumpled senseless to the ground.

3

The happy laughter of the two attractive young women who sat together on a seat in the sun brought a smile to the faces of several passers-by who were strolling beside the river in Truro one Saturday afternoon.

Their two heads were bent close together over a book of fashion-plates. One of the women, a fetching redhead, wore a costume of jade poplin with a little feathered hat perched on her upswept hair. She had put aside her newspaper to follow her friend's pointing finger.

'Oh, Rose, look.' The other girl gave an infectious giggle as she spoke. 'Can't you just see me in a crinoline like that? With all those frills I'd look like a walking tea-cosy!' Her bubbly brown curls bounced as she laughed again, almost dislodging her hat of golden straw. She clutched at it with one hand, then smoothed the yellow taffeta of her skirt over her ample hips.

'But Kate, everyone in fashionable society wears them now. Look at this picture of Her Majesty.' Rose waved the paper under her friend's nose. 'She's opening the Great

72

Exhibition and every woman there is in a crinoline.'

'Well, I can't imagine anything more clumsy,' Kate retorted as a clock chimed somewhere in the town behind them. Rose jumped up and folded her paper.

'Come on,' she said, 'time to go. We're going to be late.'

'Oh doesn't a half-day fly?' sighed Kate as they fell into step. Rose picked up the hem of her skirt as they crossed a muddy patch.

'I expect Fanny's fretting already,' she replied. 'Customers waiting and no sign of her staff — she'll be ready with the sharp end of her tongue.'

'Oh, you know her bark's worse than her bite. I used to be terrified of her when I was a scullery-maid, but now we get on all right.'

'Yes, I know. She's been very good to me, Kate. Do you remember that night when I turned up on the doorstep — ten years old, ragged, starving and worn out with walking all day?'

Kate nodded, her eyes on a small boy with a hoop who was bowling it briskly towards them on the narrow path.

'I was only just out of the orphanage myself, but I felt some important telling you what to do.' Her round blue eyes twinkled as she went on: 'How about those awful mob-caps we wore — and the sacking aprons — remember those, do you? What sights we was.'

The child with the hoop stopped to let them pass and Rose gathered her skirts to step round him.

'I'll say so. And standing in that freezing scullery scouring endless pots and pans with sand took all the skin off my fingers. But the food Fanny gave us made up for it.'

'Oh yes, I've never tasted a pasty yet to beat Fanny Laity's.'

'You know, Kate, the smell of pasties was the first thing that hit me that night when I arrived. Matt was eating one then, and he looked me up and down while I was waiting and asked me where I'd come from. I remember saying down west — near to Camborne and Redruth. I was afraid to say exactly where, in case I was sent back.'

The two girls turned a sharp corner into an alleyway which was a short cut to the main street. So narrow that it was known as 'Squeezeguts Alley', they were forced to walk in single file, and Rose continued talking over her shoulder.

'I was absolutely weak with hunger. And I must have been staring at Matt's pasty as if I could swallow it whole, because he noticed and bought me one.'

That had been after Sarah . . . and I ran away in the night. Fleeing from that great burden of guilt . . . it's all still there deep down . . . imprinted on my soul for ever . . . Rose swallowed hard. Every so often, even now, the past arose to haunt her, at unexpected moments like this and in nightmares when she would awake sweating from visions of a tiny, screaming baby tossing on a tide of blood-red murky water. She had never been back. I wonder if Joss ever knew, she thought. I see his face to this day whenever I read a book . . .

'And now you're going to *marry* Matt!' Kate's voice impinged on Rose's thoughts. 'You *are* lucky, Rose. He's a good man, is Matthew Lanyon. He's kept an eye on you ever since, hasn't he, really? And he's waited eight whole years for you to grow up.' She sighed and raised her eyebrows. 'I think that's *so* romantic. I'd be thrilled to bits if any chap did that for me.'

'You read too many penny novelettes,' Rose replied, as the image of the big, dark-bearded miner replaced the memories in her head. She gave Kate a brilliant smile which did not, however, reach her eyes. He is, she told herself fiercely, a genuinely good man. Kind, generous and sober-living. More than could be said for many miners.

And he loves me dearly.

But, whispered a secret voice deep within her, do you love him? Certainly I love the comfort of his big warm arms around me and his shoulder to lean on. I can shut out the past then, she replied. But, she sighed, was that all there was? Where was this heady 'love' so exhilarating and so precious that it had inspired great music, great paintings and poetry down through the ages? Surely there should be *more*.

Rose straightened her shoulders and lifted her chin. She had given Matt her word. She was pledged to marry him and she would keep her promise.

'Well, here we are — home again,' she said, changing the subject as the Tudor frontage of the Red Lion hotel came into sight. 'Back to work.'

'It's all right for you,' Kate grumbled, 'you've got tomorrow off as well, haven't you?'

'Only the afternoon. And I worked last Sunday when you were off on the gad — so you can't make me feel guilty about it.' Rose gave her a playful dig in the ribs and they bustled down the side of the building to the kitchen entrance. 'We'd better slip in and get changed quickly. See you in a minute.'

The two girls separated and Rose ran up

the stairs to the very top of the building. She was eighteen now and had risen from scullery-maid to second cook, but this little cell-like room was the first and only place of her own that she had ever had. Thank goodness she had remembered the Red Lion from childhood trips to Truro with Aunt Winnie.

Winnie had been a friend of Fanny Laity, who had taken in the bedraggled little waif under the pretext that she needed another scullery-maid. Dear Fanny, thought Rose with affection, reaching for a clean cap and apron. A quick drag of a comb through her springing russet hair before perching the cap on top, and she sped downstairs to the kitchen.

'Ah, Rose. You're here at last.' Rose ignored the rebuke as Fanny raised a flushed face from the oven. 'Dining-room's packed out. Give me a hand with these will you, Kate's rushed off her feet.' She hefted a tray of steak-and-kidney pies out of the oven and put them on top of the range. 'No — there's someone knocking on the door. Answer that first, you're nearest. It'll be the vegetable man, I expect.'

Nothing could have prepared Rose for the shock she received when she opened the outside door. A huge, dark man stood on the doorstep holding two crates piled high with vegetables. Other boxes stood at his feet. He loomed over her, blotting out the light, and as she raised her eyes to his Rose felt her stomach clench in the old instinctive knot of fear.

Reuben Clemo. But he was powerless to hurt her now. They were no longer children. She tilted her chin a fraction higher.

'Well, if it isn't my little long-lost cousin!' He grinned and pushed his dirty cap to the back of his head as he looked her up and down. 'So this is where you're to. And grown into such a fine young lady!' he leered.

'Reuben.' Rose acknowledged him with a nod, and bent to take some cabbages from one of the boxes to hide her shaking hands.

'Hurry up with those crates, young man,' came Fanny's voice in the background. It gave Rose confidence to face up to her cousin and satisfy her natural curiosity.

'What are you doing in Truro?' she asked. 'Live here now, do you?'

'Naw.' Reuben lifted a box of carrots over the doorstep and she stepped to one side. 'I do come to market every Saturday, see. And your housekeeper do order her veg from our stall. Doing all right, I am,' he went on, going outside for another crate. 'Likely to take over old man Rule's farm where I do work, when

78

he goes, as a matter of fact. He haven't got no childer of his awn.' He dumped the crate beside the rest.

Rose held open the door as he went to and fro.

'Do you . . . do you . . . ever see my father?' She asked, hesitatingly.

'Naw, nor don't want to neither.' Reuben spat inelegantly on to the dust of the yard. 'Kicked me out he did, or good as, after Ma died. Vidneys haven't never done nothing fer me, you included.' Straightening, he leered at Rose. 'How's yer fancy boy these days?' he remarked. 'Still see him, do you? 'Cos, you can tell him that Reuben haven't forgotten *nothing*.' His voice dropped to a menacing undertone. 'I said I'd get even with he and you and one day thass just what I'll do.'

'But that was *years* ago — we were only children! You surely can't still hold a grudge against Joss? And after what *you* tried to do to me!' Rose's voice, raised in indignation, brought a shout from Fanny.

'What's going on, Rose? Is something wrong with the order?'

'No Fan, the man's just leaving. Here's the bill.'

Fanny took the piece of paper and crossed the kitchen to add it to the spike where messages were kept.

79

'Well, goodbye cousin, you'll be seeing me again.' Reuben grinned, displaying the blackened stumps of his rotting teeth. 'Now that I know where you're to, that is.'

He clumped off across the yard. Rose closed the door behind him and leaned against it, her head swimming. All the old wounds she had thought healed had been painfully opened up in one brief meeting with her old enemy.

★ ★ ★

'Matt's down in the taproom, Rose,' said Kate, bustling in with a tray full of dishes to be washed. 'I expect he wants a pasty as usual.'

'I'll take some of these,' Rose replied, bending over the oven. 'These pasties are done, Fanny,' she called, 'shall I take them out?'

'Yes, and give that soup a stir while you're there, will you?'

Rose piled the piping hot pasties on to a tray and took the steps down to the back of the building. Abe Pengelly the landlord who, with his wife Maud as housekeeper, ran the establishment, was pulling tankards of ale. The low-beamed, stone-flagged room was thick with smoke and loud with the rumble of male voices.

'Hello, Matt. Waiting for a pasty, are you?'

'How did you guess, my handsome?' Matt's deep brown eyes twinkled. 'Smelling good they are, too.'

'Just this minute out of the oven,' Rose replied and took the loaded tray to the counter. She took out a plate from a shelf beneath it, selected the biggest pasty and threaded her way back to Matt.

Matthew Lanyon, a big brown bear of a man, was a miner at Killifreth, a few miles west of Truro. He caught hold of Rose's hand as she laid the plate in front of him.

'You're looking pretty as a picture today,' he said, eyeing her appreciatively. Rose blushed. She had long ago matured from the pinched and skinny waif she had once been. Security and regular meals meant that her skin glowed with health and her arresting colouring of burnished auburn hair and sparkling green eyes had caused many of the men around them to glance her way.

She had continued the sketchy education she had begun with Joss, by reading everything that came her way. She continued practising how to speak 'proper' by listening to and copying the customers at the Red

Lion. For the inn prided itself on being *the* fashionable place in Truro to see and be seen, and its standards were high.

The great panelled dining-room at the front of the building was patronized by businessmen and their wives, by gentleman farmers in Truro on market day, and by elegant ladies on shopping trips to the local emporia.

'Hey, Rose,' said Matt. 'Do you know that the fair's in town?'

'The fair? Oh yes, I did see them putting up stannings on the green.'

'Like to go, would you?' Matt raised his eyes to hers. 'Will and I thought we would. Bring Kate as well — I reckon Will do fancy her on the quiet.' An impish grin lit up his face. 'Never know, perhaps we'll have a double wedding!'

'Oh Matt, they've only been out together a few times,' Rose chided. 'But Kate does like him, I know. Anyway, yes, I'd love to go. Shall I slip up and ask Kate now? You'll still be here, won't you?'

He nodded, picked up his pasty in his hand and began to munch.

'I'll wait till you come back, my bird. Give me time for another pint, that will.'

★ ★ ★

82

So they arranged to go to the fair the next Saturday night. Before then, however, Rose was to have another encounter with her venomous cousin.

She had been coming back through the town with a bag of groceries which Fanny had sent her out for, and was approaching the hotel from the back, down a narrow alley or 'ope' which was not used by many people as it led only into the grounds of St Mary's church.

Reuben had been lurking in a doorway. He stepped out right in front of her as Rose turned the corner.

'Ah, there you are then, Rosie girl.' He chuckled. 'Told you you'd be seeing me again, didn't I?'

Rose gasped and one hand flew to her mouth. Struggling to appear calm, however, her voice was firm as she said:

'Reuben, what are you doing, hanging around here? You frightened me half to death.' Her heart hammering furiously against her ribs, she clutched the bag of shopping in both hands and tried briskly to push past him, seeming far more confident than she felt.

But he was towering over her like a dark wall, arms folded across his chest, and there was no way she could squeeze by. Rose halted and stamped a foot in anger.

'Why can't you leave me alone?' she said furiously. 'What do you want?'

Her tormentor gave another chuckle.

'What do I want?' He mimicked Rose's voice in a mocking falsetto. 'That's rich that is. Oh, yes, you don't know how funny that is.'

'Oh stop being so stupid and let me past!' Rose fumed. 'Fanny's waiting for these groceries — I can't stand here all day.' She clasped the bag to her with both hands and again made a dive to one side of him, trying to use the bag as a battering ram. But it was no good. Reuben shot out one hand and caught her arm in his vicelike fist.

'A bit short of ready cash at the moment, I am.' He grinned, showing the stumps of his rotting brown teeth. 'Like to help me out, would you, cousin? For old times' sake, eh?'

'Me? Give you money?' Rose was incredulous. 'You must be off your head! Now take your hands off me and let me pass.'

He made no move to do so, however, but only jerked her closer towards him. Rose took the stench of his breath full in her face and recoiled. She squirmed and tried to kick out at him, but he was as strong as an ox. Rose began to feel a twinge of real fear. She was helpless in this out-of-the-way place. She doubted whether anyone would hear her even if she screamed.

'Because I thought if you're not willing to be obliging like, I could make things really nasty for you, see.' Reuben twisted her arm and leered down at her.

'Pooh,' said Rose with bravado. 'What do you think you could do so much?' She stared back at him with her chin tilted in defiance, as a vision went through her head of all the several kinds of physical assault that he had at his disposal. With every minute that passed, she was feeling increasingly more like a rabbit caught in a trap.

Then in his small black eyes Rose saw a gleam of cunning and of calculation, which seemed to hint that her adversary was not planning an immediate bodily assault on her. There was something else coming, Rose was sure.

But nothing had prepared her for her enemy's next remark.

'I know yer guilty secret, see.'

Rose jumped, her heart in her mouth, before she realized that she *had* no guilty secrets. The man was plainly mad.

'For goodness sake stop talking in riddles and let me go. I haven't the faintest idea what you mean.'

'Don't you now?' He peered into her face

and grinned. 'Think about it, Rosie girl.' He gave her arm a shake, then snapped, 'How about the time you threw the baby in the river, then?'

Shock hit Rose like a drench of cold water and her mouth dropped open. '*Threw* her? Sarah, you mean?' She gaped at him in bewilderment.

'Yes — Sarah. Unless there was others what you seen off as well, was there?' He sniggered. 'Yer baby sister what you was supposed to be looking after and what was washed up dead.'

'B . . . b . . . but I didn't! You know I didn't! That's preposterous!' Rose's voice climbed up and up the scale. 'She crawled to the edge and . . . and . . . fell in and was swept away.' All the blood had drained from her face and she had begun to shake uncontrollably.

'And I say, prove it.' The beady eyes bored into hers. ''Twas an open verdict remember, weren't it? Nothing to say what really happened.' The eyes narrowed. ''Course, you was gone before the inquest — made sure of that, didn't yer — cleared off afore you could be caught and questioned. Oh they tried to trace you and all that, but yer pa and ma wasn't really bothered, they said you'd come home when you was hungry. But you was clever, oh yes, and you was never found. Till now.' He cackled.

On and on went the voice of nightmare as Rose, mesmerized like a rabbit by a snake could only listen, trembling in every limb.

'I could have been around that day. Might have been picking blackberries — hidden in the bushes. I could give evidence that I heard the cheeld screaming blue murder. I could say that you couldn't make her stop and you slapped her and shook her, then you lost yer temper and chucked her down. Into the water.'

Horrified, terrified, Rose screamed: 'No! You liar — you — you *evil* lying monster! You know I did nothing of the sort. I loved Sarah — *loved* her.' She burst into hiccuping sobs and sagged against the hand that was constricting her arm.

Then she forced herself to straighten up and fight back.

'They won't believe you after all these years!' she spat. 'Eight years ago! They'll say why didn't you speak up at the time. Why wait until now?'

Reuben smirked.

'At the time I kept quiet out of loyalty to my kin, see. I was only a boy and didn't know no better. Didn't want to get my little cousin into trouble. But,' he added sanctimoniously, 'it have been preying on me ever since I've growed up, but I never knew where you was to until now. And now that I've found you again, I want you brought to justice to clear me conscience, see.' He gave a great guffaw.

Rose willed herself not to faint, although the blood was singing in her ears and the walls of the alley were wavering in front of her. She swallowed hard.

'That's *blackmail*,' she whispered.

'Call it what you like, don't make no odds. Gimme yer purse,' he snarled as he released Rose's arm and tossed her from him. She stumbled a step or two then clutched at the wall for support as she put down the shopping-bag and fumbled in it. Then with tears streaming down her face she threw the purse to him. What else can I do? she howled in silent agony.

Her tormentor rummaged around, then spat copiously on the ground in front of Rose.

'Measly five bob — thass all yer got, is it?' He glared at his cousin. 'Don't you go telling me no lies, mind.' Rose nodded, thankful that she had spent the rest before he caught up with her.

''Twill have to do fer now, then.' He thrust the two half-crowns into a pocket of his filthy trousers and tossed her the empty purse. 'Git going,' he said, 'until we meet again.' He leered. 'And we will, you can be sure of that, Rosie maid. Goodbye, cousin.' Chuckling, he swaggered down to the end of the alley, then turned to raise a hand in a mocking farewell, and vanished.

★　★　★

Rose pulled herself together and walked into the hotel with knees like jelly. For the rest of the day she could think of little else than the hideous insinuations and threats made by her cousin. But she had to force herself back to the present, for today was Saturday and they were all going to the fair. She was brought back to earth at last by the sound of a knock on the door of her room. Before she could answer it Kate had popped her head inside.

'What are you going to wear, Rose?' Kate asked eagerly, her face wreathed in smiles. 'I'm really looking forward to this, aren't you?'

Rose nodded and pasted a smile on her own face. 'Well, I've got that checked tarlatan that I've never worn. I've been saving it for something special. You remember I made up that length of material I bought down the market?'

'Oh yes. The blue and emerald — that's

lovely. You are clever Rose, to make your own clothes.'

'If I didn't, I just wouldn't have so many outfits,' said Rose practically. 'I bless Aunt Winnie for that — she's the one who showed me how to use a needle, little as I was — and I learnt a lot from just watching her sewing.'

'I'll wear my pink. Will hasn't seen that before.'

'It suits you. You like Will, don't you?' said Rose, fishing. The sudden spread of colour across Kate's face gave Rose her answer and she smiled again, this time with genuine feeling.

'They're not a bit alike are they, Matt and Will?' Kate said with a giggle.

'Like chalk and cheese,' Rose agreed. 'There's Will small and wiry and ginger like he is, with freckles all over his face, and Matt huge, burly and dark. Couldn't be more different. Look, get a move on, Kate,' she added, 'I'm nearly ready and you haven't started yet. They'll be here soon and we're still chatting.'

★ ★ ★

Soon the four were threading their way through the laughing, jostling crowds towards the green. A wave of raucous music was blaring from the colourful steam-organ, augmented by the automaton figures on the front, banging their drums and clashing their miniature cymbals in time to the beat. Roaring, hissing traction-engines with brightly painted bodies and decorations of shining brass supplied the power for the organ and the rides.

Casting off her troubles at last, or at least putting them temporarily out of her mind, Rose felt a thrill of childlike excitement. She had been denied her own childhood, but now she was going to make up for it. The noise was deafening; they could hardly hear themselves speak over the din of showmen bellowing to be heard.

'Roll up! See the freak shows, the menagerie, try your hand at boxing, at Cornish wrestling.' And spend, spend, spend on anything from plaster 'fairings' to sticky gingerbread.

The four sampled the hoop-la and the coconut-shy, where Matt won a lace-dressed doll and presented it to Rose with a bow. The sight of people riding sedately up and down on the graceful 'gallopers' appealed to Rose and she pointed and mouthed, 'Shall we?' Minutes later she was clasping a twisted brass pole like a barley-sugar stick, and laughing like a six-year-old as they rode round and round. Matt, on a golden rooster beside her, leaned over and squeezed her hand, his eyes full of love. And at that moment Rose was completely happy.

The fragrance of crushed grass was everywhere, mingling with the aroma of savoury pies, frying onions and the less attractive smell of hot grease and oil from the machinery. Rose's head was whirling from all the noise and excitement and Kate at her side must have been feeling the same, for at that moment she turned to Will.

'Phew!' she said. 'Isn't there anywhere a bit quieter where we can go next?'

'How about having your fortune told?' Matt suggested from her other side. Rose shrugged. It would be a bit of harmless nonsense.

'All right.' She nodded. 'Coming, Kate?' At least she would be able to sit down for a few minutes. 'I wish I hadn't worn these new boots tonight,' she confided to Kate as the two girls approached a tent where a banner proclaimed: *Madame Leonora — the genuine Romany fortune teller. Your future revealed.* 'They're beginning to pinch.' She had been so proud of their dainty heels, but now she envied Kate her flat pumps.

'They look ever so smart, though,' said

Kate. 'You'll just have to suffer for appearances' sake!' She giggled, and Rose scrabbled for her last silver threepenny-bit as they entered the tent.

Kate was urging Rose to go first and pushing her through the black velvet curtain decorated with cabbalistic signs. It was dark inside the booth and very quiet considering the volume of noise just outside.

When her eyes had become adjusted to the dimness Rose could see a woman sitting before her, a kerchief over her head and a shawl around her shoulders. Her hands were resting on a crystal ball on the table. It was such a predictable scene, everyone's idea of a gypsy fortune-teller. Rose had been sceptical before she came in, now she almost laughed out loud.

The woman gestured with a slim brown hand and Rose sank thankfully into the chair opposite her. She met the woman's eyes and as they locked Rose felt a curious sensation. The eyes were mesmeric, haunting and timeless. The woman could have been any age from fifteen to fifty.

'Relax and give me your right hand.' The voice was low and husky with a foreign cadence. 'You can rest those weary feet for a while, yes?'

Rose's eyes widened. How did she know?

She saw you were limping when you came in answered the voice of reason, and Rose smiled. The gypsy turned Rose's palm upwards and began to mutter. A frown creased her forehead and she gave Rose a brief upward glance before tracing the lines with a forefinger.

'Born in grief,' she said, so quietly that Rose had to strain to catch the words, 'and reared in pain.'

Rose started: that much was true.

'Death has struck — and will strike again.'

A cold shiver feathered down Rose's spine and her head began to reel. Death? Sarah! Just as she had been trying to forget. But she couldn't have known — could she? The gypsy was staring into the crystal globe as if peering through a mist.

'E're you your heart's desire attain,' she finished. Then the woman dropped Rose's hand as if it were a heavy weight. She looked exhausted and her eyes had dulled as if a light had gone out behind them. Rose staggered to her feet and left in a daze. On the way out, she almost fell over Kate waiting for her turn.

'What did she say Rose? Was it good? What's she like?'

'Tell you in a minute — go on in, she's waiting.' Rose gave her friend a gentle push and sank down on to the grass outside the tent to wait for her. She could see Will and Matt in a group of people were watching a fire-eater thrust a handful of flaming torches into his mouth.

Madame Leonora's words were still ringing in her ears. As for her prophecy, well, most babies were born in grief and pain. It was Rose herself who had applied it to her own experiences. That's what fortune-telling was all about — it was the way a listener interpreted it that made it special. Madame Leonora could say the same thing to everyone.

So what about *death has struck and will strike again*? Look at it rationally. Everyone experienced bad times at some point in their life. She hadn't actually said anything personal at all — it had been Rose, again, who had immediately thought of Sarah, of the harrowing guilt, from which it seemed she would never be free. But when Madame Leonora had said '*death has struck*', she had been looking at Rose's hand just as if it *were* her fault. *And will strike again*. No! She wasn't going to be the cause of another person's death, was she? Rose shuddered, it was too dreadful to think about.

She jumped as Kate burst out of the tent, a smile like sunshine lighting up her face and two red spots of colour burning in her cheeks.

She flung herself down beside Rose.

'Ooh, wasn't it creepy!' She giggled. 'You'll never guess what she told me — and I don't understand what it means. It was all in rhyme.' Kate wrinkled her brow. 'It went like this: 'If you would your true love see, look where never grows a tree'. That's the bit I don't understand. Then she said: 'Fortune fair will follow thee, far away across the sea.' Isn't it exciting? I'm going overseas — to good fortune!' She wriggled and straightened her billowing skirt. 'Do you believe in what she says, Rose? What did she tell you?'

Rose hastily improvised some nonsense, having no intention of sharing her strange experience with Kate, and was relieved to see the men coming towards them. Kate ran merrily off to meet Will and was telling him all about the gypsy's prophecy.

Will threw back his head and roared with laughter.

'Surely you don't believe all that stuff, do you, my handsome?' He took Kate's hand and led her away. 'I bet she says the same thing to all you maids.'

Oh no she doesn't, Rose thought and smiled up at Matt as he helped her to her feet. She stumbled as one of the wretched boots gave her toe a vicious pinch, and had to grab his arm to save herself from falling. He tucked her hand under his elbow and they walked towards the exit.

'It's been a grand evening, hasn't it, maid?' said Matt as they wended their way through the town. 'It has, Matt,' Rose replied. 'I thoroughly enjoyed myself.'

They were crossing a hump-backed bridge over the little river Allen which rippled past on its way to join the mighty Fal and the sea, when Matt drew Rose to a halt and turned her to face him.

'And I've saved the best part till last,' he said quietly. 'I got the keys of the cottage today.' He bent and kissed her on the lips. 'We can be wed as soon as you like.'

Rose's stomach did a flip. They had been waiting so many weeks for the cottage at Porthtowan to be vacated that now the time had come she was shaking with nerves.

'Oh Matt,' she whispered, 'that's marvellous. But it's such a big step, getting married.'

'Not having second thoughts, are you?' he said with mock severity. Rose raised her eyes to his.

'I'm pledged to you, Matt, you don't think I'd go back on my word, do you?'

'Of course not, my bird, I was only teasing.' Matt cupped her hot cheeks between his great hands. 'How about as soon as the banns are called? We're paying rent money as from today, don't want to waste it, do us?'

Rose lowered her head and scuffed a toe.

'Something wrong, is there, my hand-some?' asked Matt.

Rose nodded. 'It's just that . . . well, I can't get married in church, Matt.'

'What?' His brows contracted into a frown. 'Why not?' he demanded.

'My parents weren't married, that's why. I . . . I'm illegitimate, Matt. And I wasn't baptised either. I'm a b — '

Matt placed a warm forefinger over her lips before she could say the word. Echoes of the familiar tune — 'Bobby Shafto' — came drifting out of the past and the hateful words that went with it rang in Rose's head.

'Then we'll be wed in chapel. Don't make no odds to me. The Methodists aren't so fussy. Weren't no fault of yours what your parents done, my bird. Leave it to me, I'll sort it out.'

Rose looked up at the steady brown eyes and the honest, loving face so close to hers and thought that to have Matt beside her for ever to 'sort things out' would be very agreeable. Common sense told her that he was the father-figure she had been denied as a child and the big brother she had never had. And the security of a home of her own, the one thing she had always yearned for, was extremely tempting. She and Matt would do very well together, she decided, and once married to this good and decent man, Reuben Clemo's threats would no longer be able to touch her, for Matt would sort him out as well.

'As soon as you like,' she echoed in a whisper, 'and I'll be a good wife to you Matt, I promise.'

Rose was preoccupied with her own thoughts on the next evening that she had arranged to meet Matt. They had been strolling through the park and had paused to sit down for a rest and to listen to the open-air concert being performed in the bandstand.

In the interval between two pieces Matt reached for her hand and said, 'Rosie, there's something I want to tell you.' Rose raised her eyebrows. 'Mm?' she replied enquiringly. The serious note in his voice made her wonder what was coming.

'Nobody don't know this, only Will,' Matt said. 'He and me was working together as a pare — a team, you know — a couple of years back, and we came upon a good little sturt. Know what a sturt is do you?'

'Of course I do,' Rose retorted. Having lived among mines all her young life she knew the local word for a sudden windfall of good luck. It was every miner's dream to come upon an unexpected lode of high quality ore. Sometimes it had been enough to set a man up for life, more often it was just a little nest egg. 'Tributers', as they were called, lived by their skill and knowledge of mining terrain by bidding at setting day for a pitch they liked the look of. They bargained for so much in the pound return on the ore they raised and, if they had picked a good pitch, were occasionally well rewarded.

'It isn't no fortune,' Matt went on, 'but I thought after we took out enough for a few sticks of furniture, we could have a bit of a trip. A honeymoon like. What do you think, bird?'

'Honeymoon?' Rose's eyes shot up in surprise. 'Oh, I hadn't thought about it. I took it for granted we would go straight home afterwards. What sort of a trip do you mean, Matt?'

'Well now, I been reading about this Great Exhibition what they're putting on up London. And I've a mind to go and see it for myself. How about it maid?' His brown eyes twinkled merrily down at her.

'*London?*' Rose could not have been more incredulous if he had said the other side of the moon. 'Go all the way to London? *Us?*' Her mouth dropped open and her eyes were round as marbles. Rose had never been east of Truro in her life and her flimsy knowledge of the nation's capital was based entirely on what she read in the newspapers and in the *Illustrated London News*.

'I don't see why we shouldn't.' Matt's jaw was set in a determined line. 'It do only cost a shilling to get in if you go on the cheap days, and the railway is running excursions.'

'What are the cheap days?' Rose asked absently, her mind turning over this totally unexpected adventure.

'Monday to Thursday. I could manage that, and you won't be working by then of course. I aren't sending no wife of mine out to work.' He chuckled and pinched her cheek. 'So what do you think?' He ran a hand through his mane of bushy hair.

Rose was gazing down at the water but seeing the Crystal Palace. 'Oh Matt — what an adventure!' She raised sparkling eyes to his face. 'We could see all the famous sights — and the fashions — and the exhibition as well. That would be *wonderful.*'

'Right then, Rosie soon-to-be Lanyon. We'll do it.' Matt seized her by the waist and lifted her high, twirling her round till her skirts billowed, to the amusement of some passing children. He kissed each of her flushed cheeks in turn before setting her down again.

Back at the inn, Rose flew up the stairs with stars in her eyes to tell Kate the news. Kate had just arrived back herself and Rose caught up with her on the top landing.

'Coo Rose, you lucky thing!' Kate exclaimed, 'You might even see the Queen herself!'

'I doubt if she'll be there on the shilling days,' Rose replied with a grin, as Kate followed her into her room and sank on to Rose's bed.

'The Crystal Palace,' Kate murmured. 'All that glass shining in the sun. It do sound like a fairytale. Do you know, Will said it do cover eighteen acres of that there — um — what's it called? Hyde Park, that's it. Fancy! That's bigger than the whole of Willie Bray's farm up on Castle Hill where we do get our milk. And he said they got real trees growing inside it and all!'

Rose was listening round-eyed. 'I'll bring back as many pictures of it as I can, Kate, and tell you every single thing. When I come to visit, of course,' she added in a small voice. For Rose suddenly realized she was going to miss her friend immensely, and all the bustle of life at the Red Lion. There would be no more popping in and out of each other's rooms to exchange confidences and gossip. Rose would soon be the mistress of her own home.

'Coo, I'm going to miss you something awful, Rosie,' said Kate as if she had read her friend's mind. 'I know you'll still be visiting, but it won't be the same, will it?'

Rose gave her a hug and replied, 'You must come and see me often. I'll feel very strange at first being a married woman, but Porthtowan's only five miles away. We'll go to and fro, you'll see.'

Deliberately changing the subject she said, 'Let's have a look at that pattern book before we go to bed. If we've got two gowns to make — yours and mine — before this wedding, we'd better get started.'

Kate's face immediately brightened as Rose had known it would, and they were soon lost in a welter of pattern books and fabric samples.

4

''Bye Rose. Goodbye Matt! All our love — we'll be thinking of you. Have a marvellous time!'

The newly-weds were clambering aboard the stage which would take them on the first leg of their journey to London. All the staff of the Red Lion, where the wedding breakfast had been held, were lining the street to see them off. Their bags had been hoisted on top, the driver stood ready with whip in hand.

Then they were off. Rose leaned out of the window waving her handkerchief until they turned a corner and their friends disappeared from sight. She sank back into her seat with a sigh and smiled up into Matt's loving face. He took her hand and squeezed it.

'Well Mrs Lanyon, so we're on our way at last.'

'Oh Matt.' Rose laid her head on his shoulder. 'Hasn't it been a lovely day!' All her doubts and fears had blown away on the warm spring breeze and their wedding-day had been perfect.

'It certainly has, and this is just the beginning, my handsome,' her husband replied. 'Have I told you how pretty you're looking in that outfit?' he whispered in her ear. Over her simply cut gown of apple-green taffeta Rose wore a mantle of russet shot with green, and a dainty straw-hat trimmed with pheasant-feathers perched on her shining hair.

'Not for about half an hour,' she giggled, 'but you can tell me again if you like.' She sat upright and took off her gloves. 'You're looking very distinguished yourself.' On Matt's big frame the shoulders of his black broadcloth suit were straining at the seams, and he was resplendent in striped trousers and a fancy waistcoat of red-and-black brocade.

Rose and Matt chatted quietly together, having a regard for the other passengers, until they reached Saltash, where they had to leave the stage and embark on the ferry-boat which would take them over the river Tamar and out of Cornwall. Rose was gazing wide-eyed at the mass of shipping thronging the broad river. Having been used to the modest traffic on the river Fal, the water here seemed to be a veritable forest of masts and spars and she was hardly listening to what Mat was saying.

'I said, they reckon it won't be long before the railway do come right down into Cornwall. There's a Mr Brunel what's drawing up plans for a bridge over the river here. Imagine a bridge big enough to carry a railway train, can you, maid?'

'I can't see that happening,' said Rose. 'Anyway, Cornwall just won't be the same if it does.'

'You can't hold back progress and new inventions, maid. That's why I'm really looking forward to seeing this exhibition,' said her husband with enthusiasm.

At Plymouth they had booked a clean room in a respectable lodging-house and by the time they arrived there they were both exhausted. Rose had been up since dawn, unable to sleep for excitement and apprehension and had felt only relief when after a meal, they retired to their shared bed.

'I reckon, Rosie, we're both too tired and wound up to — well, to enjoy our first night together — and we've got an early start in the morning,' said Matt forthrightly.

He cuddled her close in his warm embrace.

'Go to sleep my bird,' he whispered. 'We got plenty of time for that later on, haven't us?' He kissed her gently and pulled the covers over them. Rose, feeling a mixture of relief and disappointment, for she had keyed herself up for this moment, did not argue the point and they slept.

London exploded on to Rose's consciousness in a burst of noise and bustle like nothing she had ever experienced before. The traffic, the vastness of the endless streets and towering buildings, were almost overwhelming, but most of all the crowded throngs of people, many like her and Matt drawn to the capital by the Great Exhibition, were what fascinated her most of all. Smart people, shabby people and the purely destitute, all seeming to be in a desperate hurry, impinged on her brain in a riot of colour and confusion.

Matt too was overawed. Rose was clinging to his arm as if at any moment he might be prised from her and never seen again. They had found lodgings with a respectable widow in a small house in Pilgrim Street, off Ludgate Hill, where they were in a dark little room overlooking an even darker courtyard. However, it was neat and clean and the food was plentiful and appetizing, even by Rose's critical standards.

'Are you sure we can get an omnibus to Hyde Park from here?' Rose asked him anxiously. 'We've been waiting for ages. Are we standing in the right queue?'

'It's where Mrs Prentiss told us to stand. She should know.'

A woman in front of them who was holding two excited little girls by the hand, looked over her shoulder and said, 'Several of them have gone past without stopping. They were full up already. Everybody's going to the exhibition. Oh here one comes now, perhaps we'll be lucky this time.'

Conveyances of all kinds were rattling along at breakneck speed. Brewers' drays drawn by powerful shire-horses, hansom-cabs and the elegant carriages of the well-to-do, all jostled for space. Darting between them went the crossing-sweepers, risking life and limb so that the better-off need not soil their footwear or risk the hems of their ladies' gowns being dirtied.

From the top of an omnibus was the perfect way to see the city.

'Ooh,' said Rose as they settled themselves, 'I feel a lot safer up here than in the street. Look, Matt — Fleet Street where newspapers are printed.' She craned her neck as they passed down the narrow way.

'And those huge rolls of paper on that there cart must be what they use,' he replied with interest, following Rose's gaze.

As they clip-clopped and rumbled on into the Strand and up Regent's Street Rose's mouth fell open at all the theatres, shops and eating-houses, and the great emporia of the

West End left her speechless. Shops selling nothing but jewels, or furs or luxurious fabrics, leather goods, hats . . . there was no end to them.

'Oh Matt, it's like a dream — I never imagined . . . '

He squeezed her hand.

'Nearly there now, maid, this here is Marble Arch, someone just said.'

The omnibus turned a corner towards Hyde Park, and they saw it. The Crystal Palace — the nickname given to the structure by *Punch* magazine had stuck — rose like some great cathedral of light. Sunshine was striking fire from its arched and lofty central span where the flags of all nations fluttered in colourful harmony, a symbol of the peace, prosperity and global friendship which His Royal Highness Prince Albert had worked so hard to achieve.

'It's like fairyland,' Rose murmured as they entered by the Prince of Wales gate and passed into the hall itself. 'Oh, there are those trees that Kate told me about.' Rose nudged Matt and craned her neck. 'Look, three of them, growing inside the arch. Instead of cutting them down to make room for the building, they put the glass roof over them. Clever.' She smiled up at Matt but he was looking elsewhere and hadn't been listening to a word she'd said.

'See that great fountain, Rose — isn't it clever the way they pump the water round? I bought a catalogue while you were gawping.'

Rose looked indignantly at him. 'I wasn't . . .' she retorted, but he was deep in the booklet.

'We can find our way round a bit better now.' Matt glanced at the galleries running round the second floor and the innumerable side aisles and other rooms. 'Good job I did. Look at it all, maid, we could be here for a week and not see everything.'

'Aren't the flowers gorgeous — it's like a greenhouse in here,' said Rose, entranced by the scents and sounds and sights of her fairy palace.

'Well, he was a gardener, Mr Paxton. It says so here,' Matt replied, consulting the brochure again. 'It looks like a greenhouse because he based the design on a garden room he built at Chatsworth. Where's Chatsworth. Know, do you?'

'No,' Rose said absently. 'Matt, like you said, we're never going to have time to see half of the exhibits, it's just too enormous. Why don't we split up? You want to see the machinery which I don't, and you wouldn't be interested in the fancy goods that I like.'

'What? Separate? Leave you to go round on your own, you mean? Mad, are you? Matt's face was like thunder and he glowered down at her. 'You'd push your way through all these crowds, unaccompanied? Why, you're my wife.' Why, thought Rose fleetingly, did those two words suddenly sound so ominous? 'What sort of girl will people think you are, Rose? Anything could happen, you might be accosted by some low kind of man — then what'll you do?'

'Yes, I'm your wife, Matt. But that doesn't mean we always have to be clamped together, does it?' Rose lifted her chin and looked him in the eye. 'Don't worry about me so, or my reputation. Nobody up here knows me, so I don't care what they think.' There was a slightly sick feeling in the pit of her stomach. This was their first disagreement. She didn't want to have a row with Matt, but surely he was being over-protective. 'I think you're being a little bit unreasonable, don't you Matt?'

'Unreasonable?' he growled. 'Just because I'm concerned about you? This isn't Truro, you know. Suppose you get lost?'

'Buy another copy of that leaflet for me then. It's got a plan of the building in it. I can't get lost if I follow that, and we can agree on a place to meet again at a certain time.' She hated the placatory tone she could hear in her voice, but perhaps this was what married life was like.

'Oh well, all right, but make sure you don't talk to nobody. Nobody at all, do you hear me?'

'I can hear you, Matt.' Rose's voice was cold. 'I shall go to the south-east gallery in the British part of the nave — down there.' She looked up from the catalogue and pointed. 'Silk shawls, lace, embroidery and jewellery, that sounds lovely.'

'The machines what I do want to see are on the north side,' Matt replied as he turned a page. 'There: 'machinery in motion, fire-engines, steam-hammers and mills, power-looms and marine-engines'. There's an engine-house in this place too, with five boilers of a hundred horse-power each, taking the water supply round and working the moving exhibits. Just imagine the size of that!'

Matt had forgotten his previous show of poor temper and his face was alight with enthusiasm. Rose had not.

'No I can't and don't want to,' she retorted. 'That's why I suggested that we separate.'

'Are you sure you'll be all right, Rose?' he added dubiously.

'Of course I shall,' she snapped. 'You'd better tell me where we're going to meet and then take yourself off to your beloved engines.'

'Right. We'll each go off on our own for an hour, then meet at they refreshment rooms on the north end. Can you remember that? The north end, mind. And don't be late, I'll be worrying about you else.'

'Yes Matt. No Matt,' Rose replied tongue in cheek and set off upstairs to the gallery.

Surrounded by opulence and splendour, she hardly knew where to start, until her eye was caught by some magnificent Paisley shawls with sweeping fringes. Beside them was a beautiful silk scarf at least four yards long, embroidered all over with flowers. There were woven ribbons of all hues, patterned with honeysuckle, with twining convolvulus or passion-flowers.

A length of silk brocade, according to its description, contained ' . . . fifteen colours — an exquisite specimen of weaving, which required 30,000 cards and ninety-six shuttles.' Rose knew nothing of weaving techniques but it sounded as impressive as it looked. Beside it was a glowing cashmere scarf, said to have been 'purchased at the exhibition by Her Majesty the Queen.'

Rose wandered on, past sumptuous jewels, past fans with carved ivory sticks, or painted ones, or gilded. There were carved finials for

113

umbrella-handles, whip-handles, parasols. Here were fringed hangings for windows or mantelshelf — with tassels, bobbles or swags. Now carpets, clocks — it was too much. The time! Rose glanced at a mounted clock above her head. An hour had passed like five minutes and it was time to rejoin Matt.

By the time she had pushed her way back through the crowd he was already there and looking anxiously for her. Rose collapsed laughing on to the bench and sighed.

'Oh Matt, I would never have thought there were so many lovely things in the world. And that's only one tiny bit of it. Oh, my poor feet are aching so!'

'I know, so are mine. I must have walked for miles. But they machines was some eye-opener. When I think of what I got to tell Will. He'll never believe it. I tell you Rosie, down home we don't know the half of it, do us?'

Rose nodded. 'Look, there's a table free over there. I'm dying for a cup of tea.' Matt ushered her towards the round, marble-topped table beneath a potted palm.

'Fancy anything to eat with your tea, do you? They've got savoury patties, Bath buns, macaroons, and pound-cake threepence a slice.'

'A piece of cake and a cup of tea would be lovely. And Matt,' Rose lowered her voice, 'I need a halfpenny for the ladies' — um — waiting-room.'

After they were rested and refreshed, Matt produced the catalogue again and leafed through its pages.

'Shall us keep together now and go and see the stands from foreign countries? Manage it can you, bird?'

'Oh yes, now I've had a rest. We want to see as much as we can while we're here.'

★   ★   ★

They stayed until closing time and were enthralled by exhibits as diverse as swords and cutlasses from Turkey, malachite ornaments and astrakhan hats from Russia, Indian carpets, Belgian furniture, tapestry from France and a display of the Queen of Spain's jewels.

As they stumbled out at last, footsore but happy, the gas-lights were softly glowing and the lovely day was over. Central London, however, was as crowded now as in the daytime. Theatre-goers were gathering in the Haymarket and Leicester Square and the smart restaurants and clubs beginning to open their doors for the business of the night.

Although they were both exhausted, Matt and Rose stayed talking far into the night, too excited by it all to relax. At last they climbed into bed and Rose stretched out a hand to extinguish the oil-lamp. The hand shook a little, for surely tonight Matt would . . .

But he had forestalled her.

'Leave it, my handsome, I want to look at you.' And he began to unfasten the many pearl buttons down the front of her nightgown. Rose's flesh quivered. 'Not cold are you? Good,' as she shook her head. 'You know I aren't much of a one for no flowery talk, don't you, maid?' Matt said as he bent his head close and slipped one arm beneath her.

Deftly for so large a man he removed the nightgown, and beneath the covers Rose could see that he was naked.

'But I dearly love you, Rosie. I'll be a good husband and right now I want you as a man wants the woman he loves. Understand, do you?'

His eyes were dark and serious and he looked somehow different, but it must have been the dimness of the lighting, Rose told herself. Her stomach had clenched with apprehension, but Matt only folded her into his arms and drew her close. They kissed as they had done many times, but then Matt's face drifted lower until his lips were on her breasts. Rose arched her back, startled at her own response, while Matt gently stroked her quivering body.

'I'll try not to hurt you, my bird,' he whispered, 'but I've waited so long for this moment.' Then Rose saw it. Just as she remembered — hideous, bloated, monstrous! She was again the terrified ten-year-old Rose, and Reuben Clemo was pressing the whole weight of his great body down upon her. She was being stifled. She could feel the thing against her body, damp, slimy.

'No-o!'

But her screams were stifled by Matt's shoulder.

He felt her stiffen and cringe beneath him and raised himself, thinking he had hurt her.

'I'm being as gentle as I can, Rosie, but I can't wait much longer,' he panted. Then he realized that Rose was pummelling his chest, pushing him away with all her might and gasping raggedly.

'No, no, no! Oh Joss, Joss!' she screamed out in some kind of frenzy.

Then Matt caught sight of her face, and the stark terror he saw there killed his desire stone dead. Rose's skin was ashen, beads of sweat stood on her forehead and her eyes were huge pools brimming with hurt. They seemed glazed and far away.

'Rosie maid, what did I do? There, there, it's all right my bird.' Matt grasped her shoulders, supporting her with his face full of concern. Was it some kind of seizure? He knew little of women, but surely this was more than maidenly modesty?

Suddenly Rose's eyes snapped back to reality and she began to sob.

'Oh Matt — I . . . I . . . can't. You don't know . . . I'm sorry.' Swiftly she averted her eyes from his hurt and wounded face, clasping her arms tightly around herself, rocking and shuddering, with her face veiled by a tumble of bright hair.

'Oh, my Rosie, it's all right, it's all right.' He clasped her in his arms again and she turned to him then and buried her face against his shoulder, still weeping as if her heart would break. Matt let her cry herself out while he softly stroked her hair with one massive hand. 'Never mind, never mind, we'll leave it for now,' he said generously, although his own body was aching for fulfilment. 'Go to sleep, my handsome, we'll leave it until us do get back home. Things'll be different in our own place, you see.'

Rose gave a hiccuping sigh and fell fast

asleep in his arms, worn out by her storm of emotion. Sleep eluded Matt, however, for several hours, during which he wondered who the person called Joss could have been, who had obviously deeply upset Rose at some time or other. He would ask her in the morning.

But he never did, because in the bustle of packing and rushing to catch the train, for they had overslept, it went quite out of his mind.

★　★　★

Once they were home again, the Cornish way of life settled around Rose and Matt and the memory of their trip came to seem like a story which had happened to someone else. Only the many souvenirs they had collected to decorate their new home would remain to prove that it had actually happened.

Matt returned to his work at Wheal Hope and Rose set about making their cottage clean and comfortable. It was perched high on the sheer cliffs above the sea at Porthtowan, cliffs that were riddled with old workings and bare of vegetation from the poisonous chemicals in the soil left by decades of mineral mining.

'Things have been happening since we've

been gone Rosie,' Matt announced, coming in from his first core back at work. He tossed his croust bag into a corner and went through to the scullery to unhook the galvanized bath-tub from its peg. 'Water hot, is it?' he called back over his shoulder.

'There's plenty in the boiler on the range,' Rose replied.

As he sat soaping himself he went on: 'You'll never believe this, maid, but there've been a riot over to the mine.'

'A riot?' Rose put her face around the door and raised her eyebrows. 'What about?'

'Well, you know I been telling you we was all fed up with the way the mine have been neglected? It got to the stage where Captain Trenerry was near tearing his hair out trying to get something done about it, and he sent a deputation of the men to the counthouse meeting to complain.' Matt stood up and wrapped himself in the towel Rose handed to him. 'But the management wouldn't give them a straight answer. They put it off again until the next meeting and the men waiting outside saw red and started throwing stones. There was a fair old brawl, I believe. One of the men was knocked out, and it got quite nasty I should think.' He slipped a clean shirt over his head.

'So where does that leave conditions down the mine?'

'As bad as ever.'

'Can't you get a job somewhere else, Matt?' said Rose anxiously. 'I shall worry about you every time you go down Wheal Hope.'

'I'll try, but there isn't no hope of that, maid. Although tin prices are rising at the moment and everyone do say we're heading for a boom time soon, mine-managers are being very cautious about taking on men until they're sure. Besides, we're doing all right on that lode we're working — good quality ore, 'tis and don't show no sign of petering out yet for a bit.'

'I know the money's nice while we're starting off furnishing the house and everything, but don't take any risks, Matt, will you?' Rose pleaded.

'Trust me, my handsome. I been in mining for fifteen years of my twenty-six, so I aren't no beginner. I reckon I can shift for myself by now.'

'Still, just don't take any risks,' Rose repeated and returned to her polishing. She took a great deal of pride in their home, the home of her own that she had always dreamed of. However, after the bustle of settling in was over, she found that once the daily chores were done she was left with time on her hands, and she found herself wishing that the two of them would become three before too long. A baby would keep her busy and would be company for her when Matt was at work. Rose had eventually steeled herself to accept Matt's love-making without flinching and had now grown accustomed to sharing the high feather-bed upstairs with him. Matt seemed satisfied with it all, but Rose felt herself still yearning for the something unattainable which always seemed to elude her.

Their cottage was in an isolated position, set high above cliffs which plunged sheerly for 200 feet down to the tiny hamlet of Porthtowan set in the cleft of the valley below. A small stream meandered through the valley bottom to a small cove and the sea. Further out, great breakers streamed in from the Atlantic and dashed themselves to pieces on the treacherous rocky coastline. They had no near neighbours and she sorely missed the company and bustle she had been used to at the Red Lion.

Rose found a certain amount of solace in books, which she obtained from market stalls on her weekly visits to Truro for her shopping. She would have liked to discuss them with Matt and share the different ideas and points of view of other people, but although Matt feigned an interest, Rose could tell that it all went over his head, and soon gave up the attempt.

Matt was strictly a practical man and never read anything more than the newspaper. Often he would not even finish that, but would toss it to one side to go and fix the gate or dig the garden. Rose told herself sternly that he was a good husband, although she was very conscious now of the difference in their ages, and that she should be thankful to have such a man to love her so unconditionally.

Friday, however, was the high spot of Rose's week, when she would travel into Truro on the meandering horse-drawn omnibus to do her shopping and call in on her old friends at the Red Lion. Usually Fanny and Kate would snatch a few minutes to chat over a cup of tea and catch up on each other's news.

Today however, Rose arrived at the hotel to find the kitchen in uproar. Eva, who had taken Kate's place when Rose had left and Kate had gone up the scale, was sprawled, screaming apparently with pain, on a wooden settle with her foot up on another chair. Fanny was bending over her and tutting as she felt Eva's ankle, there was a smell of burning from the range and a small kitchen-maid was standing in the doorway of the scullery, staring open-mouthed at the scene.

Rose took instant action and flew to the range, pulling off a pan of potatoes which had boiled dry.

'Haven't you got anything to do?' she shouted to the wide-eyed child. 'Go and peel another panful of potatoes — right away.' The girl scuttled away and Rose turned to Fanny.

'What's happened?' she said as the older woman raised herself to her feet.

'Stop that dratted noise, Eva, you aren't hurt so bad as all that,' Fanny snapped at her and passed a hand over her flushed face. 'Oh, Rose, thank goodness you're here. Couldn't give us a hand for a minute or two, could you? This stupid girl fell down the cellar steps and twisted her ankle. She haven't broken nothing — only wrenched it.'

'I aren't stupid!' The girl protested. 'Tripped over the coal-shovel, didn't I?'

'Wasn't looking where you was to, was you, stupid,' Fanny persisted.

Rose had reached for a clean apron and cap as Fanny was speaking.

'Of course I will, Fan. What shall I do first?'

'Take that tray of pasties out of the oven, if you will. They'll be ready by now. And give that soup a stir while I go and find the witch hazel for this here foot.' She bustled off

At that moment the door to the dining-room burst open and Kate flew in, pink-cheeked and breathless.

'Oh Rose, how lovely to see you.'

Rose smiled and returned the greeting.

'Going to give us a hand, are you?' Kate asked, glancing at the apron. 'Thank goodness — the dining-room's packed. I know it always is on market day, but they all seem to have come in at once.'

She consulted her order book and came further into the room. 'I want two steak-and-kidney pies, two roast beef and a pasty.' She turned to Eva. 'How's the ankle now?' she added, as she took down plates from the vast dresser and rattled them on to a tray.

'A bit of this and she soon won't know it happened,' Fanny answered as she came forward and dabbed at the injury. 'Now, stay there and keep that foot raised. I'll try and get a cup of tea made now that Rose is here to help, bless her.'

'I'll take these orders through, Kate, shall I?' Rose offered. 'You're looking all in.'

'Oh, you're a treasure.' Kate flashed her friend a grateful smile. 'My feet are killing me. I think the worst of the rush is over, though.' She pointed to the loaded tray. 'The roasts are for Dr Hocking and his wife. The pies for a couple of boys from the public school, and the pasty is for the young gentleman in the window-seat.'

Rose repeated her instructions as she nimbly manoeuvred the heavy tray through the crowded room. She had delivered all the orders except one and was making her way towards the window when she suddenly stopped dead in her tracks.

'Rose! Rose Vidney. It *is* you, isn't it?' He scrambled to his feet to greet her.

The voice was the same, and the eyes. But how he'd changed. From the boy she had never forgotten into the most devastatingly handsome man she had ever seen.

'*Joss!*' Rose exclaimed, and the tray slipped from her nerveless fingers with a crash.

★   ★   ★

Joss had recognized Rose immediately as he caught sight of her crossing the room. There was only one vivid face with colouring like that, and the ten years since they had parted vanished as if they had never been.

She had grown into a beautiful young woman. The ragged ten-year-old urchin was now tall and graceful, her slim body swathed in a long white apron, a snowy cap perched on the bright hair he remembered so well.

Her luminous eyes, the deep emerald of an uncut gem, had widened in disbelief as he spoke to her and were now sparkling at him as she recovered herself and smiled.

'I'm so sorry. I — I'll get you another one,' Rose stammered, transfixed. She could hardly take her eyes off him long enough to pick up the tray.

'No, it's not damaged.' Joss waved a dismissive hand as he reached under the chair and retrieved his pasty. 'It'll do. Sit down and talk to me.'

Rose shook her head and glanced over her shoulder towards the kitchen. She couldn't desert them at this busiest of times. She opened her mouth to explain.

'No, of course, you can't do that,' Joss added. 'You're on duty. Look Rose, we have so much to catch up on — can you meet me when you finish?' Rose nodded. 'What time would that be?' Joss asked.

'Half past two,' she said swiftly. 'I'll see you outside this window then.'

Rose staggered back to the kitchen on legs that felt like jelly. Joss — after all these years!

★   ★   ★

Joss was punctual and they arrived together at their meeting place. He was wearing the sling

127

on his arm that she had noticed earlier, and was just about to ask what he had done when he spoke.

'I thought a stroll by the river. Does that suit you, Rose?'

'That'll be lovely,' she agreed, dismissing all thought of the things she had been going to do that afternoon. Today nothing had gone according to plan.

'So you work at the Red Lion. Do you live in?' Joss asked as they strolled along.

'No, I used to, before I was married, but I've left work now — I'm only helping out temporarily today.' Rose bit her lip. Matt had made it clear that he would expect her to be at home when he came in, with a meal waiting on the table.

'I see,' replied Joss. 'My congratulations on your marriage. Who's the lucky man?' Privately he was thinking how enchanting Rose looked and felt a pang of envy for this man, whoever he was. She was wearing a coat and skirt of rust-coloured gabardine trimmed with bottle-green velvet, and a bonnet to match. A soft mist was beginning to roll in over the water and spangles of moisture were gleaming in her hair, which she had swept up at the back.

Little tendrils curled in the nape of her neck like the down of a baby bird, and it was all that Joss could do not to stroke them, and that vulnerable and curiously childlike nape. He controlled himself by cradling his injured elbow in his good hand and turned his attention to the shipping in the busy river, where a tall schooner was in the process of off-loading a cargo of timber.

'His name's Matthew. Matt Lanyon. He's a miner.' Rose glanced up into those eyes of the astonishing violet-blue she remembered so well and her heart turned over. 'How did you break your arm, Joss?' she asked with concern, noticing the movement. 'Is it broken?'

'It's a long story,' he replied, 'but it's partly because I took up mining.'

'*Mining*? You? You're having me on!' Rose's eyebrows disappeared into her hairline and stayed there while Joss told her his story.

'I just can't imagine you as a working miner Joss, in spite of what you say,' she exclaimed as he came to the end. To Rose he would always be gentry, whatever he did.

'So that's what happened to the arm. I'm off work until it heals. I had to come to Truro to the bank today, else we would never have met.'

'It seems crazy to me,' said practical Rose. 'To be born rich, I mean, and not have to work, then throw it all away for an awful job like mining.'

'That's more or less what my father said,' replied Joss grimly. 'He hasn't spoken to me since. But do you know, Rose, in a way it was meeting you that made me see there was another side to life.'

'*Me?*' Rose turned to him in surprise. 'How do you mean?'

'Well, it made me realize what poverty and hardship existed right under my pampered nose. I thought I might be able to do some good if I understood the problems which mining families faced. So I'm trying to learn by first-hand experience.'

'But Joss, I think that's marvellous.' Rose looked at him in admiration. 'So when you inherit the Pencarrow mining interests you'll know what things are like.'

'It's doubtful whether I shall inherit anything,' Joss said drily. 'My father's cut me off, but what I'd really like to do is study engineering. I might go to night-school one day.'

'You'd get on well with Matt.' Rose smiled. 'He's mad on engines.'

'He's a miner, you said?'

'Yes. At Wheal Hope. We live at Porthtowan.'

'Wheal Hope?' Joss shot her a quick look.

'Yes, why?'

'Oh nothing.' He shrugged. 'I went down it

a while back for a look round. Shall we move on? It's getting a bit damp standing here.' He held out his good arm and Rose hesitantly placed her hand upon it. Instantly a tingle of magnetic attraction shot up her arm and she nearly withdrew it. But that would look more pointed than leaving it there. Joss seemed regardless and was strolling casually along, guiding her back over Lemon Quay and through the streets of elegant Georgian houses towards the town. As they walked Rose told Joss of her own life after Sarah and how she had run away from home.

'I asked all over for you, but when they said you'd gone, I thought that you'd run to relations or something. I had no idea . . . ' Joss opened his hand in a gesture of contrition. 'Rose, if only I'd known.'

'You couldn't have done noth — I mean anything about it.' Rose smiled. 'Do you remember how you tried to make me speak 'proper', Joss? I've been practising ever since. I don't often lapse now.'

'I noticed.' Joss returned the smile and squeezed her arm.

'I've never stopped reading, either. You threw me the lifeline that I hauled myself up with, Joss. I'll always be grateful for that.'

A silence descended. In the awkward pause, realization dawned on Rose that they were no longer a pair of innocent children, but man and woman grown. Joss would never be free of his birthright however he might try, and she was another man's wife. There could be no friendship between them now. She must get back to her shopping and her future life with Matt. Rose disengaged her hand which felt suddenly cold and made her farewells.

★   ★   ★

But it was as if fate had arranged that they should meet again. One Friday Rose, head down, came hurrying out of the hotel, for she had spent longer there than she had meant to, when she almost bumped into Joss who was passing at that moment.

'Hey — whoa there!' he chuckled, catching her arm as she staggered and almost fell. 'Where's the fire, then?'

'Joss!' Rose's face lit up like sunshine at the sight of him. 'I'm sorry — I wasn't looking where I was going. Did I hurt you . . . your arm?'

He shook his head.

'It's healing well, but I shall be off work for a few more weeks yet. Apparently there was a small fracture in one of the bones.' He was still holding her elbow, and as he steered her gently into a half-turn, he went on: 'Shall we walk?'

'Oh -er — yes.' Rose's legs were feeling like jelly, her spirits had soared at the sight of him, and she was prepared to forget all her errands if it meant she could spend a few moments in his company.

'You live at Porthtowan, didn't you say?'

Rose nodded.

'How often do you come into Truro?'

'Every Friday,' she replied, incapable of prolonged speech. She felt mesmerized by this man and could hardly drag her eyes away from him.

Joss grinned broadly.

'Oh, that's good. So do I. I'll be able to see you again. Friday shall be our day — I'll meet you here every week until my arm is healed.'

Rose gaped at him. She felt as if Joss was taking her over body and soul and that she was no longer responsible for her own actions.

'Once I go back to work,' he was saying, 'it'll depend which core I'm on. But for now, shall we say the same time and the same place next Friday?'

In a dream, Rose could hardly believe what she was doing, enchanted by his smiling face and the dark fringe of lashes which rose and fell over those fascinating eyes. But oh yes,

yes, her head was nodding. She would be there next Friday.

★ ★ ★

There followed a heady time during which Rose had eyes and ears for nothing and no one but Joss. She thought of him through all her waking hours and dreamed of him at night, longing for the next Friday to come round.

She and Joss spent their precious few hours together in tea-rooms, in the art galleries, museums and exhibitions. They browsed in book-shops and, as the weather became warmer, walked in the park or beside the river.

Rose's everyday life was separate and apart. She lived as if behind a veil of gauze and the only reality was Joss. Rose had fallen deeply and passionately in love for the first time in her life.

Now, too late, she had discovered the elusive something that was everything. That had inspired the poets and painters she admired. And it was as different from what she felt for Matt as is a painting of a flower compared with the delicate perfection of the real thing. So Rose floated for a brief precious spell on a cloud of pure happiness.

5

Joss was surprised to receive an unexpected letter from his mother, delivered by hand to his lodgings. He had heard nothing from his father since the day of his accident and similarly, nothing had yet been done to improve conditions at Wheal Hope.

He slit the envelope, pulled out the single sheet of paper and scanned it.

Dearest Joscelyn, it read, I am unable to stand this estrangement any longer. Not to know where you are and how things go with you down that dreadful mine. I think about you so much and have hardly been able to sleep from worrying. Could you — would you — be able to meet me at Matthews' Hotel in Camborne on Thursday (tomorrow) at around three-thirty? I shall send this with Carnyon the gatekeeper. If this is not convenient, leave a message at the Lodge. I shall wait until four o'clock for you.

Your affectionate Mama.

Joss smiled. The mixture of loving concern and autocratic summons was so exactly like his mother that he could almost hear her voice. Of course he would go; he bore her no ill-will and a meeting on neutral territory would in no way affect his position.

So the following day he strolled through the town and reached Matthews' Hotel at the appointed time. The building occupied one whole side of the main square. Striped awnings above the front door and the windows softened the severity of its granite façade, and potted bay-trees flanked the flight of steps to the entrance.

The Pencarrow carriage was just drawing up as Joss arrived and he crossed the road to help his mother down. Jennifer was wearing a skirt and matching fitted jacket of navy-blue corded silk trimmed with white braid. Her upswept blond hair beneath the navy straw-hat was showing a few threads of grey which had not been there before he left and there were tiny worry lines around her eyes and mouth. Joss hoped it hadn't been worry over him that had brought on these signs of ageing, but refused to feel guilty if it had.

'Mama,' he said, stooping to kiss her cheek. She clasped his hand with her gloved one and gave it a squeeze.

'Joss, it's wonderful to see you. Thank you for coming. Oh!' she started as she caught sight of the light sling that Joss was still wearing. 'Your arm — is that what happened at the — er — counthouse meeting?' Joss nodded as they went up the steps together and into the foyer of the hotel. 'Your father told me how you pushed him out of harm's way and were hurt yourself as a result. That was a very brave thing to do.'

'It was nothing,' Joss replied shortly, 'and it's almost healed. Let's go into the lounge and sit down.'

His mother settled herself on a red-plush banquette and began drawing off her gloves finger by finger.

'He also said that he wanted to call Dr Anderson and have you looked after at home, but you refused.'

'I'm a working miner, mother, and the mine surgeon is good enough for me. He did a fine job and as I say, the arm will soon be out of the dressing altogether. Shall we ring for some tea?'

Jennifer nodded. She was looking her son up and down. Joss had greatly changed. Apart from being leaner and more muscular, with brown and work-roughened hands, he also had an air of quiet assurance about him which was new to her. Her beloved eldest son was a boy no longer, but holding his own in a tough and demanding male world, and

137

secretly Jennifer admired him for it.

'So, Mama,' said Joss as tea arrived, 'why the tête-à-tête?' His eyes crinkled with amusement and he ran a hand through his thick chestnut hair before reaching for a scone which he spread liberally with butter and jam. 'Was it really because you've been missing my company, or is it another reason that brings you here?' He stretched out his long legs encased in shining brown boots, and took a massive bite.

'Er . . . ' His mother hesitated. He was more perceptive than she thought. 'Well, yes.' She lowered her eyes and played with the kid gloves on her lap. 'Actually you're quite right.' She took up her teacup and sipped from it. 'I *have* been longing to see you, but there is something else as well.' Joss smiled. He had always been able to read her mind. 'Your father,' she went on, and Joss's expression instantly changed.

'Did *he* send you?' he broke in.

'No, no.' His mother was quick to assure him. So quick that Joss was in two minds whether to believe her or not. 'But we've both been wondering about the future — your future, that is, and also about the estate as well.' She was fiddling with her napkin, pleating it into tiny folds as she went on: 'Your father is a stubborn man,

Joscelyn, as you know.'

Joss raised an eyebrow.

'You're very like him in that respect. He won't admit it, but I know he regrets his harsh words to you. Both when you left home and when you came to the meeting as well.'

Joss looked at her in genuine surprise.

'Oh yes,' Jennifer went on. 'He told me that he had to put you down because he couldn't afford to lose face in public. But then when you put yourself in danger to save him he felt so bad about it, but he doesn't know what to do to heal the rift.'

She pushed an untasted macaroon around on her plate.

'What I'm trying to say is, I know he'd really love to see you again, but he'll never climb down and be the first to admit he was in the wrong.' She raised bland blue eyes to her son's stormy ones, then recoiled as Joss thumped a fist on the table and set the delicate china rattling.

'If you think for one minute, Mama,' he hissed, 'that *I* am going crawling back to him in some attempt at reconciliation, I can only tell you how mistaken you are.'

Two elderly ladies nearby had turned to stare disapprovingly at the sound of the dancing china. They whispered and nodded behind their hands and hurriedly looked away as Joss glared at them.

'First of all,' Joss wagged a finger at his mother, 'he's got to do something about Wheal Hope. Shoring timber and ladders at least. So you can tell him from me, Mama, that he won't be seeing me until he does.'

'But Joss,' his mother was twisting a lace handkerchief in her fingers and seemed on the brink of tears, 'I know nothing about things like that.'

'It's perfectly simple, Mama, a child could deliver such a message.' Joss threw down his napkin. 'And now if you'll excuse me, I have to go.' He uncurled his long legs and stood up, towering over his mother. 'It's been nice seeing you.' He dropped a kiss on her cheek and strode from the room, leaving her staring helplessly after him.

'But Joss . . . ' she whispered as his feet clattered down the steps and away.

Jennifer had been about to warn him that he was seeing too much of that girl he had taken up with. Of course, a young man must sow his wild oats, but he had been seen about Truro with her hanging on to his arm just as if she were a lady. And that would never do.

★ ★ ★

140

'Kate, how lovely to see you! Come in.' Rose opened the door to her unexpected visitor one afternoon a few weeks later.

'I hoped you'd be in,' said her friend. 'I only decided to come last minute, and I couldn't let you know. Matt in, is he?' She followed Rose into the kitchen and shrugged off her shawl.

'No, he's on afternoons this week. Cup of tea?'

'I'd love one.' Kate settled herself in Rose's bentwood rocking-chair and smoothed down her black skirt. 'I was hoping Matt would be here — I wanted a word with him. It's about Will.'

'What about him? Not ill, is he?' Rose's face was anxious as she turned from the range.

'No, nothing like that. He's thinking of changing his job.'

'You mean he's giving up mining?' Rose stared at her in disbelief. 'What's he going to do?'

'No, not exactly, but he haven't been having much luck where he's to, down Killifreth. He been there all his working life — he followed his father down, see. But now he says he's going into the arsenic over to Bissoe. It do make more money, and he wants to put a bit by for when — when we do . . . '

141

Kate broke off and blushed.

'Oh Kate, you're going to marry him!' Rose put down her cup and clasped her hands in delight.

'Well, he haven't asked me yet, but we got a sort of — understanding — you know? But,' her face clouded, 'I'm that worried about him, Rose, it's some dangerous work. Pure poison.'

Rose looked at her friend and raised her eyebrows in concern as Kate went on:

'I've heard men say it do poison the air and poison the land so that nothing don't grow no more. And it do poison men what work in it. I was wondering, see, if Matt could have a chat to him and see if he can't talk him out of it. Ask him will you, when he comes in?'

'Of course I will.' Rose was appalled. 'I've seen — and smelt — the arsenic works, of course, and I know that arsenic's a by-product of mining, but I've never given it much thought, because I don't know anybody who works in it.' She glanced out of the window as she spoke, recalling all she had heard about the process. 'Don't they burn it off in those furnaces with very tall chimneys?'

'You mean they calciners. Yes.' Kate sipped her tea and replaced the cup on its saucer. 'The arsenic powder — it's white, like flour — gets collected in underground flues and the men have to shovel it into barrels. They don't have no protection — only handkerchiefs tied over their noses and mouths. That's all they got against breathing in the fumes.' Her face was sombre.

'What's arsenic used for?' Rose asked, curious.

'It do go up-country. They use it in lots of ways, Will says. The cotton mills do take it for fixing coloured dyes, for one thing.' Kate shrugged. 'And the farmers do use it for killing insects. A lot of it do go abroad, to America, he said, to use against boll-weevils in the cotton fields. Anyway, it's always in demand, so it's steady work, see. He's gone over there to see if there's a job going. We came down on the bus together as it's my day off.'

'Another cup?' Rose offered, rising.

'No thanks. Um — Rose . . . ' Kate looked up with an odd expression on her face. 'There's another reason too, why I came.' She looked down at her lap and twisted a handkerchief in her fingers.

Rose stared at her friend. She's actually looking *embarrassed*, thought Rose in surprise, wondering what was coming.

'Oh? What was that?' She moved from her seat on the low window-sill, where she had been enjoying the early summer sunshine on

143

her back, poured herself another cup of tea and came to sit beside Kate on one of the kitchen chairs.

'It's — it's about this affair you're having, Rose.' Kate lifted her head and looked her friend directly in the face. 'Oh, I know you'll say it's none of my business,' she raised a hand as Rose drew her brows together and opened her mouth to speak, 'but you're heading for real *trouble*, you know.' Now that Kate had taken the plunge, she couldn't stop talking and her face flushed as she let forth a torrent of words as if a dam had burst. 'Don't you realize you're making a complete fool of yourself — and of Matt too? Your precious Joss is *gentry*, Rose, he's only playing around with you. Can't you see — ?'

Rose glared at her and snapped as she broke Kate off in mid-sentence. 'Joss isn't *like* that. And anyway,' she added defiantly, 'we're just *friends*.'

'Pooh!' said Kate expressively.

'Friends,' Rose repeated. 'That's all. I don't want to fall out with you, Kate, but you said it yourself: it's none of your business, nor anyone else's.' Rose lifted her chin and her eyes flashed sparks of green fire. She jumped to her feet with a swirl of blue skirts and stood looking down at her friend's curly head.

Undeterred by this display of temper, Kate went on:

'For goodness sake, Rose, you're a married woman — not some dewy-eyed child what don't know no better.' Kate jumped to her feet. 'And what about Matt?' she turned on Rose and wagged a finger. 'Have you thought about the effect it will have on him? Because the word's getting around, you know, with you being seen all over Truro with your fancy man. It's only a matter of time before someone, out of the kindness of their heart, will mention it to him.' Kate paced the length of the kitchen and back.

'You've been in another world since Joss turned up. Matt could have noticed for himself by now. I know he isn't the brightest, but he do dearly love you, Rose. And he's too good a man to be treated like this.'

Kate paused to draw breath.

'I haven't done anything that I'm ashamed of,' Rose hissed furiously. 'I look after Matt like I always have done. If I come to Truro to see my friends, male and female, that's my business and Matt's never minded me doing it.'

'But put it like this will you,' Kate persisted. 'How would you like it if once a week Matt kissed you goodbye and went off gallivanting with another woman *friend*?

145

Would you be forgiving and turn a blind eye? I don't think so.' Kate stood with arms akimbo as she railed at Rose, the brown ringlets which framed her face fairly bouncing with her anger.

'Oh Kate, stop *nagging* — you're worse than some old *fishwife*!' Rose leapt to her feet and stamped a foot as her shredded nerves finally gave way to floods of scalding tears.

Kate, having driven home her point, was all comfort and concern. She dried Rose's face with her own handkerchief, led her back to her chair and poured another cup of tea.

After which she returned home, leaving Rose with her bubble of joy pricked and her feet meeting solid ground for the first time in several weeks.

★   ★   ★

Rose had been telling no more than the truth when she had said that she and Joss were only friends. What Kate had said, however, had struck home, and Rose was suffering agonies of conscience, knowing her friend was right, and knowing too that she was deeply in love with Joss.

She knew intuitively that Joss felt the same. In a touch, in a look. Sometimes when their eyes met the tension was like an undercurrent

146

waiting to sweep them off their fee[t] [and carry] them into deeper waters. But alway[s] [some kind] of normality would slip into plac[e] [and save] them.

But for how much longer? Rose tortured herself with the knowledge that they would have to part sooner or later, and that it would be the end of the happiest period of her life. She lay awake far into the night, her nerves in shreds, her body yearning for the impossible. Matt had made love to her in his usual fashion, taking what he needed and leaving her unfulfilled and sleepless.

Coldly and objectively Rose faced the fact that there were two courses of action open to her. She could and should send Joss away and never see him again. A shaft of desolation struck her like a physical blow at the very thought. How could she face her mundane life without him? She almost wished Joss had never come back into her life — at least, before he had, she had not known what she had been missing. But to lose him now — oh however can I bear it? She screamed silently into the depths of the night. It would be like losing a limb.

The alternative was to leave Matt. To break his heart. To break her own solemn vows. But what sort of a monster would she be to treat a man so cruelly, who had never shown her

... hing but gentle kindness and his own
...and of love? Daylight came and she rose to
face the world again, haggard, unrested and
no further forward.

Rose's guilt-ridden conscience made her
especially attentive to Matt for the next few
days, as if doing so would make up to him for
her misdemeanours. She even made an effort
to finish knitting the woollen muffler which
was to be his birthday present. It had been
thrust to the bottom of her work-basket ever
since she had met Joss, forgotten and
neglected like her husband.

The birthday came and went, and soon
Friday was looming disturbingly close. She
would have to make a decision, and soon.

★   ★   ★

Born to be a troublemaker and with a chip on
his shoulder that was fast becoming an
obsession, Reuben Clemo was adept at
keeping his ear to the ground and his eye on
the main chance, seizing any opportunity to
pick up scraps of information that could be
turned to his own advantage.

His vegetable round had been steadily
expanding and now included Great Place.
This was partly due to the affair he was
having with one of the kitchen-maids there.

Oh, there was nothing serious about it, he told himself, both of them knew that. But Janie Snell was a pert little baggage and as eager for it as he was. Added to which, she was a useful source of gossip. During the cold weather they managed to sneak off for an hour to a disused loft in the stables while the housekeeper's back was turned. Now that summer was coming they would meet in the woods.

In this way Reuben had been kept up to date with goings-on at the big house, for Janie's tongue was as loose as her morals. He had learnt of Joss's row with his father, and of his job at Dolcoath.

Today, after Reuben had pulled her down beneath him in a mossy clearing and they were lying panting in the aftermath, Janie said:

'Hey Rube, have you heard the latest?'

Reuben rolled over and seized one of her full breasts.

'No, what?' he replied as he gave the nipple a tweak. Janie edged closer.

'It's Mr Joss. He's carrying on with that Vidney girl that was. You do knaw she — some relation of yours, idden she? Ginger hair, thinks she's too good fer round here. Spends all her time up Truro.'

She pushed her lank hair out of her eyes

and laid her head on Reuben's matted chest. He was listening carefully.

'Oh yeah. Well? Go on,' he said, running a hand down her spine.

'Ooh, that tickles!' Janie giggled. 'Anyway, I knowed she years ago when she didn't have no clothes to her backside hardly. She's married and all. They do live down Porthtowan near to Ma. Her husband Matt Lanyon's a miner down to Wheal Hope. And her carrying on with Mr Joss bold as brass! Idden no better'n we for all her stuck-up airs, is she, Rube? At least what we do don't harm no one else, do it, my handsome?'

'Thass right bird, hitch yer skirt up a bit higher, thass of it. Like that do yer?'

'Ooh Rube, you are a one!' Janie purred like a kitten. 'Down a bit, oh that's lovely.' And she wriggled beneath him in delight as Reuben digested this interesting information.

A few days later he was on his way to Porthtowan.

★　★　★

'Who are you? What do you want?' Matt opened the door abruptly, not pleased at being woken up. He had been doing a week of nights and had just dropped off to sleep.

150

Rose had gone down to Porthtowan to the shop, as Reuben well knew. He had been watching the house and waiting for just this opportunity.

'I'm a friend of Rose's — related to her too, as a matter of fact. First cousins we are. Reuben Clemo.' He extended a hand. 'Pleased to meet you, Matt.'

Matt ignored the hand.

'I've heard of you,' he snapped. 'What are you doing here?'

'I got a bit of news fer you. Something important.' Reuben looked quickly over his shoulder. No good for Rose to come back yet. 'Cup of tea going, is there?'

'No. I was in bed, I've been on nights. Get on with it, can't you?' Matt said irritably and kept him on the doorstep.

'I thought you had a right to know how very friendly your wife have become with another man.' Reuben smirked. 'For a little consideration like, I could tell you his name.' He thrust both hands into his pockets and leered at the other man.

'You mean you want *money*?' Matt's face went brick red. 'Why you . . . you . . . ' Both hands flew out and he grabbed Reuben by the lapels of his dirty jacket.

They were both big men and tough from manual work, but fury made Matt the

151

stronger. He shook the other man like a rabbit.

'You'd better tell me — you evil-minded . . . foul-mouthed . . . ' Through clenched teeth came words Matt hadn't realized he knew. Reuben's head met the doorframe with an almighty crack and he sagged in Matt's grip.

'What's his name, tell me his name or I'll tear you limb from limb!' Matt hissed. Reuben weakly raised an arm in surrender. Matt flung him away in disgust and Reuben crumpled at the knees and slid to the ground in a heap.

'Joss Pencarrow,' he croaked, one hand at his throat. 'Over to Great Place.' He managed to fire one parting shot. 'I thought, when a man's being cuckolded see, he do have a right to knaw.'

'Get off my doorstep, you devil!' Matt roared and turned to go inside.

'Give my regards to Rosie,' came a whisper.

Matt slammed the door and leaned against it, panting. He was light-headed from fury as well as lack of sleep and knew he could not go back to bed now. His stomach was churning as he turned Reuben Clemo's words over and over in his mind.

Joss, he had called him. Stupid sort of name for a man, he thought irrelevantly. But he'd heard it before somewhere. Joss! That had been the name that Rose had called out the first time he . . . they . . . So this was nothing new! She must have known him for years. She had been going with him even before they were married!

What should he do? What could he do? Matt sank into a chair and buried his face in his hands. Should he face Rose and have her deny it? But what if she actually admitted it? Either way, nothing would ever be the same again. Matt saw his marriage, his home and his life disappearing like a puff of smoke. He'd be the laughing-stock of the neighbourhood — and was already, if that lout was to be believed. He would never be able to hold up his head again.

When Rose returned he was waiting for her.

'Oh, Matt? I thought you'd be in bed by now,' she remarked, passing him with a bag of groceries.

'Couldn't sleep,' he muttered.

'You're looking a bit flushed. Sickening for something, are you?' Rose rested her bag on the kitchen table and began to unpack it.

'Aye, maybe I am.' Something in his tone of voice made Rose turn and look her husband in the eye. His face was stern and set. 'You going Truro, are you, maid?'

'It's market-day Matt. You know I always go on Fridays. There are so many things I can't get in the village.' She lifted her chin and glanced at the clock on the shelf behind her. 'Time I was moving. The bus'll be here soon.' She reached for her plaid cloak which she had just taken off, and swung it around her shoulders.

'Rose, there's something I got to say . . . '

'Right, get a move on then,' she replied with impatience.

'I may be stupid, but I'm not so dumb as what I don't know what's going on — '

'Going on?' Rose, startled, wheeled round to face him, her heart pounding against her ribs. He knew then. In a strange way it was almost a relief.

'Between you and that young . . . ' He spat expressively into the hearth and glowered at her with naked fury smouldering in his brown eyes. Rose had never seen this side of him. Colour flooded her face and her legs began to tremble.

'I aren't putting up with it, Rose, understand me, do you? Hear this and take it in.' The deep eyes locked with hers and held as he went on: 'I've loved you since you was ten years old. I waited and watched you growing up into a beautiful woman — the only woman I ever wanted. I still love you more than life itself, and always will. But I won't be made a fool of. It's him or me — as simple as that. Got the message, have you?'

Rose opened her mouth to speak, to justify herself, to tell him that there was nothing more than friendship between her and Joss, that she had never been unfaithful, nor broken her marriage vows — but Matt raised a brawny hand to prevent her.

'Just don't say nothing. Go and do your marketing — and *just* your marketing.' His voice was dangerously quiet. 'If you aren't back on that there early bus, then don't bother to come back no more, Rose. Because I shan't *want* you back, see?' He turned on his heel and left the room, leaving Rose rooted to the spot and shaking like a leaf in the wind.

Silence fell. Rose clapped a hand to her mouth. Matt had never spoken to her like that before. He hadn't even given her a chance to reply — to put her side of the story! Condemning her out of hand! Ready to believe the worst of her! Whipping herself into a fury which served to smother the small voice of her conscience, Rose gritted her teeth and clasped her cloak about her. If that's the way he feels then let him, she said grimly. And she slammed the door loudly behind her.

All the way to Truro as the lumbering

horse-bus dragged its way up hill and down, Rose continued to seethe. How dare Matt speak to her like that! Chastising her like a naughty child. Delivering an ultimatum without giving her a chance to answer back. Serve him right if she *didn't* come back. See how he would like that — coming home to an empty house and no meal on the table or clean shirts in his drawer. He would soon be *begging* her to come back then.

★　★　★

Joss could tell that something was wrong as soon as saw the set line of Rose's mouth and the misery in her eyes.

'What's the matter?' he asked with concern as he joined her on the bench where she was sitting, under a rustling sycamore tree in St Mary's Square.

'Oh Joss,' Rose's lower lip trembled. She half-turned in her seat and clutched his arm. 'It's Matt. He's heard gossip about us. You know what wagging tongues are like. And he thinks the worst.'

Joss squeezed her hand.

'I suppose it was bound to happen,' he said grimly. 'People are never happier than when they're making mischief. I wonder who told him. Did he say?'

Rose shook her head.

'I never thought to ask,' she replied. 'For one thing I was too upset and for another, Matt never let me get a word in. Joss, he wouldn't let me explain or . . . anything . . . ' Tears welled out of her eyes and began to creep down her pale face.

Joss pulled her to her feet.

'Look, let's get away from here and go somewhere where we can talk. I've got Captain stabled at the George. Now that this arm is so much better I can ride again. Captain was the only luxury I didn't give up when I went down the mine.' He smiled and gently cupped her cheek. 'Come on. You can ride up in front of me. We'll take the coast road and stop off there for a while. Then I'll drop you back to Porthtowan.'

There was little chance of conversation as Joss gave Captain his head and they went spanking along above the azure water. Sea-campion and cushions of thrift flowed down the cliff-side in a stream of white and shell-pink. The scent of gorse in flower filled the air with coconut, and its brilliant gold mingling with the purple of heather made a regal carpet beneath the horse's hoofs.

The ride was utterly exhilarating. Rose leaned back into Joss's embrace and closed her eyes. Her hair and cloak streamed out behind them and she was acutely conscious of being cherished and cared for. Wrapped around as she was by Joss's strong warm arms, the colour came back into her frozen face and her spirits lifted in spite of everything.

Joss reined the horse in at last and turned into a narrow track which led to Wheal Hope cove, just around the point from the mine. Here he dismounted and lifted Rose down. They looked at the sandy beach below and their eyes met.

'Shall we?' Joss asked, and Rose nodded. He tied the reins to a sturdy gorse bush and extended his hand.

The cove was deserted and peaceful. The tide was far out beyond the reef of rocks which fringed it on the western side, and a golden crescent of smooth sand stretched down to the water. The sun was just peaking the black cliff behind them and everything sparkled, newly washed and clean. The air was fresh with the crisp tang of salt and seaweed about it, and was growing warmer by the minute.

They strolled out from the shadow cast by the cliff into a patch of sunlight. Small pools set among the rocks were still and deep, hiding the secret life below the water with delicately coloured weed of coral, russet and brilliant green. Joss sank on to a comfortable slab and tugged at Rose's hand, pulling her down beside him.

'Now tell me all about it,' he said, not releasing her hand. He gave it a squeeze with his big, warm one and Rose's taut nerves began to unwind. It was impossible not to relax in this glorious spot, with the soothing sound of lapping waves all around.

So she unburdened herself of her row with Kate, of Matt's terrible ultimatum and of her own misery. Joss listened in sympathetic silence until she had finished.

'No one believes me, Joss, no matter how often I tell them the truth. That we're *not* — well, doing anything wrong, you know? That we're just old friends.' She turned her head and met his eyes. Joss nodded thoughtfully and sighed, then he lowered his eyes to scuff in the sand with the toe of one boot.

A silence fell between them. Rose had been trailing one hand in a tiny pool in the rock beside her and she idly pulled out a strand of emerald seaweed.

'That's called 'mermaid's hair',' she remarked absently as she wound it round her finger. The weed immediately lost its fern-like beauty. 'That's just what I feel like myself — a bedraggled, stringy mess.' Her forlorn and desolate expression tore at Joss's heart and he slipped a comforting arm around her waist.

'It's exactly the shade of your eyes,' he remarked, 'and you're not the least bit bedraggled. Rose, you are beautiful,' he added and his voice dropped to a whisper. 'Oh my poor little mermaid!' His voice was husky with emotion, and Rose turned swiftly and buried her face in his shoulder as the scalding tears came flooding down her face, and then she was in his arms.

With a gentle finger Joss dried first one eye and then the other, before bringing his mouth down to hers in a long and lingering kiss. The sky reeled above her as Rose gave herself up for lost, drowning in the depths of those violet eyes and the desperate longings of her own body.

Deep down, the one part of her brain still capable of rational thought was screaming defiance at Matt. You didn't believe me before — it was you who drove me to this. Now I'll give you something to *really* worry about. And as she returned Joss's kiss with a passion all the fiercer for being so long denied, the seaweed fell from her fingers and slipped back into the water, immediately regaining its former beauty and grace.

'Over here,' said Joss softly. He half-carried her towards a tiny cave tucked underneath the cliffs. The floor was strewn with minute crystalline fragments of crushed shell — opal, pearl and pink, gleaming white and iridescent blue. The sun's rays shone through the cave mouth and it was warm and dry inside. Joss gently pillowed Rose's head on a sandy bank and stretched out beside her. His hands were firm and warm as they removed both her clothing and his own, and they lay for some time with their eyes locked as their hands explored each other, touching, stroking, marvelling.

'Oh, my Rose, I've waited so long for this,' Joss murmured, combing his fingers through her bright hair. Rose was in another world where nothing mattered but the two of them and this moment. Here in this rocky fastness with the pounding surf echoing the throbbing of her own heart and the calling of sea-birds all around, she was a different person, her true self, and need pretend no longer.

Then the floodgates of all their pent-up emotions suddenly burst and carried them away into those deeper waters she had been both longing for and dreading. Joss's long, sensitive fingers aroused feelings inside Rose's being that she had not known existed and raised her soul to heights of bliss of which she had never dreamed.

Sky-clad, with the song of the surf in their

ears and the warmth of the sand beneath them they were just two more of nature's children, sharing their love in the way of all natural creatures since the beginning of time. And like other wild things, their ultimate cries of rapture were carried on the wind to mingle with the fluting calls of the great sea-birds that wheeled above them.

Afterwards they fell asleep, exhausted by the strength of their emotions, and it was a long time before they began to stir. By now the sun had long passed overhead and the air was cooler. Rose sat up and pushed her hair back from her face. Joss lazily pulled his clothes towards him and began to dress, helping Rose with hers. When at last they emerged from their paradise, the sun was indeed way past its zenith and was sinking slowly towards the western sea.

Rose saw it with a lurch of her heart. The bus she should have been on had departed hours ago and she realized that from this moment her life would never be the same again. But as Joss bent to place his lips against her throat and a shiver fluttered through her body, Rose sighed with contentment. She could face any problems to come, with the thought of this glorious day to sustain her.

Joss raised his eyebrows at the sight of the

sinking sun and turned to Rose with concern on his face.

'Look how late it is, Rose. What about Matt? Would you like me to see you home?'

Rose firmly shook her head, her own face grave now.

'That would only make things worse. I must face up to this on my own, Joss.'

His mouth came down fiercely on to hers in one last, long kiss before they turned to climb back up the cliff path together, arms around each other's waists, reluctant to draw apart until the very last minute.

6

Matt was in a state of emotional upheaval as he strode across the springy turf on his way back to the mine. Rose had not returned on the early bus, and he was worried sick about her. He told himself he had been too hard on her — too hurt and too angry to listen to her side of the story — he had believed what that lout had told him, every word of it, and had flown right off the handle.

But it was only because he loved her so much. For all he really knew it could all have been a pack of lies, but he had acted first and only started to think about it afterwards. Suppose Rose had taken him at his word and really left him? How could he bear it? He would have to find her, make it up, for how could he live the rest of his life if he had lost her?

It was very quiet and the June sunshine was warm on his back. The sea was a pure forget-me-not blue and the grass beneath his feet was full of small wild flowers. Tiny blue butterflies hovered about them like cut-out scraps of sky. But Matt saw none of this natural beauty. He trampled them beneath his boots as he strode along the cliff path with his head down, oblivious to anything but the image of Rose's face.

Laughing, tender, childlike, vulnerable, excited, all her varying moods and expressions played behind his eyes and he could not free himself from them.

'Oh my Rosie,' he sighed aloud.

Matt was jerked abruptly out of his reverie by the chink of metal on stone. Then he stopped dead in his tracks as a huge chestnut stallion loomed over him, blocking the narrow path.

'Hello boy,' he said cautiously, stepping round the animal. It was the most beautiful piece of horseflesh he had ever seen. Standing a good seventeen hands high, it had the delicate legs and finely muscled lines of a thoroughbred. Worth a small fortune. What the hell was a valuable animal like this doing wandering loose on the cliff edge? Had it shed its rider? Had someone fallen over? Then Matt caught sight of a thorny branch entangled in the reins. He lifted them and removed it.

'So, you were tied up and broke free, did you?' he murmured, stroking the velvet nose. The horse looked back at him, its eyes full of intelligence, fringed with long black lashes that any girl might have envied, and blew softly.

Matt gathered up the reins, walked the horse a short distance and tied it firmly to a fence-post. Maybe its rider was not far off. He went along the way the horse had come from and walked almost a mile without seeing any signs of life. He would be late for core at this rate, he thought crossly, and was about to give up the fruitless search.

By now he had come to the place known locally as 'Devil's Lair', where sheer cliffs of black rock plunged 200 feet over a yawning abyss to the boiling sea below. Many a vessel had foundered here. Black fangs of rock jutted out of the water ready to trap the unfortunate, and strong currents always tugged and sucked around their base.

As Matt approached the edge and peered cautiously over, he fancied he could hear voices in the distance. Then, rounding a bend of the track and coming towards him along the cliff-path he saw a young couple, chatting and laughing together with their arms entwined around each other's waists.

His wife and her lover. Blood surged to Matt's head and danced dizzily behind his eyes. With a savage roar he launched himself towards them.

'Whore! Whore! You . . . you . . . *trollop*,' he bellowed at Rose, seizing her arm and flinging her to the ground.

'Take your hands off her!' Joss yelled, coming for him. Matt's great fists, each the size of a small ham, flailed the air as he threw himself at the other man. Joss ducked and the first deadly left-hander caught him a glancing blow on his scarcely healed shoulder. Joss flinched and, recovering from the disadvantage of surprise, he tried to dodge his enraged opponent as the two men circled each other like wild animals, Matt waiting for an opening to knock Joss senseless, Joss trying to defend himself as the two men teetered on the very brink of the chasm.

'Stop! Stop! Joss — Matt — *stop it*!' Rose screamed. They were so near the edge that she could hardly bear to look, yet paradoxically could not tear her eyes away from the ghastly nightmare scene. She clapped a hand to her mouth, sick and horrified, but powerless to halt either of them.

Matt was deaf and blind to everything but the urge to crush the other man to pulp. Joss was more agile than he was and had learnt to use his feet during boxing lessons, but this was no gentleman's fight. Maddened with rage, Matt was panting for breath and gathering himself for another onslaught of hammer blows.

Joss had managed to bloody Matt's nose

but he was handicapped by his arm which was sending out signals of excruciating pain no matter how he tried to shield it. Then Matt returned a hefty blow which landed squarely on Joss's old injury and he heard the crack of splitting bone as it opened up again. Screaming in agony, Joss clutched at his arm and Matt took the opportunity to follow it up with an upper-cut to his jaw. Joss hurtled backwards over the cliff and disappeared. Matt, coming to his senses at last, teetered horrified on the edge for a long moment, then with a howl which echoed eerily after him, also plunged sideways and down.

Rose's agonized scream echoed from the black walls of rock, and a pair of nesting gulls flew startled into the air, adding their own raucous cries. Shaking in every limb, she crawled to the brink and looked over. Both men had come to rest on a jutting outcrop of rock about half-way down. One was lying with arms outflung like a rag-doll, the other was struggling into a sitting position. Which was which Rose had no means of knowing. Both men had been wearing dark clothing and they were too far away to make out their features.

Rose's throat was so dry that her tongue felt too big for her mouth and she could not swallow. She dragged herself up on to legs

168

like jelly and gathered her skirts high, as she ran stumbling and gasping towards Wheal Hope.

★　　★　　★

They came running as soon as Rose raised the alarm, with ropes and tackle, with blankets and planks for makeshift stretchers, with horses and a cart. The miners of Wheal Hope were well used to accidents and to dealing with sudden emergencies.

'Don't you fret, missus, we'll soon have they up,' panted the first man to reach the scene. Rose had come back in the cart they had brought for transporting the injured men. Or the bodies, cried a small inner voice. No! She would not listen, could not bear to imagine the unthinkable. Of course they would be all right. Both of them. These bustling, capable men would rescue them.

They were going over the edge now on ropes and pulleys, two of them sliding down the sheer cliff as if they did it every day. Rose stood like stone, one hand to her mouth as the rescue party reached the first injured man and signalled to those on the top to stop paying out the rope.

They perched precariously on the tiny ledge, looking down at the motionless man. It was only just wide enough to hold the four of them. From this height they all looked like dolls to Rose, or match-stick men. She watched transfixed as each successive wave washed a little higher over their feet. At last one man managed to hoist the casualty over his shoulder in a fireman's lift. The other gave the signal to raise the rope and began to guide the carrier as they started the long slow haul to the top.

All of a sudden however, as Rose watched helplessly from above, a huge wave propelled by a freshening breeze and the incoming tide, washed high over the rocks at the foot of the cliff. It reached up a huge tongue as far as the ledge and as she screamed aloud, licked at the other man like a ravening animal and swept him headlong into the abyss. In an instant he had disappeared from sight in the swirling water.

Her mouth was too dry to call out again, her scream had become a hoarse and throaty quaver of sound that was at once drowned by the seabirds' calling, as she stared transfixed at the spot where the man had disappeared. The roiling water had completely swallowed him up and now continued to hurl itself against the unyielding rock in a fury of lashing spray. The other men had seen it too and there were hoarse, urgent shouts as another rescuer prepared to go below. But no one could have battled with that maelstrom and survived.

And which of them had it been? Matt or Joss? Rose had bitten a thumbnail to the quick before the rescuer had risen far enough up the cliff for her to recognize who it was he carried. Then her soul lifted in an uncontrollable surge of relief and joy as she saw that it was Joss. At the same moment she knew with a sickening lurch of her stomach that Matt had been swept away. The seesawing of such raw emotion was too much, and Rose turned aside to retch helplessly into a stand of heather bushes nearby.

The rescuers were over the rim at last, panting and gasping beneath their load. But as they gave up the burden into other outstretched arms they hardly paused for breath.

'More rope,' one grunted before slipping over the edge again to help his colleague, who was nearing the bottom of the cliff.

'Hurt bad, is he?' asked one of the miners, coming forward as Joss's still form was being laid on the makeshift stretcher. 'Looks like it,' he added solemnly, staring down at the motionless figure.

Rose recovered herself and dropped weakly to her knees beside Joss, impatiently pushing her hair out of her eyes. All the pins had scattered in the heather.

'Is he dead?' She grabbed the stranger's arm. 'Tell me he's not dead!'

'I don't think so, missus. He's badly, but I believe he's breathing.' The man had an ear to Joss's chest. 'I think your husband'll be all right, my dear.' He straightened up. 'The mine doctor's on his way now.'

Rose glanced up at the sound of approaching hoofs, then down at Joss. His face was a thready mass of blood and broken skin where the rock had ripped it as he landed. One eye had swollen and was a mass of purple bruising. That must be where one of Matt's punches had landed. Rose flinched at the sight of the unnatural angle of his arm. It was obviously broken again. Her stomach heaved afresh at the thought of the pain he must have suffered. He was better off unconscious — when he came round his agony would really begin.

When, or . . . if. Panic gripped her and she seized one of his hands in hers.

'Oh Joss, speak to me!' Rose laid her other hand on his cold forehead and groaned. 'Don't die, don't leave me,' she pleaded. But beneath the dirt and blood the beloved face was colourless, almost grey, and his lips were blue and bloodless.

'He — he's not my husband,' Rose gulped. 'My husband's still down there somewhere.' The man looked curiously at her. 'Well, anyroad, the doctor will see to he now, and the men are down there searching for the other fellow. Best stay out of the way, missus,' he warned. 'They'll bring him up as soon as they can.'

The man's face was grave. He wants me out of the way because they know Matt is . . . is . . . Rose moved away and sank on to the soft turf. She buried her face in her shaking hands. The horror of it all was almost too much to take in. Shock had numbed her senses and she was beginning to shake all over. She felt cold to her bones, although around her the sun still shone warmly down. Bees were still humming merrily among the clumps of sea-pinks at her feet too, just as if nothing untoward had happened at all.

The mine doctor had finished examining Joss and they were lifting the stretcher into the cart.

'Where are you taking him?' Rose scrambled to her feet and called after the men as they whipped up the horse and the cart began to move.

'Great Place, missus. To Mr Pencarrow's home, see.'

Wait — she had been going to say — wait for me, I'm coming too, but had stopped herself just in time. For she could have no part in this — to the rest of the world they were nothing to each other. Joss was being taken further from her by the minute and there was nothing Rose could do about it.

The mine doctor, seeing her distress and misinterpreting it, came across and laid a hand on her shoulder.

'Mrs Lanyon, why don't you go home and wait for news of Matt there? They may be some time looking for him — even perhaps waiting — er — until the tide turns . . . '

If they're searching for a body. Rose could finish the sentence for him.

'All right, Doctor, I will.'

'Is there anyone who can come and keep you company? Friends, neighbours, relations perhaps? Anyone I can call for you?'

'You're very kind, but no. I shall be quite all right, thank you. I have friends in Truro that I can turn to if necessary.' Suddenly the need to be alone was overwhelming.

'Well, at least let me give you a lift home. Jessie's back is broad enough for both of us.'

Rose accepted the extended hand. She couldn't get back to the cottage fast enough. To hide her anguish from the world, to weep alone. For herself, for Joss and for her wronged husband whom she might never see again.

★ ★ ★

When a sudden knock came at the door, Rose jumped as if shot. She scrambled up from the bed where she had been lying, hastily tidied herself and ran to open it. Dusk had fallen; she had not realized how much time had passed, but now the blue haze of a summer night lay over sea and sky.

On the doorstep stood the village constable, and the miner who had gone down the cliff a second time to look for Matt.

'Mrs Lanyon. Good evening.' The policeman removed his helmet and tucked it under his arm.

'Mr Curtis.' Rose's hand went to her mouth, 'and?' She turned to the other man.

'John Richards, ma'am.' He briefly clasped her hand.

'Wh — what — it's Matt, isn't it? Have you found him? Is he . . . ?'

'May we come in?' asked the constable.

'I'm sorry, of course.' Rose stepped aside. 'Please do.' She ushered them inside and closed the door, then led the way into the parlour.

'I'm afraid I've got some disturbing news,'

he went on. 'Shall we sit down?'

He's not very old, thought Rose irrelevantly, and he's hating having to do this. She watched the shining black boots scuffing at her bright rag-rug, and the constable's hands twisting his helmet round and round. The burly miner was perched on the very edge of his chair, looking as if he would rather be anywhere else at all than in this position.

The policeman cleared his throat.

'I have to tell you, ma'am, that the rescue party have found a body washed up on the shore near where your husband fell. We have every reason to believe that it is his.'

Rose clapped both hands to her face. She had started shivering again.

'Oh Matt,' she whispered.

'I'm so sorry,' he added.

'Thank you.' Rose's response was automatic.

'The body has been taken to the mortuary of course. And when — er — that is, when you feel able to, we would like you to come and identify it formally, if you will.'

Rose shuddered, then nodded. The policeman rose to his feet.

'I have to be going now, ma'am, but Mr Richards has something else to tell you and will stay as long as you need his company. Don't get up,' he raised a hand as Rose began to move. 'I can see myself out.'

Rose looked gravely at the other man who was sitting, eyes cast down to his lap where he clasped his cap in both hands as if to gain reassurance from its familiarity. Slowly he raised his eyes to her face and cleared his throat.

'I'm afraid this is going to be another shock for you, my dear,' he said gently.

Rose, wide-eyed, clutched her shawl tightly around her, for she felt she would never be warm again, and waited apprehensively for a further blow.

'When we reached the ledge at first, we found Mr Joss was hurt bad. He were unconscious, see.' He paused and wiped one hand across his face. 'Your husband, he had a great gash on his head and we was wondering how bad he were too, and which one we should send up first.' The man's face twisted with anguish and he swallowed hard. ''Twas a terrible thing to decide upon because the sea was rising so fast, we all knew in our gut that there weren't no way we was going to make it back in time for a second go.' His face was drawn and haggard as he plucked at his cap and relived the dreadful scene.

Then he raised his head and met Rose's eyes.

'But your husband died a hero, missus, I

can tell you that. He insisted that Mr Joss should go and he would wait behind, and we couldn't do no other than leave him. 'I'll be all right,' he said, though I could see he were losing blood some fast.' The man paused then added: 'Mrs Lanyon, the last thing he said — just as we was going — was: 'Tell Rosie I love her.' He shouted it loud, over the noise of the sea, and then something like: ' . . . I can't . . . ' that I couldn't catch. Then when we looked back we saw this great wave come up and break right over him.' The man's voice broke. 'Then he were gone.'

★ ★ ★

For the next few days Rose lived in a world of her own. Moving like an automaton, she dealt with the stream of people who came and went with condolences and words of help and comfort, for Matt had been well-known and liked. She knew she must have slept and woken, even sometimes have eaten, but all through a kind of curtain which divided reality from the world of her thoughts.

Thoughts that whirled restlessly through her mind, and the incessant inner voice which would not leave her in peace. It was all your fault! it said accusingly. Because of your selfishness you sent one good man to his death and left another fighting for his life. You heard what John Richards said — the last words your husband spoke in his life were words of love for you. And you were too besotted with another man to appreciate what you had until you lost it!

And, went on that small relentless voice as the knife turned in the wound, you do realize that Matt sacrificed himself for your sake, don't you? So that you and Joss could be together. When he insisted on sending Joss up first, Matt knew perfectly well that the rescuers would never make it back to him before the tide rose. And he said; 'I can't.' Did he mean, 'I can't live without her?' Oh God, had he *deliberately* slipped off that ledge? What did you ever do to deserve a man like that? . . . Stop it! Stop! Rose sobbed with her hands over her ears as she tried to stifle that persistent voice that would not be silenced.

What kind of monster was she? Rose shuddered. She had driven her kindly, loving husband to his horrific death, and left the love of her life a broken man. And for what? A few short weeks of the most perfect happiness she had ever known. And would never know again. For Matt's sacrifice, far from leaving her free to be with Joss, had had quite the opposite effect. With the memory of this constantly on her mind, how could she ever find happiness with Joss again? Or happiness at all?

Because of the guilt. It enmeshed her like a web of grey fog, its invisible strands sapping her will, the weight of it bowing down her shoulders so that she walked like an old woman, hardly raising her eyes from the ground. Take what you want from life, says Fate — and pay for it. She had read that somewhere and now knew exactly what it meant.

★ ★ ★

Eventually the world intruded and Rose was forced to face what it demanded of her. First of all she was required to go to the mortuary and identify Matt's body.

It did not take long. It was Matt and yet not Matt who lay there on the slab. His body was unblemished and not repulsive in any way. He looked younger somehow, and at peace. And totally removed from her.

Rose stared down at the waxen features. She had shared her life and her body with this person but, she admitted at last, never her heart, nor her mind. Those had always belonged to someone else. She stifled a sob and turned away.

Then there was the inquest. 'Just a formality, of course,' they told her as more of the endless days and nights dragged by. Would she ever be free of this waking nightmare Rose wondered, as the verdict of 'Accidental Death' was eventually returned, and she prepared herself to face the funeral at last.

★   ★   ★

As Rose stood in the churchyard during the interment with the scents and sounds of summer all about her, she felt that the only cloud in that sky of flawless blue was hovering directly above her head and accompanying her wherever she went.

She had often wished that she had been able to get on with Matt's family. It would have given her the support of an older woman whom she could turn to for comfort and advice, and friendly sisters-in-law would have provided her with the female companionship which she lacked. If she had had anybody to whom she could have unburdened herself it would have helped.

But Matt's widowed mother had never accepted Rose. Jealousy and possessiveness had combined in her rejection of her prospective daughter-in-law from the very beginning and now, who knew what rumours regarding her were circulating around the close-knit village community? Rose glanced towards the black-clad figures of Phoebe Lanyon and her two daughters clustered together at the graveside, all dabbing their streaming eyes, and wished that she could cry. She had not really wept yet. Her grief, overlaid with the searing guilt, was too deep to be assuaged by tears.

As the ageless words of the service drifted over and around her, Rose had a sudden memory of the time when Matt had brought her for her first and only visit to his home before they were married. He had warned Rose how difficult his mother could be.

'She never got over Pa's death, not really,' he confided, 'and she clings on to me, see, as I'm the only one left at home. But I got two married sisters down in the village who do see her every day.' He paused with one hand on the gate, and lowered his voice. 'Thing is, she always thought I would wed Mabel Harris from next door — that's her best friend's daughter. I've known Mabel all my life and she's a nice enough girl, but there wasn't never anything like that between us. So I told Ma straight — I'm going to lead my own life. And she didn't like it. Anyway, there we are.'

Phoebe had not attempted to veil her open

hostility to Rose. A tall woman with a thin face, her grey hair was screwed into a knot at the nape of her neck where it was skewered with steel pins. She looked Rose up and down with her lips compressed into a thin hard line, and ushered them into the parlour.

This was so cluttered with furniture and knick-knacks, Rose recalled, that she was almost afraid to move in case her skirt should sweep some ornament from its place on the occasional tables or the bamboo whatnot. Rose sat down on an over-stuffed *chaise-longue*, and after some small-talk, which mostly consisted of Phoebe grilling Rose as to her antecedents, her family and her life until now, Matt followed his mother to the kitchen to help with the tea-things. On the wall near Rose's seat hung an ornately embroidered text in a wooden frame with cross-corners. *Thou, God, seest me* it proclaimed. Rose shivered in the chilly room.

Maybe she had been meant to hear the voice which came drifting up the passage. Certainly Matt's mother made no attempt to lower it, and had left the parlour door open.

'My dear Matt,' came the peevish voice. 'How can you tie yourself to she for the rest of your life? Little nobody like that. Look where she do come from, and there's something funny about her background what

183

she isn't telling, I'll be bound.' For Rose had given only a sketchy outline of her early life.

'Hold your tongue, Ma. We do love each other, we're going to be wed and that's that. I'd liefer it were with your blessing, but it don't make no odds. Rosie's my girl, Ma, and that's the end of it.'

'Pah! Even if you didn't want Mabel, the ideal wife for you she'd have been, you could have had your pick of all the village maidens — and you have to go and fall for the likes of she!'

The venomous voice rose and fell, while Matt stood firmly up to her. It was a long time before he appeared with the tea-tray, but it had given Rose a chance to wipe away her tears. There followed a stilted and uncomfortable time before they could decently make their escape. Phoebe Lanyon had not come to their wedding, only the sisters, who had been polite but not over-friendly. Rose knew that Matt had often gone to visit his mother after their marriage, but he had rarely mentioned her name.

Neither did Rose. She could still hear her mother-in-law's nagging voice haranguing Matt from down in the kitchen that day. '. . . Bewitched you she have with those great green eyes. Better watch out you don't cross she, boy. She do look as if she could ill-wish you sure enough if she put her mind to it.'

Catching Phoebe's eye across the grave now in a glance that was hastily averted, Rose caught her breath at the hate it conveyed. Maybe the woman believed that her prediction had come true. Rose was suddenly reminded of Madame Leonora the gypsy fortune-teller and her prophecy. *Death was here and will be again* was what she had forecast. And she had been right. Rose shuddered convulsively and clutched her cloak tightly about her although the sun was blazing down with noonday heat. After mingling with the other mourners and responding absently to their murmured condolences and handshakes, Rose left the churchyard immersed in her own thoughts.

★ ★ ★

What next? she asked herself as the future suddenly yawned before her. She would have to move out of the cottage of course, for she had no income now and very little in the way of savings. Through the grey fog which still engulfed her Rose heard the inner voice once more. You'll have to face up to it, Rosie girl, you're on your own again. So what are you going to do with the rest of your life?

7

Rose paid the rent on the cottage for a further few weeks and as a temporary measure returned to the Red Lion to decide what to do next. To stay on in the cottage would be unbearable: she could never escape the memories there, but the bustle of the hotel would provide a distraction. Besides, there was nowhere else she could go.

So she found herself back in one of the tiny attic rooms as if she had never been away. But nothing was the same. She didn't belong here any more. She didn't belong anywhere. She had nothing. The home of her own that had been Rose's dream all her life had vanished like the rest of her dreams.

Not even her old easy companionship with Kate was the same. They were still friendly, but guarded with each other. The two who had shared their secrets and dreams, who had been almost as close as sisters, were now polite but distant. Rose knew that Kate blamed her for Matt's death, although of course this was never mentioned. She was kind enough to Rose and often kept her company in the evenings. During the day

186

Rose pottered about in the warmth and bustle of Fanny's kitchen doing odd jobs to help out, or wandered aimlessly around Truro on her own.

After a while her thoughts began to turn to Joss. How was he? Was he thinking of her? How serious were his injuries? Did he know what Matt had done and why? She knew that Joss had survived the fall, from the report in the local paper concerning the serious accident which had befallen the squire's eldest son, along with many sincere wishes for his speedy recovery. But she needed to see for herself how he was, to say goodbye and to explain that there could be no future for them now.

At first she had hoped for a message from him. But when none came she assumed he must be too ill to write. So the only way she was likely to find out was to call at Great Place in person. It wouldn't be easy — to the rest of the world she and Joss had no place together, and the gap in their social standing was unbridgeable, but Rose was not the sort to give up without trying.

★　★　★

It was a four-mile walk to Great Place after she had left the horse-bus which had brought her from Truro. A lovely walk, through lanes frothing with wild flowers. Swags of pink and white dog-roses hung in the hedges and the trees were full of birdsong. It was a beautiful day, the sun was shining benignly down and fantastic cloud formations like puffs of whipped cream floated overhead. Rose took it for a good omen. She was going to see Joss — surely no one could turn her away on such a glorious day as this — and her spirits, so long down-trodden, experienced the first little lift for many weeks.

Great Place was set in a wooded valley and surrounded by parkland. Rose turned into the carriage-drive, on either side of which fallow deer were grazing. She had never seen these dainty animals before; she paused to lean on the railings and watch them while she took a rest. Although it was now mid-morning, no one was about in the gatekeeper's lodge as she passed it and walked down the rest of the drive. The way was flanked now by rhododendron and hydrangea bushes, and soon she was approaching the house itself.

In spite of its name it was not a large house by county standards, resembling more the family home which it was, than a showpiece. But to Rose it looked big enough to be formidable. A circular gravel carriageway surrounding a lawn swept up to the main entrance. A raised terrace was bisected by a flight of granite steps, its severity softened by flower-filled urns, leading to a pillared portico and the front door.

All Rose's instincts were telling her to go round to the back, to the kitchen door and ask one of the servants what she so desperately wanted to know. But why should she? She was calling as a friend of Joss's and as such she would use the front door. Rose stiffened her resolve and straightened her hat, shook the dust from the hem of her skirt and reached for the bell-pull.

The door was opened by a stiff looking housemaid in an immaculate uniform of black and white. She looked Rose up and down, glanced beyond her for the visitor's non-existent carriage and pursed her lips.

'Yes?' She raised an eyebrow. Rose took in a deep breath.

'Please tell your mistress that Mrs Rose Lanyon is here and would like to speak to her.' She stood her ground and outstared the maid.

'You'd better come in,' the maid said grudgingly. 'Wait here.'

Rose followed her into the hall. She sank on to a carved wooden chair with a seat of Berlin wool embroidery and eased her aching feet.

'You're to come this way,' said the maid, returning. 'Madam is in the small drawing-room.'

Jennifer Pencarrow had been sitting at her bureau, deep in the letters she was writing when the maid had announced: 'There's a young person to see you, ma'am. A Mrs Rose Lanyon.'

'Mm? Oh, show her in, will you,' she had replied without raising her eyes. Now she sanded the last of her correspondence, replaced the pen and ink in their silver holders and turned to face her visitor.

Jennifer saw a young woman with anxious green eyes huge in her pale face, wearing a hat of common straw over her springing auburn curls. She took in the girl's obviously home-made gown with its cheap trimming and noticed the dust on her boots.

'I don't think I know you,' she said, rising and smoothing down her skirt of mulberry silk. Expensive lace fluttered at her throat and sleeves as she indicated a chair in the window.

'No, we haven't met, ma'am,' Rose replied. Expecting the other woman to join her, Rose sat down, but Jennifer remained standing, toying with the bobble-fringe of the long curtains.

Rose immediately felt at a disadvantage, but she tilted her chin, straightened her back and looked the woman firmly in the eye. Her throat was so dry from nervousness and the long hot walk that her tongue felt too big for her mouth, but her voice was even and composed as she said:

'I'm a friend of Joss — Mr Joscelyn — and I've come to enquire how he is recovering after his accident.'

'You're a *friend* of his?' Jennifer's eyes narrowed, then widened as understanding dawned. This was the little chit that Penelope had been talking about. Her sister lived in Truro and had bumped into her nephew several times, according to her, with his 'friend' on his arm.

'Rather a common sort, dear,' she had said as they were sipping tea in the Pencarrow drawing-room, 'from the working classes. Perhaps you should have a quiet word with Joscelyn.'

And something else was filtering through now, too. Comprehension gleamed in her eyes as Jennifer snapped: 'Did you say your name is Lanyon?'

'Yes.'

Incredulous the other woman gasped.

'That lout who attacked my son and half-killed him was called Lanyon!' Her eyes bored into Rose as she added: 'I think you have some explaining to do.'

'That was my husband,' Rose admitted quietly. 'But won't you tell me please, how Joss . . . '

'Your *husband*? Do you mean to say that you are a married woman — and in spite of that you have been carrying on a . . . a liaison with my son? Have you no decency, girl, no shame at all?' The older woman was pacing up and down the room in agitation, gesticulating with her hands as she went.

'Joss and I are old friends,' Rose murmured.

'Friends? Pah!' Her voice dripped contempt.

'I knew Joss before I ever met my husband, but we . . . lost touch.' Rose's voice tailed off. This woman would never believe a word of her story.

'Get out of here. Back to the gutter where you belong,' Jennifer hissed through clenched teeth. 'I won't have the name of Pencarrow dragged through the mud by you any longer.'

'I'll go when you've told me how Joss is and not before.' Rose succeeded in keeping her voice level.

'How dare you! You don't deserve to know.' She turned on her heel and looked Rose in the eye. 'But if it will speed your departure, I will tell you that his poor arm is broken again and his whole body is a mass of cuts and bruises. His right eye is closed and they think his face may be scarred for life.' Her mouth shut in a tight, hard line.

'I'd like to see him,' said Rose determinedly. 'Will you let him know I'm here?'

Jennifer's face turned the same colour as her gown and she looked about to explode.

'Of all the cheek! You hussy. When it's all your fault he's lying there in this terrible state!'

'At least ask him if he'll see me?' Rose heard the note of pleading in her voice and hated herself for it, but this was her only chance.

'He's still heavily sedated and in no fit state to be disturbed, even if I consented.' The lie slipped out easily enough. Actually Joss was much improved but why should she tell the little chit that? 'Which, considering the circumstances, is hardly likely. You have a lot to answer for, Mrs Lanyon. I just hope you're satisfied.' Her lip curled in disgust. She crossed the room and tugged at the bell-pull. 'Now go, and don't you ever come here again. Just keep well away from my son in future.'

'I'll only do that when I hear from Joss himself that he doesn't want to see me,' Rose hissed, her eyes snapping sparks as the maid entered.

'Show this person out,' snapped the other woman.

So Rose found herself on the terrace with the great door thudding shut behind her. But she wasn't going without a fight. She hadn't come all this way for nothing. She slipped down the steps and round the corner of the house behind a screen of rhododendrons. Here she scrabbled in her reticule for pencil and paper, hastily scribbled a note and found a threepenny-piece to go with it.

Rose peered cautiously through the bushes. The coast was clear. She left her hiding-place and crept like a shadow around to the kitchen quarters at the back of the house. Just as she reached the door it was flung open and a kitchen-maid appeared on the step carrying a bucket of potato peelings.

She jumped at the sight of Rose and pushed a strand of her lank hair back from her face with a grubby hand.

'Wha — who — ' she began and Rose instinctively put a finger to her lips. Then she flourished the money under the girl's nose and slipped the note into her free hand.

'Would you see that Mr Joscelyn gets this personally? Give it to him and no one else. You understand?'

The girl's plain face was a picture of astonishment, but she grabbed the coin and buried it in a pocket of her stained and greasy apron.

'All right, miss,' she said and did the same with the note. Rose disappeared around the corner and Janie Snell, on her way to tip the peelings on to the gardener's compost-heap, gave a sly and knowing grin.

★   ★   ★

'Hey, Rube,' said Janie later that day, 'take a look at this here.' They had met in a wood on the outskirts of Great Place, in a clearing surrounded by immense pine-trees whose needles had formed a thick and springy carpet beneath the pair.

'I'd rather look at you, my handsome,' Reuben leered. 'Get your clothes off.'

'Wait a bit, I mean it. This is important.' She dragged forth Rose's note from her skirts and waved it under his nose. 'That Vidney girl — Lanyon — she were round to Great Place today. Snooping about outside the back door she were, and when she saw me she says in that stuck-up way she got: 'Would you see that Mr Joscelyn do get this personal-like,' and she gave me threepence. Well, I can't read it, can you? I thought you'd be interested.' She handed over the paper.

'You're a good maid, Janie, I'll thank you

proper in a minute. Now, what's all this here?' Reuben screwed up his eyes and squinted at Rose's writing. 'Trouble is, bird, I can't read it neither!' Janie giggled and wrapped both arms round his waist.

'Don't make no odds though, do it?' Reuben gave a great guffaw, tore the note to shreds and stuffed the pieces down a rabbit-hole.

★   ★   ★

It was now several weeks after his beating and Joss had recovered sufficiently to sit up and take notice again. There had been internal injuries which had only been discovered by the doctor's examination, and he was still confined to bed. The smaller cuts and grazes on his face had now healed, but there was a livid weal running from his right eye to his cheekbone where a sharp stone had added to the split already inflicted by Matt's fist. And his left arm was in plaster again.

'You're looking better today,' his mother remarked, sweeping into his room as he pushed aside his empty breakfast tray. 'You've recovered your appetite as well, I see.'

'I feel a lot better,' Joss replied. 'Mama,' he said hoisting himself further up on the pillows, 'has — er — anyone been asking after me while I've been out of action?'

'Oh yes,' said Jennifer, 'almost everyone we know has been calling or writing, Aunt Penelope was here only yesterday, you remember, and not for the first time. Then there was . . . '

'That's not what I mean,' Joss interrupted. 'Has anyone whom you *don't* know been here? Or are there any messages you've forgotten to give me?'

'Why should there have been?' inquired his mother blandly. 'Were you expecting something?'

'Oh no, nothing. It doesn't matter.' Joss sighed and sank back on to the bed. 'When do you think I'll be allowed up? I'm fed up with being an invalid.'

'It depends on Dr Anderson, dear. When he's sure the internal bleeding has stopped. But you're going to have to be very careful for a long time. You realize that, don't you?'

Joss growled something unintelligible.

'I want to write a letter, Mama. Get someone to bring me the things, will you?'

'Of course I will dear. I'll send Bates up with them right away.'

★   ★   ★

Some time later that day Jennifer was passing through the hall and stopped to riffle through the outgoing mail, which was always placed on the round table outside the dining-room door to await posting. Her eyes gleamed as she noticed the thick cream envelope addressed in her son's bold black handwriting, and she swiftly removed it from the tray. Later in the privacy of her own drawing-room she held it to the candle-flame which she kept for melting sealing-wax and watched it shrivel away to nothing.

'Bates,' she said later to the butler, 'if any mail should come for Master Joss, will you see that it is passed to me. He must not be worried with trifles, it will only hinder his progress. I will decide what is proper for him to see until he is fully recovered.'

'Yes, of course ma'am.'

Why doesn't she reply? Joss fumed, a prisoner in his own home. Three letters and she's ignored every one. I can't believe it of Rose. Visions of her lovely face, and of the precious hours they had shared before their lives were torn apart, tortured him night and day. Obviously she's prostrated with grief over Matt's death. She must have loved him deeply after all. Probably regretting her little 'fling' by now. So that's all it was to her — a diversion. She was just playing with me. And I thought — oh Rose, my love . . .

As the dreary days came and went with still

no word from Rose, Joss became deeply sunk in depression and cared little any more about getting up and about, staring listlessly out of the window as summer turned slowly into autumn and there was still no word from her.

'Why didn't he reply to my note? Or the two letters I posted, either?' Rose cried in anguish, alone in her tiny room. 'He doesn't want to have any more to do with me, that's why. I'm nothing but trouble. Kate was right, he was only playing with me all the time. And I thought — I thought . . . Oh Joss, my love.' Her bottom lip trembled and scalding tears ran down her face.

Once started, Rose could not stop weeping. The tears she could not shed after the tragedy now poured streaming down her face. She wept for Matt, for Joss and for herself. For lost opportunities and for her drowned little sister of long ago. She wept for a long time, until when at last the tears abated she was left weak but cleansed by the healing flood, and the numbness that had been part of her since Matt's death had been dissolved away. It was time now for her to face up to the future.

★ ★ ★

Eventually Joss's physical wounds mended, but the emotional scars had gone deeper and would never cease to hurt. Life, however, had to go on, and he must decide what he was going to do with it.

Mining was now out of the question. He would never be strong enough to cope with it now, even if his job was still available. But of course it wasn't, he'd been away far too long for that.

However, what he had already learnt from his mining experience made Joss even more determined that his father was going to do something about Wheal Hope. Since he had been ill an uneasy truce had been called between Sir Robert and himself and they were on speaking terms again, if not exactly cordial ones.

'You haven't forgotten it's the twins' coming of age next month, have you, Joss?' His mother turned to him at the breakfast table one golden morning in late September. Mentally she noted how changed he was since his accident. He had lost weight, there was a new, bleak look about his eyes, and his face had lost any remaining traces of youthful roundness. The profile turned towards her could have been carved out of granite.

'I had, actually.' Joss lowered the newspaper he had been reading and rasped a hand over his face. He was growing sideburns to hide the scar which refused to disappear, and they were itching. 'What are you planning, Mama?'

'Oh, I think a party, don't you? Your own was such a success, wasn't it. All the county families came and we had a wonderful time. Do you remember?'

'It seems like a lifetime ago,' replied Joss drily, suddenly feeling the weight of his twenty-seven years. He rose and pushed back his chair. 'But if that's what you want, I'm sure that's what we shall have.'

And a party was the last thing he felt like. Joss swept out through the house and round to the stables to saddle up Captain. He had taken to riding every morning as a means of strengthening the lazy muscles which had been weakened by weeks of inactivity. Several times he had been tempted to ride over to Porthtowan, but pride had made him grit his teeth and head in the opposite direction.

By the time the twins' birthday came round, the celebration party had turned into a full-scale ball. Joss came downstairs that evening to find a huge fire blazing in the open grate of the panelled hall, where servants were passing through with trays of drinks. He helped himself and strode on through a doorway and down a corridor into the long drawing-room which had been cleared of furniture for dancing. Upon a raised dais set with potted plants and trailing greenery, a small orchestra was playing. The room was full of colour and gaiety and Joss could not prevent his spirits from rising a little as his foot began to tap in time to a waltz.

The chandelier above shimmered and gleamed, its light refracting from the ladies' jewels and adding lustre to their splendid gowns. As they dipped and twirled they resembled so many butterflies in a flower-garden.

Joss was feeling slightly uncomfortable in a cut-away coat of bottle-green over tightly fitting black trousers, with an embroidered waistcoat. Snowy linen gleamed at his throat and wrists. He hadn't dressed up like this for years.

'Joss dearest, you look quite splendid.' His mother was talking to a grey-haired woman in purple, and a pale, thin girl in blue satin frills and pearls.

'You're looking very fine yourself, Mama,' he replied, inclining his head towards the two women.

Jennifer smiled, knowing he was right. She did look her best, in a gown of deep blue shot with gold which shimmered as she moved. It was new for the occasion and had cost a small fortune from a top London couturier. During the period of its fitting she had stayed in the capital for a few days and replenished her everyday wardrobe as well. It had seemed the economical thing to do. Her piled blond hair, cunningly arranged to conceal the grey areas, was decorated with a sapphire clip, and a choker of the same gems blazed at her throat.

'This is Mrs Agar and her niece, Miss Emma Robartes. My eldest son, Joscelyn.'

Joss bowed and mouthed the right responses, then felt duty-bound to dance with the girl, an insipid little thing with sandy hair who blushed deeply as he led her on to the floor.

'Do you live locally, Miss Robartes?' Joss politely enquired as she twirled beneath his arm.

'We are from Lanhydrock, near Bodmin,' she replied, adding with a pronounced lisp: 'but I'm prethently thtaying with my aunt near Redruth.' Obviously trying frantically to think of something to say in her turn, the little figure fluttered her eyelashes and murmured: 'What a very thplendid occasion thith ith — I *am* enjoying it tho.'

'Indeed, I'm so glad,' Joss replied, after which the conversation lapsed and he was thankful when the dance ended and he could return the limp little creature to her aunt's side.

Joss ignored the quadrille which followed

and crossed the room, where he could see his brothers talking with a small group beneath a potted palm. The two lively youngsters had turned into elegant and poised young men, something which hit Joss forcibly as he saw them in all their formal attire in this setting.

His brothers were just through university and had only arrived back that morning from touring Europe with a group of friends. As Joss had been out all day, this was their first real meeting since before his accident.

'Joss!' Edward spotted him first and Joss strode over to greet him.

'Edward.' He grasped his hand. 'And Anthony.' He clapped the other twin on the shoulder. 'Congratulations on this very special occasion. It makes me feel pretty ancient to think of you two reaching your majority.'

Edward's face still retained a hint of the mischievous boy he had been, reflected in his impish grin and twinkling dark eyes. Anthony was more serious by nature and was self-consciously smoothing a newly cultivated moustache.

'So, now that you've reached this great milestone, what are you going to do with the rest of your lives?'

'I've got some great news, Joss.' Excitement coloured Edward's cheeks. 'I haven't had a chance to tell you, but I've been commissioned into the Thirty-Second. I leave to join them at Bodmin in a fortnight.'

'Marvellous! Congratulations again.' Joss helped himself to a drink from a passing maid and raised his glass to his brother. 'I'm sure a soldier's life will suit you down to the ground. You always were a dare-devil, eh, Anthony?' He winked at his brother. 'Always up to some sort of mischief.'

'I'll say,' Anthony chuckled. 'Eddie was always the ringleader, with me tagging on behind. The things we got up to! There was never one like him for dreaming up stunts — and landing us in hot water too.' He took a swig of his drink and turned to his twin. 'Do you remember the time when we built that tree-house down in Oak Wood?'

'And persuaded the kitchen-maid — what was her name — ?'

'Beth.'

'That's right — to be our damsel in distress up in her castle tower. Anthony was the wicked ogre who had imprisoned her . . . '

'And you were the handsome prince riding up on your pony. Then you scrambled up a rope to rescue her — only the branch broke and you both landed in the stream! I can hear that poor girl's screams still.' He chuckled and Joss listened, amused.

'She was terrified that the housekeeper would dismiss her for spoiling her uniform. Poor child.'

'But we smuggled her in and kept the woman talking while she fled up to her room.'

Joss smiled with his brothers as they told their tale, but he felt one step removed, and envied them their closeness.

'So it's the army for Edward. What about you, Anthony? Have you any plans?'

The young man's face fell, and he looked down into his drink as he swilled it round in his glass.

'No, not really.' He sighed. 'The trouble is, I'm not particularly good at any one thing. I'm not ambitious, nor brave enough to fight in battle. I'm happiest in the country, out with the horses and dogs, but I can't make a career out of that.'

'I see. Well don't worry, old fellow, you don't have to decide right away. I'm sure that something will turn up for you.' Joss turned to go. 'I want a word with Father actually. Did I see Mr Evans the banker with him just now?'

'Yes, he's here with his family, but he went into the study as if they were having a private talk.'

Joss looked over his shoulder.

'Oh, there's Mr Evans, just coming out. I'll

go and see Father now.' He nodded to the banker as he approached. 'Good evening, sir.'

While the banker was greeting the twins, Joss excused himself and went towards his father's study. He found him nursing a bottle of whisky and looking like a man who has already had enough to drink. Robert was slumped in an armchair, his heavily jowled face flushed and puffy, and the hand holding his glass was shaking.

'Oh, Joss. What do you want?' he growled.

And it's nice to see you too, thought his son. Aloud he remarked:

'Are you all right, father?' With diplomacy he added: 'You're not looking — er — very well.'

'Sit down, boy.' Robert indicated a chair. Joss sat, regarding his father with concern. 'Have a drink.' Robert proffered the whisky bottle.

'No, thanks, and if you don't mind me saying so, you've had enough as well.' Joss pointedly removed the bottle and placed it on a side table.

His father gripped the arms of his chair and looked him in the eye.

'Something's come up,' he said abruptly. 'You'll have to know sooner or later, so it might as well be now.'

Joss crossed one leg over the other and folded his arms.

'Oh yes? What's that?' He was expecting some tale of tenant trouble or other minor problem about the estate. Certainly nothing had prepared him for the reality.

'I'm ruined,' said his father.

Joss's jaw dropped and his brows shot into his hairline with amazement.

'What do you mean, *ruined*?' He waved an expressive hand. 'Here you are, entertaining the cream of the county families out there, and you tell me there's no *money*?' He snorted in derision.

'It goes back a long time,' Robert muttered, 'when you boys were growing up. A lot of outlay — expensive schools, sports equipment and suchlike, then 'varsity. And your mother always liked nice things. Clothes, jewellery, entertaining. Keeping up appearances . . . and staff . . . it was endless.'

Joss listened to this catalogue with mounting horror and a sick feeling of apprehension in the pit of his stomach.

Robert shrugged his shoulders and spread his palms wide.

'What could I do? Shares were falling, mining slumped when the gold rush started and the market tumbled. So, there was nothing else for it . . . I had to mortgage the house.'

'*This* house? You mean, it doesn't even belong to us any more?' Surely it can't get any worse, Joss thought, his head spinning as he tried to take in the enormity of what he was hearing. 'And hasn't done for years?'

His father slowly shook his head.

'I hung on and hung on, didn't tell your mother. Hoped things would get better, but they didn't. And now Evans has been here tonight with an ultimatum. He wants a promise of regular payments or he'll take possession. We shall be out.' He paused and drummed the fingers of one hand on the arm of his chair. 'So I asked myself, what are we going to do?'

He leaned forward, his arms on his knees, and looked his son squarely in the eye. 'I only came up with one solution. And it concerns you, boy.'

'*Me?*' Joss exclaimed.

'You.' Robert wagged a finger for emphasis. 'You're going to have to find a rich young woman who's wealthy enough to bail us out, and marry her for her money. It's the only way we are going to get out of this mess.'

Joss's eyes widened in astonishment, then he snorted.

'Me? Marry? You must be joking. I shall

marry whom I choose, when I choose.' He looked scornfully back at his father. *If only*, he thought with a pang. In his mind's eye Joss saw the love of his life, and a spasm of pain crossed his face. He sprang to his feet and began to pace up and down.

'But think about it,' came the relentless voice of his father at his back, drowning out his dreams. 'You're the one who's always going on about improvements to the damn mine. Money's going to have to come from somewhere, else it'll have to close down. I haven't got capital to keep this place going, let alone any mine.' He heaved himself upright and unsteadily wove a path across the room until he had joined his son in the window embrasure.

Placing a heavy hand on Joss's shoulder as they looked unseeingly out across the lawns and flower-beds below, Robert drew in a long breath.

'Think about all the staff here who would lose their jobs,' he persisted. 'Think about the tenants. Think about your mother — can you imagine her living in poverty? It would kill her.' Joss caught a whiff of whisky-laden breath as his father looked up into his face. He flinched.

Joss turned away from the window and Robert returned to his chair, sinking back into it with a heavy sigh.

'You're the only one who can save them all, Joss. I wish it were otherwise but . . . ' he shrugged. The spread hands said it all. Hopeless, it was hopeless.

Joss's head began to pound. He could hardly take in what he was hearing. He had to marry an heiress — just like that. Any heiress! If it wasn't so incredible it would even be funny.

He turned on his heel and stared down at his father for a long moment. Then:

'Why *me*?' he said, knowing as he spoke that he was clutching at straws. 'You do have two other sons, you know.'

'Bah!' Robert said with annoyance. 'Couldn't trust either of *them* with a responsibility like this.' He shook his head and tutted. 'You know as well as I do — they're still little more than children in spite of this great occasion today. Not a serious thought in their heads.' He glowered into the middle distance.

Joss had known the answer before he spoke. Now he knew that the nightmare was really beginning. He could feel its tentacles closing in on him, strangling him and all his hopes for the future in one suffocating web of horror.

'But you can't do this to me!' he cried, beating a fist into his open palm. 'It's *blackmail*, moral blackmail. Turning me into some kind of cold and calculating money-machine!'

Robert's red-rimmed eyes met his own for a second, then slid away as he examined the toe of his boot.

Joss was blazing with indignation and fury. How could he, a completely innocent party, have been forced into such a position as this? How could he have had the misfortune to be born to this pathetic, drink-sodden hulk of a man before him!

Joss opened his mouth to say all these things and more, but before his rage exploded into words he took another look at his father. Robert was sitting motionless, like a deflated balloon, all his old pomposity beaten out of him.

He seemed to have physically shrunk since his admission of failure. His face, formerly so choleric, had taken on a greyish tinge and he looked an old, old man.

So it really is up to me, Joss thought, as the realization hit him that their previous roles of father and son from this moment would be reversed. He was now the stronger of the two and would have to shoulder the responsibilities which had up to now been his father's.

'I need to think,' he said tersely, and left the room. But he already had an idea of what he was going to do.

There's no time like the present, so the cliché went. And if this distasteful business had to be faced, what better opportunity could there be than this moment? As he had pointed out to his father, half the gentry of Cornwall with their daughters were under his roof right now. Joss made his way back to the ballroom and sought out his mother whom he eventually found in the conservatory, eating an ice and temporarily alone.

'Joss! I haven't seen much of you this evening. Don't you think it's going well? Are you having a good time?' She moved along the wicker seat to make room for him beside her.

Hands in his pockets Joss slumped beside her next to a tub of geraniums and stretched out his long legs.

'Never better, Mama,' he snorted. The sarcasm, of course, went unheeded.

'Good, good,' she murmured and tapped a foot to the lilting music floating out from the dance floor.

'Tell me something, Mama,' said Joss, his eyes on the dancers swirling past the connecting door. 'Which of those young ladies is the wealthiest in the county?'

'What a strange thing to ask, dear. Well, I don't know — let me see.' She tapped the

213

ivory sticks of her fan against her knuckles in thought. 'There's Caroline Lemon of Carclew, and little Emily Basset from Tehidy — her father is big in mining, but I should think that really it would be Emma Robartes. She's quite wealthy in her own right, I believe, from a relation on her mother's side. You know who I mean, don't you?' She turned to him. 'I introduced you to her earlier.'

Joss's face dropped. Among all the other pretty girls here tonight, of course it would be her.

'I know who you mean, Mama,' he said with feeling.

* * *

Joss pursued his courtship of Emma Robartes with relentless determination on his part and delighted incredulity on hers. Assiduously he called on her at her aunt's home in Redruth, bearing flowers and small gifts at intervals. He sat in the stuffy drawing-room making polite conversation and drinking endless cups of tea while Emma fluttered and dimpled artlessly at him.

The boredom of the conventional small-talk was only equalled by the irritation of the girl's lisping voice. It was 'Joth' this and 'Joth' that — soon, he glowered, it would be: 'my fianthé' and eventually: 'my huthband.' Could he stand it? Savagely Joss squeezed a cucumber sandwich to death and knew he would have to.

When, after a few weeks, Emma returned to Lanhydrock, Joss patiently continued his courtship there, riding the thirty miles or so each way in all weathers. Feeling disgusted with himself and lower than the humblest crawling creature on earth, he asked for her hand in marriage as soon as it was decently possible.

8

A knock on the door of her room momentarily startled Rose, who had, as usual lately, been sunk in thoughts of her own problems.

'Come in,' she called out hastily as Kate entered with such an air of suppressed excitement about her that Rose wondered what was coming.

Her friend flopped down on to the bed as she had always done in the old days when there were confidences to be shared, and held out her left hand.

'Look, Rose,' she said simply. On her fourth finger sparkled a dainty ring.

'Kate! You're betrothed. You and Will — at last!' Rose was immediately jolted out of her own misery by the expression of pure joy that shone out of Kate's eyes and lit up her face like a beacon. She generously hugged her friend and added: 'I'm so *pleased* for you both.'

'Thank you, I knew you would be.' Kate looked down at her hand and twisted the ring around. 'But I feel a bit awkward being so happy when you . . . you . . . '

'Oh don't be silly,' Rose said briskly. 'I know I haven't been the best of company, sunk in my own woes, but this is just what I need to cheer me up. When will the wedding be?'

'Well, quite soon, maybe in only a fortnight.'

Rose's eyes widened in surprise and for a moment she thought the worst.

Kate must have read her thoughts because she said:

'No, it's not for the obvious reason — there's something else I have to tell you.' She looked up, her expression suddenly serious. 'You see Rose, we — we're going to emigrate.'

'*Emigrate?*' Rose couldn't have been more surprised if Kate had grown wings and flown through the air. 'Where . . . where to?'

'To Australia. Imagine it, can you? Will says that's where all the opportunities are to. A challenge, he says, a whole new life. And a man can make a fortune on the copper-fields. First he said he would go on ahead and send for me after — but I said not likely, I'm coming too.'

Rose smiled at Kate's determined face.

'As if I was going to get married and watch him sail away without me,' Kate added indignantly. 'One day we'll come back and settle here, he says. But I don't know how many years that'll take.' There was a hint of shakiness in her voice.

Rose squeezed her hand.

'He's a good man is Will,' she said with sincerity. 'And he's got himself a treasure in you. I wish you all the best luck in the world.'

'It'll be some adventure though, sure enough. But one thing I'm really glad about, it'll get Will away from that there arsenic works. I hate him being up there — it must be damaging his lungs with all them fumes — but he just laughs at me for fussing.'

'Men are all the same,' said Rose with the voice of experience. 'Matt never took any notice of me either, when I used to worry about the conditions down Wheal Hope.'

'Do you know, Rose,' Kate said, 'I thought of something strange the other day. Remember, do you, ages ago when we all went to the fair that day and the gypsy told us our fortunes? She told me a sort of riddle about finding my love 'where no trees grow' and I couldn't make head nor tail of it.'

Rose nodded, unwilling to think about what the woman had said to her.

'Well,' said Kate earnestly, 'Will have turned out to be my true love — and in that poisonous old place where he works to there aren't no trees — not even a blade of grass neither, come to that. And here we are going 'far away across the sea' just like she said! Struck me all of a heap it did, when I thought about it. Funny though, isn't it? Just as if she really *did* know.'

A cold shiver ran down Rose's spine, but outwardly she only shrugged.

'It must be only coincidence, Kate,' she said, trying to convince herself as much as her friend. 'You've just made it fit. That's how fortune-tellers make their money, out of gullible people like us!'

★   ★   ★

It was nearly the end of October, a warm and golden Indian summer which seemed set to last indefinitely. Rose was still undecided what to do with the rest of her life, apart from the fact that she would soon have to start earning her living again. A return to the kitchen of the Red Lion held no charm for her — it was too full of memories. But Rose would not admit, even to herself, that the real reason why she was dragging her feet was, simply, Joss Pencarrow.

For in spite of everything, the long silence, his ignoring of all her letters, not a word or a message from him after Matt's death — and that had hurt — Rose knew that Joss would only have to lift his little finger and she would go running to his side as if nothing had happened. She would hate herself for it, but she wouldn't be able to resist.

So why doesn't he? enquired the small voice within her. She stifled it and went out to buy a local paper. Reading it later in the quietness of her room, the answer suddenly became glaringly obvious. It leapt out at her from the page as if it had been printed in letters of fire ten feet high.

'The betrothal is announced, and the marriage will shortly take place, of Mr Joscelyn James Pencarrow of Great Place, and Miss Emma Louise Robartes of Lanhydrock.'

I never knew he was called James, Rose thought irrelevantly, before shock set in and she began to tremble. She felt icy-cold and sick. This explained everything — the gaps — the silence. It was all over, for ever. Joss was of course gentry, as everyone had warned her, and she'd refused to listen to them, convinced that he loved her. Now he was marrying a girl of his own class and proving them right. What a fool she had been.

Her own mind was made up now. In the

minutes since she had read that announcement, Rose had decided she had to get completely away. From Truro, from Porthtowan, from her memories and from her mistakes, and make a fresh start.

She surprised herself when she discovered that what she really longed to do was to go back home, to her roots. To the gritty mining district where she had been born, in spite of the dreadful childhood she had had there.

Sunk in the past, Rose recalled her drunken father, slatternly step-mother and the constant poverty in which they had all lived, and shuddered. It had all culminated in the horror of Sarah's death. She forced herself now to think of the tragedy from an adult perspective, and found that with distance she could do so at last without the harrowing guilt that had accompanied her through her early life. For she had only been a child herself when it had happened, far too young for the responsibilities that had been forced upon her, and now the time had come to lay that guilt aside once and for all.

Thinking like this brought back to her the recent threats and blackmail from her cousin Reuben. Rose had neither heard nor seen anything of him since then, and could only pray that something else had come up to take his mind off her.

But there had been some happier moments amid all the horror. Rose's mouth curved in a wistful smile at the thought of the summer days she had spent with Joss on the sunny hillside, herself a skinny little urchin and he the boy she had always worshipped.

And what had she done with her life since then? she asked herself bitterly. One good man had gone to his death because of her, and the love of her life had turned out to be a god with feet of clay, who had betrayed her bitterly. Rose's mouth tightened into a grim line. Oh yes, she had learnt some hard lessons, and would return a sadder and a wiser woman because of them, but return she would, revisit the scenes of her childhood and lay the ghosts of the past for ever.

★　★　★

Rose snapped back to the present. She was a good cook. She could find employment somewhere in Camborne surely? Or Redruth, its twin mining town. She was still only twenty-two and if she sold the contents of the cottage she would have a substantial sum of money to start her off. She could go and stay in lodgings to begin with, and then maybe get a little room of her own. It was all falling into place.

Once these decisions were made, Rose could not wait to get started. The best cure for a broken heart, she told herself, was to keep busy, and this gave her the push she needed to perform the last heart-rending task still looming over her. That was going back to Porthtowan, turning out the cottage and finally vacating it.

* * *

Kate had offered to help and they booked the services of a carter to transport Rose's furniture and belongings to a temporary store in Truro. As they stepped inside, the familiarity of her home hit Rose like a blow in the stomach, and without Kate being there to urge her on she would never have had the heart to begin.

They had brought packing-cases with them in the hired van and as the man carried them in, Kate whipped a large apron round her waist and handed Rose another.

'Right,' she said firmly. 'China and ornaments first, I think. Let's put they in this tea-chest, Rosie.'

Rose did as she was told and they worked hard for over an hour. Into the chest went the wedding-presents they had received. A splendid clock from Will and Kate which had stood on the mantelpiece in the parlour, a flower-sprigged tea-service from the staff of the Red Lion, linen and cutlery from Matt's sisters. Apart from the gold band she still wore, these things were the only proof that she had been married at all. Rose firmly closed the lid on them.

By now most of the cupboards and shelves were clear. However, the most heart-rending task of all was still to be faced. Sorting through Matt's clothes. Now Rose could not prevent the tears from falling. The scent of him lingered still on his jackets and waistcoats and even on his shirts, along with the distinctive fresh smell of clean linen which has been dried in the open air.

Rose buried her face in an old jersey. It was still moulded to the shape of Matt's body and she could almost feel those huge and gentle arms enfolding her — and she had treated him so badly. And for what? Now I have nobody left. Oh Matt! Oh Joss!

Rose dried her eyes on a corner of her apron and went on methodically folding and stacking. Clearing away the detritus of a life so briefly shared. Of her first and only real home, which had been the culmination of her childhood dreams. Soon it was done. It had only taken one day's work to wipe out the evidence of their two years together. Soon nothing would be left in this place to show that they had ever been.

'All done?' Kate's practical figure appeared in the doorway. 'We've got through very well. Still have the van for another hour if we want it.'

'Well, that's all the big things shifted,' Rose replied, 'but I've still got a mass of papers to go through — old bills and things like that. Kate, it'll take far longer than an hour. What I think I'll do is sleep here for one last night before I give up the key, and sort them out now. I can have a makeshift bed on the floor for one night.'

'Are you sure?' Kate looked doubtful.

'Yes, positive. But I'll have a lift in the van with you as far as St Agnes first, and then walk back. There's something else I want to do before I finally leave.' Rose paused and bit her lip. 'I'm going down to the churchyard, Kate.'

'I'll come with you if you like.'

'No thanks.' Rose shook her head. 'You go on to Truro and I'll see you tomorrow. And thanks for all your help, Kate.' She squeezed her friend's hand. 'I'm really grateful. I couldn't have faced it without you.'

'Oh, gus on, of course you could.' Kate's lapse into the Cornish vernacular was her way of shrugging off any show of deeper feelings.

225

She took off her dusty apron and shook it vigorously out of the door, keeping her back to Rose for a minute. Then she bundled it up and turned to go.

'You're ready now, are you?' Rose nodded and they left the house together.

★ ★ ★

Rose left the van at St Agnes near the parish church, then trod the grassy pathways between the rows of silent headstones. Birdsong was all around her and there were wild flowers among the grasses, sighing in the soft wind. There would always be flowers and the song of birds she thought, as she stood for a long time in the peaceful spot looking down at her husband's grave. Not so with people, though. On the day of the funeral Rose had still been in such a daze of shock that she could remember little of it, but in this place she could say her last farewell to the big and brawny man she had married.

'Oh Matt, I'm sorry!' She was weeping. 'You were too good for me. You gave me all that you had and you deserved a better deal in return.' Rose wiped a hand across her face. And this seemed such a tiny plot for so large a man.

James Matthew Lanyon
1824–1853

She read aloud,

> Rock of ages, cleft for me,
> Let me hide myself in thee.
> R.I.P.

Rock of ages. Matt had spent his working life toiling among rocks deep underground. Now he would be there for ever. Rose straightened her tired body and turned to leave.

Deep in her own thoughts, she strolled along the top of the cliff before returning to the cottage. The slanting sunlight of late afternoon brightened the patchwork of small fields inland, their colours constantly changing as the clouds raced overhead. In seconds, mint-green turned to olive, corn-gold to ochre, while spotted cows in neutral black and white grazed peacefully. Rose saw none of this natural beauty, though she was conscious of how sweet the fresh air smelled after the hot and dusty work they had been doing all day. For now she was thinking of Joss.

Foolish or not, she had to make one last visit, on this day of farewells, to the place

227

which held such bitter-sweet memories. To Wheal Hope cove where so much had happened — for this place had known their moments of greatest bliss and had also been the scene of their most appalling tragedy. As Rose walked the cliffs she saw Joss's face in every stone and bush beside the path which they had taken so often together, and heard his laughing voice in every wave which crashed and died upon the shore.

She made her way down the familiar steep track to the beach and sat for a long time on the flat slab of rock where Joss had first called her his 'mermaid'. It seemed such a long time ago. A mermaid, a magical, mystical creature of the sea. Rose gazed out over the deep and swelling ocean, over the great white horses that came rolling forever shorewards, tossing their silver manes high, and almost saw her riding on the surf. Her tossing hair was caught in the tossing spray and her slim green body was in the curve of an emerald wave.

★　★　★

Joss was making the most of his last few hours of precious freedom on this, the eve of his marriage, as he cantered along the cliff-top above Wheal Hope cove with his head full of memories. Without conscious

228

thought he reined in the horse as he came to the fork down to the beach, slid from its back and tied the reins securely to a fence post. He stood for a long time grim-faced and lost in thought, his eyes on the shifting sea below, before he turned down the track. He would take one last walk along the sand to the cave and lay all the ghosts of the past, before putting that part of his life firmly behind him and embarking on his future as a married man.

★　★　★

Rose shook herself back to the present and stood up to leave. When, half-turning, she suddenly came face to face with Joss at the bottom of the cliff, it was as if her thoughts had conjured him up. She gasped in disbelief, hands clapped to her face as the old familiar pounding of her heart began.

He was thinner, paler and somehow older-looking. On his beloved face was a tracery of small worry-lines and he had grown side-burns which she hadn't seen before. All this Rose noted in the split second as they both stood rooted to the spot, eyes locked. Then overriding all of that, Rose saw again that stark message: 'The betrothal is announced . . . '

'Rose!' Joss said. 'Oh Rose, my love.' And he opened wide his arms, as if fully expecting her to fly straight into them.

'Don't *touch* me!' She hissed and she bared her teeth like a small cornered wild creature. Like an animal too she cowered away from him and Joss, his face a picture of astonishment, let his arms drop to his sides. The sea-breezes had loosened Rose's hair which was blowing across her face in great coppery strands, and lifting the corners of her shawl. She grasped it in her crossed arms and folded it about herself as if in pain.

'I saw that announcement in the paper,' she flung at him through gritted teeth. 'How *could* you, Joss? After all we . . . we've been to each other. When I thought that you . . . loved me . . . ' Then her lip curled in disdain. 'Kate was right all along but I wouldn't listen to her. She said you were only p-playing with me . . . ' Rose's voice faltered and broke as she choked back angry tears.

Joss stepped forward, grasped her elbows and held her in a grip of steel. Rose swayed to and fro as she stamped a foot and tried to free herself.

'Why didn't you answer all those letters I wrote to you?' he demanded, shaking her. Rose stopped struggling and stared dumbly at him. What letters?

'Letters? I didn't get any letters. But I wrote to *you*. I came to Great Place and your mother wouldn't let me see you. So I left a note, then I posted two more . . . '

'You *called*? But, but . . . ' Joss released her and spread his hands in bewilderment. 'No one told me — and I thought you didn't care. That you had truly loved Matt and blamed me for his death, and — oh Rose, I'm so *sorry*.' He looked down at her with his heart in his eyes.

'And now you're betrothed to Emma Robartes!' she spat at him. Bitterly she added: 'It didn't take you long to forget me, did it?' Rose hung her head and twisted her hands in the fringe of her shawl lest he should see the tears which were pricking her eyelids.

Joss took her by the shoulders again, gently this time.

'Rose, look at me.' He put one finger under her chin and raised her face to his. 'It's not what you think — I *do* love you, and only you, but . . . ' At the sight of her eyes, great sea-green pools of pain, he broke off, overcome by the force of her misery and lacerating himself for causing it.

'Tell me you're not going to marry her, then. Tell me that, Joss Pencarrow.' Rose angrily stamped a foot and glowered at him.

'I can't do that,' Joss whispered. His face

was bleak and his expression as stony as the granite cliffs above them. Once more he gathered her to him and wrapped both arms about her trembling body, ignoring her protesting struggles. All at once he felt her slacken and lean into his shoulder. All the fight had gone out of her.

'Say it,' she said again in a whisper.

'I love you, Rose,' he said, deliberately misunderstanding her. Joss rested his chin against her glorious hair and breathed in the freshness of it. Then before she could open her mouth again he placed one hand firmly at the back of her head and brought his own lips down on to hers in such a kiss that Rose's legs buckled, she completely lost her balance and the two of them sank together on to the soft sand at their feet.

This time their love-making was rough, savage almost in its intensity, as they tried to express feelings it was impossible to put into words. They clawed at each other, pinched, bit and scratched, rolling over in the dry white sand, tearing at each other's clothing in their hunger for this union which would be their last.

When it was over they both lay in silence, drained by their passion, exhausted, desolate. Joss's eyes were closed. Rose raised herself on one elbow and gazed down at his beloved features, imprinting them on her mind, storing up the image to take with her and sustain her in the wilderness which would be the rest of her life without him.

She put her lips close to his ear in one last hopeless plea.

'Tell her you've changed your mind, Joss. Don't marry her.'

'I have to,' said Joss, reaching for her again, 'because . . . '

Rose's head jerked up as she bit him off in mid-sentence.

'*Have* to?' she cried, clapping a hand to her mouth as she jumped to the wrong conclusion. 'Oh no, that's even *worse!*' Her howl of anguish as she imagined Joss making love to Emma as he had with her, echoed around the cove and was carried far out to sea. She wrenched herself free and was off and away, skimming across the sand like a wraith before Joss was fully aware that she had gone. By the time he had staggered to his feet, dragged on some clothes and set off after her, Rose had fled right across the cove and was half-way up the footpath, almost out of sight.

'Ro-se!' Joss yelled, 'come back, wait!' But she was out of sight and hearing now, lost to him for ever. Joss sank down on to the mermaid rock and buried his face in his hands.

★ ★ ★

Seared to the depths of her soul by Joss's apparent betrayal, Rose would have set off there and then if Kate and Will's wedding had not delayed her. In the circumstances, she could hardly leave before they did.

Kate looked charming in her simple wedding-gown of self-striped ivory taffeta, and blissfully happy as she and her husband left the church for the wedding-breakfast at the Red Lion. The newly-weds were to stay at the hotel for a couple of nights before leaving for their journey half across the world.

'We shall get the stage as far as Plymouth,' Kate told Rose as they sorted and packed the clothes she was taking with her, 'and sail from there. Phew — that pile can go to one of Fanny's charities.' She tossed a couple of skirts on to the growing heap on the floor. 'She's involved in all sorts of things like the 'Relief of Distressed Gentlewomen' and that.'

'It looks as if they're going to have quite a windfall,' Rose said with a smile. There were more clothes on the floor than Kate was packing. But her friend was lost in a world of her own.

'Will says there's a new emigrant depot in Plymouth where we can stay for sixpence a day. Our ship's called the *Java*.' She stopped

234

folding underwear and a dreamy look came over her face as she clasped a couple of nightgowns to her. 'Oh Rose, I can hardly believe all this is true. I've never been out of Cornwall in my life — and now to go all that way. It do frighten me stiff to think of it.'

'Nonsense,' Rose said stoutly, 'you'll have your husband to look after you.'

Kate giggled.

'My husband. It sounds some funny when you say that.'

'Did somebody mention me?' Will poked his freckled face round the door. 'My wife, was it?' He grinned as Kate burst out laughing. 'I came to say that I've sent on that great trunk with my tools in, and your pots and pans.' He turned to Rose. 'We're taking as much household stuff as we're allowed and plenty of clothes for both summer and winter. We don't know what we shall find when we get there.'

'It's a big undertaking, Will. But you've got each other — you'll be all right,' Rose said. The wistfulness in her voice went unnoticed by the other two.

'Any road,' said Will cheerfully, 'I suppose mining's pretty much the same wherever you are. I saw a fellow this morning, Kate, what went up to Plymouth to see somebody off. He said it's a good thing to buy extra food to take on board for the voyage. We can get that in Plymouth afore we sail.'

Kate finished strapping her hamper of clothes and pushed it towards him.

'That's the last of the boxes Will, thank goodness.'

Kate took a tearful farewell of them all next day and she and Rose parted with promises to write. Rose waved her handkerchief until the coach was out of sight, then buried her face in its folds and wept. She felt more alone than ever now. Also, she no longer had any reason to delay her own departure. The sooner she left for her own new life, the better.

★　★　★

Joss and Emma Robartes were married on a dull and dank November day. A chilly mist hung over the churchyard, which remained cheerless even though the pealing of its bells announced that this was in fact a joyous occasion. The steady drip from the elm trees overhead and the mournful sigh of the thin wind stealing around the corners of the church seemed to echo Joss's mood as the Pencarrow carriage drew up outside and he and Anthony, his groomsman, alighted.

He spent the duration of the service in

another world. Beside him at the altar Emma, in a froth of silk and white fur, looked almost pretty, but as Joss took her hand in his and made his vows, the unreality of it all persisted. This smooth, sandy head bowed in prayer beside him should be one of glorious, singing auburn. The china-blue eyes should be the sparkling brilliant green of his only love. And this delicate, doll-like figure should be that of his vibrant, passionate Rose. The sense of nightmare came back and he was suffocating in these bonds which were not of his own making, but which he could hear himself promising to honour and obey.

Before he and Emma settled into Great Place to take up the threads of daily life however, Joss made a stand. He made it clear to his father that having been forced into marriage to save the older man's face, Joss expected him and his mother to move out of Great Place into the substantial dower house which stood nearby in the grounds, if only out of fairness to Emma. To his surprise, Jennifer made no objections and he silenced his father's initial bluster by threatening to tell his mother the truth.

So Joss now found himself saddled with the estate, something which he had never wanted and had gone through a great deal to avoid. Bitterly he wondered what had ever made him believe he could break away from his roots and change the position he was born into. At the back of his mind, however, he still had not given up all hope of becoming an engineer some day. He had to have a dream to cling to, to get him through the rest of his life.

Emma took up the reins of domestic management with an efficiency which surprised Joss at first, until he realized that all her life she had been in training for nothing else. For marriage and the running of a home, of course, was the aim of every well-bred young female.

She seemed competent at handling the servants and drifted serenely about the house, changing the furniture and ornaments around and putting up new curtains. At first she had come to Joss to involve him and ask his permission, until he tactfully explained that he had no interest in such things and gave her *carte blanche* to do what she liked. It kept her happy and left him alone with his own work.

Then Joss installed himself behind his father's great desk in the steward's room and immersed himself in account-books, rent-books, ledgers, letters and bills, some of which had remained unpaid for several years.

It was all in a state of utter chaos. Robert had, as he confessed, left everything to his steward, merely signing papers when necessary. Now Joss painstakingly ploughed through it all, with a thoroughness which kept him in the stuffy, cluttered room for several weeks. Until one day he at last emerged from the mountain of papers with a clearer idea of how things stood financially.

With the help of Emma's money, which of course was now his to spend as he wished, Joss paid off the most pressing of the outstanding bills. The annuity which came to her from a deceased great-aunt was a generous one, and would with careful handling take care of the mortgage repayments. Joss breathed a sigh of relief and allowed himself to relax for the first time in months. They seemed to be over the worst. His next move was to search out his brother Anthony. For Joss had an idea.

★   ★   ★

He found Anthony in the stables where he spent so much of his time.

'Ah, Joss,' said his brother, 'what brings you so far away from the paperwork?' He gave one of his warm, lazy smiles as he looked up. Standing in one of the stalls, he was examining the hoof of a carriage-horse. In the next stall, Captain snuffled and whickered a greeting as Joss entered.

'I needed some fresh air and intelligent company.' Joss grinned as he ran a hand over Captain's nose.

'You mean the horse, of course,' his brother chaffed.

'What else?' Joss retorted. 'Seriously though, can you spare me a few minutes up at the house, or are you too busy?'

'I've just noticed that Fancy's got something in this hoof. I'll tell one of the grooms, then I'll be right up.'

'I'll see you in the study.'

Joss took his time on the way back. The air was mild for January and a few bulbs were already shooting up in sheltered places. Down on the lake ducks squabbled among the reeds and a few birds twittered in the leafless trees.

Anthony joined him behind the great roll-top desk.

'This looks vastly neater than when I saw it last,' he remarked.

'You're right. I've been through the whole lot with the proverbial fine-tooth comb.' Joss thumped a pile of ledgers. 'That's why you haven't seen much of me, and I've hardly seen daylight for weeks.' He stretched out his legs and folded his arms across his chest as he regarded his brother. 'Now, I want to have a chat with you about a few things.'

Anthony's eyebrows rose.

'The first might come as a bit of a shock.' Joss paused before adding: 'I've dismissed Sam Reed.'

'*Dismissed* him? But he's been steward here since . . . for ever . . . I can't remember how many years!'

'Exactly. He was getting lazy and complacent. And actually, I have my doubts about his total honesty.'

Anthony's brows shot up.

'Really? In what way?'

'I found discrepancies that he couldn't explain — he bluffed and blustered his way around them. Nothing I could put my finger on, you know, but I had this hunch. So I convinced him it was time he left.'

'I shouldn't think that went down very well, did it?'

Joss shrugged. 'I gave him a better reference than he deserved, and he went quietly enough. Which rather confirmed my suspicions.'

Anthony's eyes widened.

'So what did Pa say about that?'

'He doesn't know yet. He asked me to sort things out for him, so the decisions are mine,' Joss replied firmly.

'Not ill, is he?' Anthony asked. 'Only it's so unlike him to give up the reins like this.'

'No, he's all right, but he's getting older all the time of course, and when he got into a muddle with bills and money-matters I think he panicked a bit. And he wasn't getting the help he should have had from Reed, either. But it's all straight now.' Joss glossed over the matter. He had not told his brothers the full truth on the basis that the fewer people who knew of it the better. Certainly he did not want his mother to get any inkling of the truth. 'But what I'm coming to now concerns you,' he added.

'Me?' Anthony looked totally mystified.

Joss looked his brother in the eye.

'You're a countryman, are you not?'

Anthony nodded.

'You love Great Place, you get on well with the tenants, you're keen on agriculture and interested in progressive farming methods, is that not so?'

'Certainly.' Anthony nodded. 'But why the inquisition?'

'This.' Joss indicated the pile of books and papers. 'I want you to take over as estate manager.' Anthony's jaw dropped and there was a silence as he digested the news.

'Think about it,' Joss said. 'You're the ideal man for the job. I've got other ambitions and I find this sort of thing tedious.'

Anthony's face suddenly lit up and he

242

straightened in his chair, hanging on Joss's every word. Joss had known what he was about before he had spoken and had carefully rehearsed what he would say to his younger brother. Anthony had a sensible head on his shoulders and a shrewd brain which was being under-used at present.

'Oh, Joss I'd like nothing better! It'll give me something worthwhile to do.' Beaming all over his face, Anthony jumped to his feet and began to pace up and down. 'And I shall be able to go on living here.'

'It won't be easy,' Joss warned him. 'You've got to get the estate making a profit again. There are still outstanding debts which must be met. But they can be. I want the home farm made really productive. I want you to look into the rent-books of the tenant cottages. Rents haven't been raised in my lifetime and they're just not realistic any more. Do any repairs they need, of course, and then charge a fair rent. You know the people, they like you, they'll listen.'

Joss paused for breath. Anthony nodded slowly as he took it all in.

'You'll need help,' Joss went on. 'I'll leave it to you to appoint an assistant. Come to me for anything you need or if you have problems you can't solve. Otherwise you have a free hand. Think you can cope?'

'I shall enjoy trying,' said Anthony modestly, 'and thanks, Joss.' They shook hands across the table.

'If all goes as well as I think it will, I shall soon be thanking you.' Joss grinned.

9

Having arranged to share some of his huge burden had cheered Joss considerably and he whistled as he rode towards Wheal Hope and a meeting with Jack Trenerry. He hesitated for a second at the entrance to Wheal Hope Lane, where the roof of Rose's home was just visible from the road. He glanced down the track. For an instant an expression of naked longing stole over his face, to be firmly banished as he kicked up the horse and rode on his way. Determined to think of other things, Joss began to reflect on the stupendous news that Emma had announced the previous evening.

They had been sitting in the drawing-room after dinner, he with the newspaper and she with some embroidery. Joss had been deep in the financial columns studying stocks and shares, when Emma had crept up to him and unexpectedly perched herself on the arm of his chair. Joss looked over the top of his paper with surprise, then laid it to one side as he saw the look on her face.

'Joth,' said Emma with such a sparkle in her eyes and an air of suppressed excitement about her that it made her plain little face almost pretty, 'there'th thomething I have to tell you.' She paused, linked one arm through his and laid her head on his shoulder. 'I've waited until now to be quite thure.'

Joss's paper slipped to the floor as his brain started working overtime. He had an inkling of what might be coming before Emma lowered her eyes demurely and went on:

'I went to thee Doctor Anderthon thith morning and he confirmed what I'd thought mythelf. That I'm carrying a child.' She raised her head and met his eyes. 'Oh Joth!' She took his hand and squeezed it. 'We're going to have a little one!' Then a hint of anxiety wrinkled her brow as she added: 'You are pleathed, aren't you, Joth dearest?'

Marvelling, for he had never considered the matter and had had no idea at all of her condition until now, Joss gaped at his wife, then put both arms round her shoulders and clasped her to him, lifting her from the arm of the chair on to his lap.

'Of course I'm pleased, Emma darling, that's *wonderful* news!' he said with sincerity. 'Me — a father!' Joss kissed her upturned face, then lifted her gently to her feet and stood upright. 'Come and sit down properly — and put your feet up — here you are.'

And as he put a footstool before her chair,

Joss looked with concern at the delicate frame of this doll-like woman who was his wife, and wondered with a touch of concern how she would stand up to the rigours of childbirth.

'We're going to have to take special care of you from now on . . . ' And they had spent the rest of the evening talking of domestic arrangements and nursery equipment.

★ ★ ★

A dog ran barking out of a farm gateway and brought Joss back to the present. Settling Captain back into his stride, Joss grinned to himself and thought about the coming child. He had never imagined himself as a father but the more he grew accustomed to the idea, the more appealing it became. A son? He would like a son. He could teach him to ride — and the boy could learn all there was to know about the mine as he was growing up. Maybe he would take a real interest . . . they would be companions when he was grown . . . But a little girl would be all right too . . . Joss snapped out of his dreams. Here was the mine.

He dismounted, entered the office and looked around. It was empty.

'Hello!' he called but there was no reply. Joss scowled — where was the man? He perched himself on a corner of the desk and impatiently swung a booted foot.

Then came the scrunch of footsteps outside.

'Sorry, Joss,' the mine captain said, 'I got called away.' He came through the door with a wide grin on his face.

'You're looking very pleased with yourself,' Joss remarked, surprised. 'What's up?'

The man tramped over to the table and tossed his battered old cap on to it.

'I just been down the fifty-fathom level. The pare working that stope have found a new lode in an old outcrop what they were blasting.' He rested both hands on the table and leaned on it as he gave Joss a shrewd and calculating look, his face serious now. 'It could be something big, Joss. It have got all the signs.'

'Are you sure?' Joss's eyes widened.

'Pretty sure. Sure as I can be till they get in deeper. Only,' he shrugged and spread his hands as he stepped away a few paces, 'it's the same old story. They'll need timbers for shoring of it up before they can start — and 'tis a brem awkward old place where to get to. But just think, boy.' He faced Joss with a gleam in his eyes. 'Tin prices are rising, there's talk of a boom-time coming — like I say, it could be big.'

Joss's stomach did a flip of excitement.

'I'd trust your judgement any time, Jack.' He clapped him on the shoulder. 'But we've got to persuade the adventurers to back us as well. I'll call a meeting — you can put it to them yourself — as soon as possible I'd say, wouldn't you?' The other man nodded and did a thumbs-up in reply.

★　★　★

Joss was not looking forward to the meeting at the counthouse, but he gave an impassioned speech backed up with sound evidence of ore-samples and diagrams and it went far better than he'd expected. The general opinion seemed to be that Jack was right; there was an upsurge in tin prices and the investors had been getting better returns on their shares lately than for several years. Some of them could also be heard reckoning among themselves that maybe a new young face at the helm might be a good thing.

'We've done it, boy! Well done — you handled they wily old businessmen like a trouper!' Jack was ecstatic as he clapped Joss on the shoulder afterwards.

'I just hope they don't have second thoughts,' Joss said, wiping the sweat from his brow. He was as delighted as the mine

249

captain. 'Let's not count our chickens until the money comes in, eh, Jack?'

But come in it did. And it gave Joss huge satisfaction to set off with Jack to purchase some of the essential items needed for the mine. They had decided that timber and ladders were the first priority, and eventually, if funds could rise to it, a larger and more efficient pumping-engine.

The two men were in high spirits as they set off for Harvey's of Hayle. Harvey's Foundry were boiler-makers, timber-merchants and suppliers of mining equipment in general. The two men were travelling in Jack's horse and cart so that he could bring back a few of the smaller things immediately, and leave an order for the timber and ladders.

'Never thought the day would come,' Jack grinned, his filthy old pipe clamped between his teeth. Joss returned the grin. Neither had he.

As they entered the foundry yard they had to step around a massive completed boiler, looking like a stranded whale, which lay awaiting transport to the mine which had ordered it. The two men stopped and Jack went off to tether the horse before coming back for a closer look. His thumbs stuck in his braces and his drill coat flapping open, he looked the iron monster over.

'She's a beauty, isn't she?' he remarked, puffing on the pipe and rocking back on his heels. 'Ninety-inch, idden she, boy?' he called to a pale-faced lad in shirt-sleeves and a tattered waistcoat, who was passing with a barrow of scrap-iron.

'Yes sir.' The youth stopped and touched his cap as he caught sight of Joss. 'Boss do say it'll take twenty pair of horses to shift her,' he added, his eyes round with awe.

Joss had crouched down to examine the complicated arrangement of brass valves and tubes which sprouted from the top of the boiler and was trying in his mind to link them up with the diagrams he had seen in his study books.

A terrific din was coming from the far side of the yard where men were working on a smaller version of the boiler at their feet. The clang of hammers on iron was deafening, as four men were assembling its metal panels and riveting them together. Behind them through the open door of the smithy, they could see a huge fire blazing where more panels were being forged.

'Come on, Jack, it's wood we came for.' Joss nudged his companion with an elbow. 'Let's get on with it. Maybe one day we'll be ordering one of these beauties to drive our new pumping engine.'

'I certainly hope so, boy,' said Jack with feeling.

★ ★ ★

Rose took her hand-luggage and boarded a train for Camborne, leaving her trunk to be sent on later. She had decided to look for employment in this gritty mining town which was closest to where she had spent her early childhood, for with maturity had come the realization that this was where she had always belonged. What had she been thinking of to imagine that she could ever have had a future with Joss Pencarrow?

A snatch of song ran through her mind, a children's hymn that she had heard somewhere. How did it go? . . . 'the rich man in his castle, the poor man at his gate. God made them high and lowly, and ordered their estate . . . all things bright and beautiful . . . ' Quite so. In other words, what chance did either of them have against the will of the Almighty? Rose bit her lip and set off down the street.

She stayed for two nights at Matthews' Hotel in the town centre while she scoured the town for lodgings and employment. A cook perhaps, for a decent family — a live-in post would be ideal and she had good references supplied by the Red Lion. Rose bought a local paper and scrutinized the Positions Vacant columns. She also put her name on the register of a couple of agencies as an assistant cook.

At one interview, however, the haughty matron who examined her impeccable references, looked Rose critically up and down and stared calculatingly at her shining hair and glowing green eyes. Then she pursed her lips.

'No, Mrs Lanyon,' she said and handed Rose's papers back to her. 'You tell me that you're a widow, and quite frankly I'm afraid that you're far too physically attractive to join my staff. I have a husband and three sons, you see, and it would be a constant worry to me in case you should strike up a — liaison — with any of them. I have to be very careful whom I employ. I'm sure you understand.' She gave a thin-lipped smile. Rose took in the plump figure and plain, puffy face and understood perfectly.

'I do understand that you are making insinuations as to my moral character,' Rose retorted, flushing, 'without the slightest grounds for doing so. Presumably if I were old and ugly I would be a good enough cook, would I?' She tilted her chin defiantly and glared at the other woman, whose eyes widened.

'I think you need to remember your place, young woman. No employer, least of all me, is likely to tolerate that kind of insolence. Good day to you.'

And Rose found herself fuming, outside on the doorstep. After several more humiliating failures, she was eventually taken on by a couple with six children below the age of ten. Here she found she was expected to toil all day and half the night doing work which could not by any stretch of the imagination be called cooking. She left of her own accord with no references. Finding congenial employment was proving harder than she had anticipated.

At last Rose had to settle for a job in a bakery run by a couple with four children. They lived over the shop in a tiny house squeezed between a jeweller's and a pawn-shop. The wife, Ellen, was a dumpy, motherly sort, garrulous and always busy. Her husband Bill, thinner and quiet, was nevertheless the ruling force in the household, to whom everyone deferred.

But it was not the living-in position for which Rose had hoped, and she had immediately to lay out some of her capital on finding somewhere to live. Eventually she found a bedsitting-room in a big double-fronted house on the far edge of the town. It meant that she would have over a mile to walk each way to her work, but she thought it worth the effort, for the house faced west and looked out over the fields and woodland of the open countryside.

'My husband and I are getting on in years,' said Alice Pascoe. Her prospective landlady was a stout and well-corseted matronly woman who had to pause several times to catch her breath as they climbed the stairs, 'and we decided to let out the top two rooms which we never use. This one is vacant at the moment, my dear.' She opened the door to a large, airy room with a high ceiling and striped maroon-and-cream wallpaper. Dark red chenille curtains hung at the bay window and the bed in the corner looked comfortable, neatly tucked into its red counterpane.

Rose looked around with approval. Alice had crossed the room and was pulling aside another heavy curtain which screened an alcove in one corner.

'There's a gas ring here and a kettle, as you can see.' Rose also noticed wooden shelves holding a couple of saucepans and a few utensils. It would be ideal for her needs. She smiled and nodded.

'I think this will suit me very well,' she said, 'providing the rent is reasonable.'

'I'm not out to make a huge profit,' the

woman went on, naming a sum which Rose thought was very fair. 'It's good to have the rooms used and kept aired, and truth to tell, I like a bit of company in the house too. We're very quiet here, just Jim and me.'

She bustled out on to the landing again and pointed down the passage. 'The bathroom's at the end there, and the WC. You'll share with the other tenant, Mr Taylor. Such a nice young man he is, and very quiet in his comings and goings.' Rose smiled politely. 'He's a mining surveyor, from St Just. Left his wife and family behind while he came up here and found a job at Dolcoath. It seems that the mines down that way are failing because of the drop in tin prices, and work is scarce. Now he's looking for somewhere for them all to live and can't find a house anywhere.'

'I noticed how crowded the town is,' Rose replied. 'I tried a lot of places before coming here. Some of them are disgracefully over-crowded. One house I looked at had a couple with five children, and the wife's mother, all sleeping in one bedroom. They were offering me a shared room with three other young women, and there was no sanitation at all. I could hardly believe it.'

Rose saw again in her mind's eye the tiny,

back-to-back cottages with their broken stairs, windowless rooms and stomach-churning smells and thanked her lucky stars that she could afford something better than that. Looking around at the gleaming woodwork, warm carpeting and shaded lamps she added: 'This house is like a palace compared with that.'

Alice nodded vigorously.

'A lot of out-of-work miners less well-off than Mr Taylor have been pouring into Camborne lately, because Dolcoath is so huge they think they can get jobs there, and they all have to live somewhere. The town's becoming quite a slum, I'm told.' She wrinkled her nose. 'Of course I never go out on the streets, there's no need. The tradesmen deliver and my dressmaker calls — I never have to expose myself to the common mob at all.'

'I'd like to move in right away, if that's convenient,' Rose broke in. She suppressed a burning desire to tell this haughty woman that she had come from just such a background herself and that she had every sympathy for the hard-working 'common mob'. However she needed this room, so she bit her lip and kept her thoughts to herself. 'I've brought a few things with me and my trunk will be following.'

'That will be lovely, my dear.' Alice inclined her head. 'Here's your key. I'll leave you to settle in now.' She turned back from the head of the stairs to call over her shoulder. 'And do let me know if there's anything you want. One of us is always here, you only have to ask.'

'Thank you, I will.' Rose quietly closed the door and sat down on the bed to take stock with mixed feelings of her new life. Glad to have found a room and a job, but heartbreakingly lonely, bereft of all that she had held so dear, and with an unknown future yawning once more before her.

★   ★   ★

The worst of the winter weather was over in Cornwall, although the rest of the country was still beset with rain and gales, and by the middle of March, daffodils were flowering in cottage gardens. 'Lent lilies' the old people called them — and the hedges were full of primroses.

It was then, as if to disprove all these signs of spring, that the biggest epidemic of influenza for years chose to strike, and was soon sweeping the county. Brought in at the ports used by sailors from all over the world it spread like wildfire, bringing death and the fear of death to rich and poor alike. Children and the elderly were worst affected, but few were immune to its virulent breath.

Schools were closed, churches emptied and people stayed indoors, hoping to escape the infection, but still the numbers affected grew and the death toll mounted.

Since her marriage, Emma Pencarrow had been taking her responsibilities as lady of the manor very seriously. She had been making regular visits to the sick and elderly of the village and saw no reason to stop doing so at this time of crisis when they needed her more than ever.

'But I *mutht* go, Joth,' she protested when he found her climbing into the carriage with a loaded basket over her arm. 'Old Mithith Thnell ith bedridden. You know her daughter Janie who wath one of our kitchenmaidth hath juth died, don't you? It'th no more than my duty, Joth.'

'Then I shall go. Give me the basket Emma. That's right. To expose yourself to infection would be pure foolhardiness. And in your condition too!' He dragged it from her arm.

'But Joth . . . ' wailed his wife.

'For goodness' sake, I'm perfectly capable of offering my condolences and delivering these things.' He held out a hand to help her from the carriage. 'You know what a delicate constitution you have, dear. It would be sheer folly to go down to the village — just asking for trouble. And you must think of the baby, as I said.'

'Well, of courth, if you forbid it . . . ' She obediently descended the steps, lowering the fur-trimmed hood of her blue woollen cloak as she came.

'I do,' Joss replied, trying not to snap. He had been planning to ride over to Wheal Hope that morning to see if the supplies had arrived yet. 'Now go indoors and stay there.' He softened the command by adding, 'You're too unselfish a person for your own good, Emma, you know. Always thinking of other people and neglecting yourself.' He dropped a peck on her cheek, jumped into the carriage and bowled away down the drive.

★　★　★

In spite of Joss's concern, however, a week later Emma became confined to bed with a high fever and a racking cough. Dr Anderson was sent for and Joss's fears were confirmed when he came downstairs and beckoned Joss into the study, carefully closing the door behind him.

'I'm afraid it's influenza, yes,' he replied to

the question in Joss's eyes. The doctor passed a hand over his weary face. He hadn't seen his bed for more than a couple of hours at a stretch since the epidemic had started.

'A drink?' said Joss with sympathy. The doctor nodded and sank into an armchair. 'Just a small one, plenty of water. Wouldn't do to go breathing whisky fumes over the patients — as much as my reputation is worth.' He took a sip from the glass Joss passed him and placed it on a side table. He looked into Joss's anxious face and went on:

'It just has to run its course now. There's nothing I can do until the fever breaks. Keep her covered up — she's delirious now and tossing about, poor child. The baby is unharmed, however; there's a strong heart-beat there.' He turned to fasten up his bag. 'I'll send for a nurse to stay with her, shall I? She needs professional care — this is more than the housekeeper and the servants can manage.'

'Please, if you would,' Joss replied. 'Get the best you can, won't you?' He paced the floor, unable to settle. 'You see, Anderson, I blame myself for this,' he blurted as he turned haunted eyes towards the other man. 'I'm sure in my own mind that I brought the infection home to Emma.'

'You? But you haven't been ill, have you?'

The doctor sipped his whisky with obvious appreciation as Joss told him the story of his visiting the sick. 'I was trying to shield her by going myself — but I must have been the carrier, you see.'

'No, no, don't be so hard on yourself, Mr Pencarrow. The infection is everywhere — in the very air we breathe, I believe. You mustn't blame yourself now.' He swallowed the rest of his drink at a gulp and rose to his feet. 'Must go,' he murmured, 'so many others to see, you understand. My next call is to your gatekeeper in the lodge house. I'll send his boy to fetch Nurse Perkins. She'll come right away, I'm sure.'

'Poor Daniels, I heard that both he and his daughter are sick.' Joss came forward to see the doctor out.

'I'm sure I've no need to tell you that your wife is gravely ill, Mr Pencarrow,' the doctor said as they shook hands. 'The crisis should come tonight,' he added, 'then it will go either way. I pray to God that it will be the right one.'

★ ★ ★

But God must have had other plans. It was just after midnight when Emma suddenly screamed out in her delirium: 'Joth, Joth,' and when he seized her hand, for he had been dozing in the chair beside her, she raised her head from the pillow and stared straight at him.

'Hold me,' she whispered. 'Oh Joth, I love you,' she added, her eyes fixed and staring. She reached out trembling hands towards him. 'Tell me you — love me . . . ' she pleaded with tears in her eyes. 'Tell me . . . '

'Of course I love you, dearest Emma,' he lied, wrapping her closely in his arms. And with a smile of content lighting up her ravaged features, Emma gave a small sigh and sank back on to the lace-trimmed pillows. In a few moments Joss could hear her deep, even breathing. The fever had broken, then. His relief was so great that Joss put his own head down on the bed and fell into a sleep so profound that it seemed like hours before he was awakened with a start by Emma's movements.

Joss struggled to shake the sleep from his head and opened his eyes. Then his stomach clenched. Emma was out of bed. Like a small pale moth in her white nightgown, she had fluttered over to the window and pulled aside the curtain.

'Emma!' Joss's throat was dry and his voice hoarse. 'You shouldn't be out of bed. Come back here this minute before you get cold.'

Emma seemed not to have heard him however, as she pulled aside the curtain and looked out at the night sky. Then she sat down on the window-seat, tucked her legs up beneath her and softly began to sing a nursery rhyme.

'Twinkle, twinkle, little thtar, How I wonder what you are . . . ' Emma chuckled to herself in a childish giggle, before jumping down from the sill and crossing the room to tug at Joss's hand. 'Papa, Papa, come and thee — all the beautiful thtars in the thky . . . '

Joss quailed and his blood ran cold. For the voice was that of a little girl, a carefree and innocent small child.

'Up above the world tho high,' she crooned, 'like a diamond in the thky . . . '

Appalled, he turned and ran for the door, clattering down the stairs two at a time as he shouted for someone — anyone — to come and tell him what was happening. The nurse who had just arrived in answer to the doctor's summons was standing in the hall removing her cloak, and gaped at his dishevelled figure and frightened eyes.

'Mr Pencarrow!' She hurried to his side and placed a hand on his arm. 'Your wife — she's not . . . ?'

Joss shook his head irritably.

'No, no. Go to her right away. I have to get Anderson back here, quickly.' Leaving the outside door swinging, and the woman looking after him in astonishment, he raced down the drive and was just in time to catch the doctor as he emerged from the cottage.

★ ★ ★

'I'm more sorry than I can say to have to tell you this.' The doctor turned exhausted eyes to Joss as he quietly closed the bedroom door and they began to descend the stairs. 'But I'm afraid the fever has turned your wife's mind.'

It was the news that he had been dreading, but still Joss stared blank-faced, unbelieving, willing the man to be mistaken. It must be only a temporary delirium, wasn't it? Emma would recover, of course she would. But deep down he knew. Had known from the first moment she had slipped so suddenly out of bed and back into childhood.

'It — it'll be permanent, you mean?' Joss swallowed.

The doctor nodded. 'I've come across it before — this regression into childhood. It's as if the mind has retreated from the pain and suffering into a remembered happier world of the past. Joss, I'm so sorry.' He gripped the younger man's arm, all formality removed by the desolation on his face. 'This may sound a foolish thing to say, but your wife will be happy, you know, in her own little world. Nurse Perkins will stay as long as necessary, and in the morning I suggest we talk things over after we've both had some rest. She will need full-time professional care, you see. There is an — er — excellent institution in the county, you know . . . ? Until the morning then.' He picked up his hat and cane and trudged slowly out to his carriage, looking as if he had the cares of all the world on his bent and weary shoulders.

Joss too had to get outside, he could no longer stay in the house, let alone in the same room as the small, pathetic figure of his wife. There was nothing he could do for her and his agony was terrible. He left the sickroom to the nurse and went quietly downstairs and out into the night.

The sky was clear and full of stars, as Emma had remarked. In the cold, crisp air they sparkled and winked, remote, unchanging and uncaring. Joss strode through the grounds and down to the lake. Hands thrust deep in his pockets, shoulders hunched, he walked like an automaton, hardly heeding where he was going.

Don't blame yourself, the doctor had said. But he did blame himself, not only for

Emma's illness and for the loss of her reason, but for tearing the girl away from her family in the first place. They had only been married for four months! Four months and he had destroyed her. Condemned her to spend the rest of her life in an institution! What a cold, calculating monster he had been. He had used her — an innocent girl little more than a child — for her money. And she had loved him!

Emma had loved him and obeyed his wishes in everything and he hadn't appreciated her goodness, hadn't even noticed it because his head had been full of Rose Lanyon! Joss raised outspread hands to the unheeding sky and groaned. Oh Emma, I'm sorry, sorry. But I did it for the best of reasons! he cried.

A graceful crescent moon was sailing above the leafless trees, serene and calm. Life is full of choices, she seemed to say. And choices have consequences we may not foresee. What's done is done and there can be no going back. Now his wife was deranged, unhinged, demented. He flinched at the words which rained down on him like hammer-blows, but the situation had to be faced.

Joss wrestled alone with his private demons until the darkness began to lift and a pearly hint of dawn appeared in the eastern sky.

Then he retraced his steps, threw himself on to his bed and tossed and turned until morning.

* * *

Work at the bakery was hot, arduous and meant long hours on her feet for Rose. She arrived at six in the morning when Bill Potter, who had been up all night, retired for a few hours' sleep.

While Ellen was occupied with children and domestic tasks, Rose would take out the last batch of loaves, set out the day's fresh produce and open the shop. The establishment doubled as a bake-house and there was soon a steady stream of customers bearing covered dishes to be cooked in the great oven which was never allowed to cool down.

Between customers, Ellen, with Rose's help, mixed and prepared the cakes, buns and pasties which would provide the following day's supplies, for Bill dealt only with the bread and would bake them all together during the night.

* * *

Rose was leaving the bakery after work one evening when Reuben Clemo detached himself from the wall against which he had been lounging, and fell into step beside her.

He had lain low for so long that Rose had convinced herself that her old enemy must have given up tormenting her after all. And this assumption that she was safe at last, made the shock of seeing him now doubly great. Her heart lurched painfully in the same old way, and then began to beat faster as Rose realized that she was as vulnerable now as she ever had been as a child. There was no Matt to protect her any more, and no Joss either. She was alone in the world and had left the few friends she did have, behind her in Truro.

Reuben walked on the outside of the two of them, squeezing her against the shop-fronts as they passed, for Rose had refused to slow her pace. Dusk was falling and a damp chill hung in the January air. On each side of the street, shop assistants were pulling down their blinds and closing up. In the market, the stall-keepers would be selling off their remaining produce at knock-down prices. Rose had been on her way there before this unexpected confrontation, hoping to get some bargains to take home for her supper.

'So this is where yer to,' her cousin began in conversational tone. 'Wondered where you'd got to this time. Been looking all over

Truro fer you, I have.'

Rose ignored him and kept walking. There were still plenty of people about, this was a busy street, he couldn't do anything here, could he?

'Times are hard this time of year,' remarked her tormentor. 'Aren't getting so much coming in now the summer veg are over. Could do with a bit extra to tide me over the winter, like.' He sidled closer and gave her arm a vicious pinch. Then as Rose jumped and whirled round, something suddenly snapped inside her.

She was seething with anger. Red-hot rage boiled up in her, she was sick and tired of being harried by this disgusting creature. All her life she had gone in fear and trembling of him. Now let him say and do what he liked. Rose would face that when she had to, but right now she was going to make a stand. Rose screamed at the top of her voice and at the same time raised herself on tiptoe and raked her fingernails as hard as she could down her cousin's face.

His jaw dropped in total surprise at the onslaught and a surge of satisfaction brought a sparkle to Rose's eyes. As she felt the sickening rasp of his day-old stubble beneath her fingertips she could hardly believe her own daring, and her spirits continued to rise.

When red trails of blood begin to stream down his face, however, Reuben bellowed with rage like a wounded animal, and came at her with both fists flying. Rose had been expecting this and nimbly dodged out of his reach. She knew that the actual pain she had inflicted was minimal beside the damage to his pride and self-importance and that if he ever caught up with her again in the future, she would have to fear for her life. But it had been well worth it.

A crowd had gathered by now and soon a police constable was pushing his way through the curious onlookers, notebook in hand. Well used to street brawls, for the mining town was never free from knots of drunken miners looking for a fight, he calmly took in the scene.

'Well, what's going on here, then?' he said.

'This ruffian attacked me, officer!' Rose cried, making sure of getting her story in first. 'He made an improper suggestion,' she went on with a minimum of truth, 'and I had to defend myself.'

'That's right — I heard her scream out,' said one woman, nodding her head so vigorously that her black bonnet almost fell off.

'So did I — dunno what the world's coming to — do you? When a young woman idden safe on the streets these days, going about her law-abiding business.' A bent and white-haired crone lifted her walking-stick and waved it in the air for emphasis.

'Great bully!' she shouted. 'Ought to be 'shamed of yerself.'

'All right are you, my handsome?' chimed in another, younger woman, placing a hand on Rose's arm and looking into her face with anxious brown eyes. Rose nodded and smiled at her.

'Yes, really, thank you I'm quite all right now.'

The woman glowered.

'Dirty great lout, ought to be locked up — put him in the clink fer the night, officer, I should. Teach the brute a lesson, that would.'

'I never!' Reuben roared as he was being led protesting, away. 'Never did no such thing. I never touched her! Making it all up, she is, little liar.' He gave Rose a glare that made her blood run cold, but she felt such a great surge of satisfaction at having taken action at last, that it scarcely mattered.

★　★　★

Although she had chosen her lodgings for their comfort and agreeable surroundings, Rose was now regretting the long walk to work every day. She found herself arriving

272

back in such a state of exhaustion that she was able to do little more than collapse into bed, ready to set off again before daybreak the following morning.

Bitterly cold weather set in as the winter gales brought showers of sleet on their icy breath, and the contrast between the hothouse atmosphere of the bakery and the chill which struck out of doors, left Rose with a semi-permanent hacking cough. At work she sucked lozenges to disguise it, fearing that if the customers noticed and objected she would be forced to leave. She was constantly tired, her back ached and her whole body felt heavy and sluggish.

On one occasion at the end of a particularly busy day, when she had been on her feet for the best part of ten hours, Rose opened the fire-door to shovel in more coal. She recoiled as a blast of heat caught her full in the face and took her breath away. It set her coughing uncontrollably and when she straightened up the room began to sway around her. Rose dropped the shovel with a clatter and fainted clean away.

When she came to she was lying with her feet up on a *chaise longue* in the Potters' living-room at the back of the shop. Ellen came bustling in with a glass of water which Rose sipped gratefully, and perched on the end of the sofa as Rose drank it.

'Oh, thank you, Ellen, that was lovely. I'm sorry to be such a nuisance — I can't think what came over me.'

'I know what it's like,' the other woman replied. 'None better.' She leaned closer and said confidingly; 'I was just the same when I was carrying my youngest — always passing out, I was.'

She took the empty glass and stood up. 'When's your baby due, then, dear?' she asked.

10

Rose gasped, all the colour draining from her face, and launched into a spasm of coughing.

'B — baby?' she spluttered. 'But . . . ' Then it all clicked. The nausea, the tiredness, the sluggishness. And that absence of her monthly courses which she had put down to emotional stress and the recent upheavals in her life. How stupid she'd been!

'Didn't you realize, dear?' said Ellen gently. Rose shook her head.

'I've noticed this past few weeks that your figure's changing.'

Rose had naïvely thought that she'd been putting on weight. She had been eating more of the day-old bread and buns that the Potters gave her to take home, and fewer cooked meals because she was always so tired.

'Anyway, you have a bit of a rest until you feel better. We're not all that busy at the moment. I'll go and mind the shop.' The other woman bustled away.

'Thank you, Ellen, I shan't be long.' Rose began to do some rapid mental calculations. It was now the middle of December. Matt had died at the end of August. It should be due sometime in May, presumably. Then she clapped a hand to her mouth in shock. For how could she be sure that it *was* Matt's child? August indeed — what about that last day with Joss on the beach? That had been in October. So in that case the baby would be due in July.

But how could she be sure either that it was Joss's child? She had been married to Matt for two years, and could already have been pregnant before he died. But, said a small voice, why hadn't you conceived before? Sheer coincidence, Rose replied. But the fact was, she had no means of knowing until the baby arrived. Until she could see who it resembled.

But — a baby! How was she going to cope with it? She couldn't go on working with a baby to look after. How would they live? She would have to save every penny she could from now on. The few months would fly. Rose's head was spinning again as she thought of all the problems which lay ahead.

But a warm and tender feeling had sprung up inside her for this tiny living creature that she had never suspected was tucked underneath her heart. A little person — someone of her own to love and be loved by. Oh, how she needed someone of her own! Rose wrapped her arms about herself and as a radiant smile smoothed the worry-lines from her face, she knew she would do anything, suffer any hardship if she had to, to protect this delicate new life.

★ ★ ★

The first blow came about six weeks later. Rose knew she had been getting slow and clumsy as her body became heavier, but had not been prepared for the confrontation with Ellen Potter that occurred one evening just as she was leaving.

The shop had just closed. Ellen finished pulling down the blinds.

'Rose,' she said suddenly, 'sit down a minute. I have to talk to you.'

Rose perched on a stool behind the counter, only too glad to be off her feet for a minute. Ellen stood awkwardly beside her.

'It's Bill,' she began. 'He's asked me to tell you. More — well — *seemly*, coming from another woman, he thought. The fact is Rose, that you won't be able to go on working here much longer. He won't have it, I'm afraid.'

She noticed the colour drain from Rose's face to be replaced by a white, pinched look and her heart went out to the girl. But what Bill said was law, and he was quite right really. They couldn't jeopardize their own business and their own livelihood for the sake of an employee.

'It's now that you're . . . well . . . showing so obviously,' Ellen said. 'It's the customers, you see. We have quite a decent class of trade here and Bill doesn't want them upset. He says it isn't — nice. Not seemly is what he said. I'm sorry my dear, but I'm sure you understand.'

Rose gathered the remnants of her tattered dignity together and looked the other woman in the eye.

'Oh, of course. I understand perfectly, Ellen. And I wouldn't dream of embarrassing either of you.' Rose's chin came up.

'You can stay until the end of the week, naturally.'

'I'll go now,' Rose's face was set. 'It'll be more *seemly*, won't it.'

'But I didn't mean . . . ' Ellen blustered. 'Have you anyone to help you? Friends? Family?'

'No, I'm all alone,' Rose replied. 'But I shall manage.'

'I would let you live here until the baby is born if it was up to me, but you know how difficult . . . ' Her voice trailed away and she spread her hands in a shrug. Rose knew Ellen Potter was good-hearted enough in her way, but she was right, there wasn't an inch of space to spare in their house as it was.

So Rose took the little money owing to her and trudged back to her room.

* * *

One bright spot that slightly lifted her spirits came with a letter from Kate which had been forwarded to the post office and was awaiting her collection. Rose went straight out again to fetch it, then sat down on her bed and slit the envelope in eager anticipation.

Dear Rose she read,
I am taking the opportunity to send this via a Falmouth Packet vessel which we met in port. Although we've only been at sea for three weeks, it feels more like three months. Our quarters are cramped and stuffy and the rules we live under are strict.

There is a daily timetable which starts at seven in the morning when we have to get up, dress, shake our bedding to air it and sweep our deck and under the berths (that's ship language for beds!) before breakfast at eight. We go to bed at ten.

The days are long and very boring with

little to do, so tempers are easily frayed. Fights break out over nothing. Two Irishmen were clapped in irons this morning for fighting over a woman.

Will and I have made friends with another Cornish couple, from St Just. The father is a miner too and they have two small children. Children fare badly, both from the lack of fresh milk and from constant outbreaks of fever. Three little ones have died already. Oh Rose, it's heartbreaking to see those tiny bundles sliding into the sea!

We survived a terrible storm a few weeks ago when our boat shipped a lot of water. At one point our deck was awash with water pouring down the hatchway from above, and when I saw our baggage floating in it I was terrified, thinking we should all be drowned.

At least I haven't been afflicted with the sea-sickness which has prostrated most of the women — (and some men!) — and I try to make myself useful to those who are.

When the weather permits we have a band in the evenings, with dancing on deck. The crew try to keep our spirits up. I try not to think of Cornwall, which I sadly miss, but must look forward not back. We

have about five more months at sea. I'll write again whenever I can send mail.
Affectionately,
Kate.

Rose wiped her eyes which were streaming, and blew her nose. She had heard her friend's voice as clearly as if she had been in the room, and the thought of Kate's cheerful face and bubbly character made her feel worse than ever. She would have given all that she possessed at that moment to pour out her troubles to Kate and receive her friend's support and some of her practical common-sense advice. Frightened of the future, all alone and friendless, Rose badly needed someone to talk to, and she wept harder than ever when she realized that it was quite possible that she and Kate would never see each other again.

★   ★   ★

Joss had sent for Emma's mother as soon as her mental condition had been confirmed. Maude Robartes was thin and slight, with a permanently anxious look about her, and the pale colouring which her daughter shared.

'So I'm afraid the situation is irreversible,' Joss repeated, wiping a hand across his brow.

'I made sure she was seen by several specialists, and they all say the same thing.' They were sitting in the high-ceilinged drawing-room, its walls hung with new paper which Emma had chosen, and tastefully furnished in shades of cream and green. Maude was huddled beside the tiled grate in which burned a roaring fire, while Joss stood with an elbow on the mantelshelf beside her, one booted leg crossed over the other. Emma, seated on a stool at the far end of the room, was cradling a doll which had been left behind by the housekeeper's grandchild, and which she had seized upon with delight.

Her mother stifled a sob, dabbed her eyes and straightened up with a rustle of her burgundy taffeta skirt.

'Oh, the shame of it,' she whispered. 'Whatever am I going to *tell* people . . . ?' She fidgeted with the cream lace fichu at her throat. Joss, fuming, took in a breath and for once held his tongue.

'Of course, in my opinion,' Maude wailed, 'Emma was too delicate for marriage in the first place.' She twisted the handkerchief in her hands. 'She should never have — '

'Married a brute like me, do you mean?' Joss's voice was dangerously quiet and his eyes flashed blue sparks. 'It's all my fault, is it?' he growled. He detached himself from the

282

fireplace and paced across the room.

The woman looked discomfited and a little colour appeared on her chalk-white face.

'No, of course not, I didn't mean it like that. Forgive me. I'm so upset.' She held out a hand in a feeble attempt to placate him.

'So are we all, madam,' Joss said tersely. 'But what I can't understand,' he went on, striding back across the room and towering over her, 'is why she calls me her 'Papa'. Have you any idea?'

Maude Robartes looked up to meet his eyes and twisted her damp handkerchief between her fingers.

'My husband died when Emma was six, as I'm sure you know,' she said. 'Emma was devoted to him and he doted on her. When he died so suddenly in the riding accident, the shock was such that I don't think she ever really got over it.

Children keep their feelings close to themselves and I couldn't get near to her to talk it over. She just withdrew into herself and never voluntarily mentioned his name again, she missed him so badly. I think she never stopped grieving for him even when she was a grown woman, although of course it never showed.'

She glanced at Emma who was tossing the

doll in the air and catching it as she laughed up into its face.

'Perhaps now that she has returned to childhood,' another tear rolled down Maude's face, 'it's natural that she should look for him again. And as you are the only male figure she knows, then in her eyes you are her father.' She glanced at Joss and shrugged.

Surprised at the perception of this woman whom he had written off as an empty-headed snob, Joss looked down at her with new respect.

'Yes,' he said slowly, 'I see. I can believe that.' His eyes rested on the figure of his child-wife and, as if sensing his gaze, she looked over and smiled sweetly back at him. Joss swallowed down the lump in his throat.

He coughed, and sat down in a velvet armchair opposite Maude.

'Now, apart from seeing Emma of course, I've asked you here today in order to discuss future plans. About her — um — the coming child.' He picked at a loose thread on his jacket-sleeve and avoided her eyes. 'The doctors tell me there's no reason why Emma shouldn't give birth in the normal way.' Joss raised his head and solemnly met the woman's eyes. 'But of course she will be totally unable to care for it herself. She won't suffer by having it taken away from her, as she will be just as content with a . . . ' he glanced across at his wife and his eyes were tortured, 'doll. So, I've been going over and over the alternatives ever since this happened and I've decided that — with help from the living-in staff whom I shall engage — I'm prepared to bring up my child myself.'

Maude stared at him for a long moment, then slowly nodded.

'I admire your courage,' she said at last. 'It will be an enormous undertaking, but I would help you in any way I can, of course. I shall want to be part of my grandchild's life too.'

'Of course,' Joss replied. A small silence fell before he went on: 'In the meantime, Dr Anderson has suggested that Emma should go into a — um — sanatorium.' He refused to use the word 'asylum', unable to face its connotations of tormented souls in straitjackets confined to their padded cells. 'St Lawrence's, at Bodmin. Conveniently near Lanhydrock, so you will be able to visit her frequently.'

He looked Maude in the eye. 'Unless of course,' he added on second thoughts, 'you would prefer to have her at home and care for her yourself.' The last thing he wanted to do was tread on the woman's toes and appear to be settling everything without consulting her. She was Emma's mother, after all, and should be involved, if only for the sake of courtesy.

But Maude shook her head and her eyes filled with alarm.

'Oh no — no. The . . . stigma, you know.' Joss snorted in disgust as she added: ' . . . Far better that she should be cared for by experts. The — ah — hospital would be much the more acceptable option.'

Then the tears began to flow again and she clutched at Joss's arm.

'She must have the best of care, of course. Anything that money can provide. I'll see to it, Joss. Please let me help. Darling Emma — she's my only daughter and I've missed her so much since she was married. Now, in a strange way, she'll always be my little girl for the rest of her life.'

Joss absently patted her hand as she rose to leave.

'I'll come and see her often. As her 'Papa' of course,' he said grimly as he showed her to the door.

He returned to his seat and his thoughts took a leap forwards into a bleak future, one where he would remain married in name only for the rest of his life to a child who believed that he was her father.

Joss ground his teeth and swore under his

breath. This was to be the cross he had to bear, then. Not content with piling guilt upon guilt, it seemed that fate was also going to wrestle him into the ground and take delight in trampling him underfoot.

Restlessly he rose to his feet again and paced the room, hands thrust deep in his pockets. His one consolation was in the prospect of his coming son, or daughter, but he quailed at the very thought of the problems that bringing up a motherless child entailed. His mind was in turmoil, he had to talk to somebody or he would go stark, raving mad himself. He turned on his heel and made for the estate office.

★   ★   ★

Anthony looked up in surprise as Joss came thundering in and banged the door behind him. He was sitting at the great desk going through a pile of rent-books, but seeing from his brother's manner that something was badly wrong, he laid them aside and stood up to meet him.

'What's up, Joss?' With concern he laid a hand on his brother's arm and guided him into a deep leather armchair. Anthony perched on the edge of another and added: 'Emma's not taken a turn for the worse, has she?'

'Oh, no.' Joss gave a hollow laugh. 'How much worse could she be, for goodness sake?' He spread his hands wide and his face was haunted. 'Anthony, I've got to talk to someone or I shall go mad too. You see, it's all my *fault*.'

Anthony looked blankly at him and ran a hand through his flop of brown hair.

'What do you mean, your fault?' He frowned. 'How can it possibly be *your* fault?'

Joss fidgeted with the tasselled fringe of a cushion.

'You don't know the half of it,' he said with a sigh as he shifted restlessly in his seat, 'but I should have told you in the first place. It concerned you and Edward as much as me, but Papa wanted it kept quiet in case Mama got to know . . . '

'Joss!' Anthony broke in, 'you're not making any sense. Slow down and start at the beginning, will you. *What* should you have told me?'

So Joss launched into the whole story of their father's financial ruin, of how he had been forced into marriage to save the estate and of the mind-numbing guilt which had engulfed him since Emma's illness and its consequences. Anthony heard him through, his eyes never leaving his brother's face. By the time he had finished, the cushion was in shreds and Joss hurled it forcefully across the room. Then he buried his face in his hands and silence fell. Anthony left his chair, placed a comforting hand on his brother's shoulder and began to pace the room.

'Now, Joss, listen to me for a change.' He wheeled round and pointed a finger. 'Did Emma have any inkling that you married her for her money?'

'No! Of course not,' Joss's head shot up as he replied with indignation. 'I was hardly going to tell her that, was I?'

'Then she must have loved you and believed that you were in love with her, right?'

'Er — um — yes.' Joss nodded. 'Yes, she did. Actually, it was the last thing she said to me that night. Before — before her mind went.'

'So, in that case,' Anthony went on — like a barrister questioning a prisoner in the dock, Joss thought, 'she was perfectly happy in her married state?'

'I suppose so,' his brother replied with a touch of irritation. 'What's that got to do with anything?'

'It's got everything to do with it.' Anthony stopped his pacing and returned to his seat. Gesturing with his hands he faced Joss and went on: 'We've established that Emma loved you, thought you loved her, and was happy in her marriage. *I* know that she enjoyed being mistress of Great Place, not only because it was what she had been brought up to do, but also because she used to talk to me quite a lot.' Joss's eyes widened. He hadn't known that. His brother looked him squarely in the face.

'She told me more than once how kind and generous you were, and how you let her do what she wanted to the house,' Anthony added.

Joss's mouth opened in surprise. 'She did?'

'Oh yes. And what I'm coming to is this. The only one who has really suffered from all this is you, Joss.' Anthony wagged a finger. 'And I'm more sorry than I can say that things have turned out as they have for you. You didn't deserve to be saddled with all that responsibility in the first place and I admire you immensely for all that you've done. But there's really no reason to go on flaying yourself unnecessarily with guilt over Emma. Do you understand me?' He ran his fingers through his floppy brown hair and looked closely into his brother's face.

Joss stared back at him for a long moment, then slowly he nodded his head.

'I believe I do,' he said at last. Then; 'She's going into a . . . a home, you know.'

'The best thing for her,' said Anthony

briskly. 'She'll have the greatest care taken of her, the best that money can buy. And she'll be happy, Joss, because she doesn't know that she isn't normal. Do you see?'

Joss nodded again and this time there was a lightening of his expression.

'Anthony, you're right.' He thumped a fist into his open palm. 'I can't tell you what a relief it's been to talk it all over. I *can* see the whole thing differently now. I'm grateful,' he said gruffly and shook his brother's hand.

'A pleasure.' Anthony rose to his feet and gave a mock bow from the waist. 'I rest my case,' he said. As they both laughed, the tension was broken and the talk turned to other topics.

'How's the estate business going?' Joss wandered over to the desk and glanced at the papers there.

'All right so far.' Anthony came to stand beside him and stood gazing out of the window. 'I thought I might offer the eldest Daniels boy a job as my assistant.'

'Tom? Ah yes, that's a good idea. He's a bright youngster, more intelligent than the rest of them.' Joss thrust his hands in his pockets.

'That's what I thought.' Anthony nodded, his eyes on the drift of early snowdrops beneath the trees of the parkland. On the circular lawn a solitary blackbird was hunting out worms and the leafless trees beyond made a dark frieze against the pale blue of the sky. 'He takes an interest in everything and gets on well with people. I think he'll do.'

'Well, I won't take up any more of your time, old man. See you at dinner.' Joss turned as he reached the door. 'And Anthony — thanks,' he said gruffly, closing it quietly behind him.

★ ★ ★

Since Rose had lost her job at the bakery, she had been living on as little as she possibly could. She sadly missed the day-old bread and cakes which had been a 'perk' she had come to rely on, and bought the cheapest and most nourishing food each day, telling herself that she had to eat for the sake of the baby.

She had become adept at acquiring less than perfect vegetables and fruit left over in the market at the end of the day, and haggling at its stalls for the cheapest cuts of meat or fish. She walked everywhere and dreaded the time when she would have to pay out for new boots. On the market stalls she also picked up some little second-hand garments and blankets for the baby.

Rose's constant headache was finding the rent money every week. She hoarded her fast-dwindling funds, begrudging each penny she spent, fearful that the day would come when she would no longer be able to pay it and would be turned out. She tried to take in sewing, but there were so many hard-pressed women in straitened circumstances like her own that work of any kind was almost non-existent.

As the months went by she was reduced to pawning the few articles of value she had left. The clock that had been a wedding present from Kate and Will was the first to go. It paid the rent for a few weeks, but Rose doubted that she would ever be able to redeem it.

Thinking of Kate led Rose to call at the post office on the way back and, as if wishing had conjured it up, found a letter from her friend waiting to be collected. At last she sank into a chair and eased her heavy body. She was becoming more and more tired, finding the effort needed to go out for food more trying every day. However, this would take her mind off her own troubles for a few minutes.

Rose eagerly tore open the letter. She had not been able to reply to the first one as Kate had still been travelling. Perhaps she was settled by now.

Copperfield Mining Co., St Lawrence, Queensland, Australia was the address at the head of the letter. So they had arrived safely, thank goodness, thought Rose.

Dear Rose,

At last after five months on board ship we have arrived! Three weeks ago we entered Keppel Bay. However we were not permitted to set foot on the mainland for another three weeks, during which we were kept in quarantine on Curtess Island, just off the coast. A tedious time. Eventually we left Keppel Bay for Broadsound in a steamer, then on to St Lawrence.

Then we headed out into the bush. What an adventure! We had to sleep on the ground during the eight-day journey and bake our bread every night. Those with children had to carry them on their backs and we were all exhausted by the time we at last reached Copperfield.

It's a ramshackle place, I'm afraid, but we are determined to make the best of it. Will and some of the other miners we made friends with on board ship have knocked together some two-roomed wooden shacks with just earth floors and roofs made out of branches of wood.

I do my cooking out of doors and we

have goats that provide us with meat and milk. They live on the rough grazing where other animals would not survive. Fresh water is scarce. The whole place is covered with abandoned shafts and piles of stones and waste — a bit like Cornwall.

We have at last got our mineral lease from the mining company and can start prospecting in earnest. We are both in good health and spirits and hopeful. I often think of you and envy you still being in Cornwall. It will always be home to me. Write soon to the above address, I long for news. Will joins me in sending fondest love.

Kate

Rose wiped away her tears and wished again, futile as it was, that she had her friend by her side to chat to. She went to the window and looked out at the pale sky. The trees were rapidly unfurling their new leaves for it was early May now. Spring flowers were dancing in the cottage gardens and in the lanes the hedges were full of primroses. Rose leaned her head against the glass and sighed.

Soon came the time which she had been dreading for months. Her scanty store of money would not cover the rent. Rose had nothing left to pawn. The last thing to go, which had been a heart-wrenching decision, had been her wedding-ring.

All she had left were the clothes she stood up in, the baby garments, and a precious handful of small change. She picked up the pathetically small bag and took leave of her landlady with the excuse that she needed to live nearer to the town. Rose held her chin held high and made no mention of the dire straits that she was in. She still had her pride.

Her heart was in her boots, but there was no other way out. She would have to go to Gas Lane and try to find somewhere there. This malodorous street was the sink in which dwelled the very poorest of the poor. It was the notorious abode of 'women of the night', thieves and paupers. Little more than a narrow alley behind the respectable shopping streets, it was overshadowed by the two huge gas-holders from which it took its name, and was seldom free from the noxious fumes which emanated from them.

Despite the cramped and tumbledown condition of the tiny cottages, they were nevertheless divided up into even smaller tenements where whole families lived cheek by jowl with each other. Men, women and children all herded in together, the maximum number of souls crammed into the minimum living space, with no water, no sanitation and no hope. Landlords were now demanding whatever outrageous sums they liked, for accommodation was increasingly hard to come by as more and more out-of-work miners flocked to the town daily.

A woman leaning against the doorpost looked Rose up and down as she approached and stared at her bag of belongings. She was clutching a baby in a ragged shawl. A listless child sat on the step at her feet dabbling in the rubbish-filled gutter.

'Looking fer a room are you, my handsome?' she asked, a spark of hope lighting up her eyes.

Rose slowed down and stared back at her.

'Maybe,' she replied with caution. 'Why?'

'Got one going here. You can share with two other maids if you've a mind to. Got one bed spare, I have. You're lucky — idden nothing else in the street, I can tell 'ee.' She shifted the baby to the other hip and straightened up. 'Come us on in, I'll show un to 'ee.'

What did she have to lose? Rose picked her way with distaste over the detritus and followed the woman inside.

Her heart sank even further as the woman led the way up a flight of filthy stairs on to a dark landing and flung open a door.

'In here. But you'll have to keep your

mouth shut, mind.' She turned sharply and looked over her shoulder at Rose. 'If Gus ever found out I was sub-letting he'd take the rent-money off me — I aren't supposed to do it see. And if any one do ask, you're my sister, all right?'

Rose nodded and swallowed. The last thing she wanted was to be mixed up in anything shady.

The room was marginally cleaner than Rose had expected, although the windows were covered with grime, and a rag had been stuffed into one corner where the glass was broken.

Three rusty iron bedsteads took up most of the space, two together under the window and one on the far side. There were a few nails knocked into the wall where various items of clothing hung and a piece of broken mirror was propped on a shelf above them. The floorboards were bare and on a rickety table stood a wash-basin and ewer. That was all.

Rose nodded dispiritedly, not trusting herself to speak for fear she should break down. But she had lived in poverty before and this was not too far removed from the conditions of her childhood. Ruefully she reminded herself how she had chosen to come back to her roots. But not quite so realistically as this. She looked the woman in the eye.

'How much?' she said.

The sum was little enough, but nevertheless her remaining money would last only for a week or two. Perhaps, she thought forlornly, something would turn up by then. She nodded.

'I'll take it,' she said. As if she had any choice.

★ ★ ★

A few weeks later and the harrowing time of Joss's self-loathing was over at last. The cliché that time is a great healer loses none of its truth with being well-used, and one day Joss discovered that the clouds had lifted. He would never neglect Emma, he would continue to take the long road to Bodmin to visit her at least once a week in all winds and weathers, but life had to go on and he had work to do. The time had come to take up the threads again.

He would ride over to Wheal Hope and see if the supplies that he and Jack Trenerry had ordered had arrived yet. Joss's realization that this had been his destination on the day he had done Emma's sick-visiting in her stead, failed for once to stab him with the familiar pang of guilt, and he even whistled cheerfully as he saddled up Captain and headed for the mine.

Joss never came this way without thinking of Rose, and instinctively turned his head to glance down the lane where she lived as he came to the turning. But he never caught so much as a glimpse of her. Today, however, the happy laughter and high-pitched voices of children at play held Joss's attention. The sounds must be coming from Rose's cottage, it was the only one in the lane. He longed to see her, and although the shadow of Emma would be forever hanging over them, surely they could be friends again?

He could not prevent himself from turning the horse's head and following the noise around the corner. As he looked over the gate he could see three children playing in the patch of back garden. One was sitting on a home-made swing, being pushed by another, while the third was tumbling on the rough grass with a puppy. A plump woman in long white apron was hanging out washing near the house. She had seen him staring, he would have to speak to her.

'Pardon me, madam, I'm — er — looking for Mrs Lanyon,' Joss improvised. She dried her hands in her apron and crossed the yard towards him.

'Mrs Lanyon don't live here no more, sir,' she said. 'Turned out she were, after her husband died, see.'

'Turned out?' Joss suddenly felt light-headed and could only repeat the woman's words parrot-fashion. He swallowed hard. It had never occurred to him that Rose had lost her home. It was obvious now, but preoccupied with his own problems as he had been, he had always taken it for granted that she was still here. He forced himself to appear calm.

'I didn't know that,' he replied. 'Do you know where Mrs Lanyon is living now?'

'No sir, I don't. I didn't never know she neither. The house was empty when we came. My husband do work down to Wheal Hope, see. That's how we got it.'

'Yes, well, thank you,' Joss said, cutting her off in mid-flow. He tossed a couple of coins to the children who were now clustering around their mother's skirts, waved goodbye and turned back towards the road.

He was overwhelmed by a feeling of *déjà-vu*. This had all happened before. *The baby died, mester, and she runned away. Her husband died sir, and she's gone away.* Oh, Rose, where are you?

As the horse wandered at will, Joss's brain was madly racing. Truro, the Red Lion

— that was the obvious place. That was where she had gone twelve long years ago.

He set off right away.

★ ★ ★

Joss stabled his horse and entered the dining-room of the hotel, where he took a seat in the window. The last time he had sat here Rose had dropped his pasty on the floor. He passed a hand over his eyes. A young woman was standing beside him, an order-book in her hand.

'Yes, sir?'

Joss looked at her closely. She was a stranger.

'I'll — I'll have a pasty, please. And can you tell me . . . ' he called after her as she turned to go, 'if Rose Lanyon is anywhere around?'

Eva, the kitchen-maid, now promoted to Kate's position, raised wide eyes at the question and shook her head.

'Oh, no sir. Rose don't work here no more. She left after — did you know her husband died?'

Joss nodded. 'Left? Why did she do that?'

'Oh,' the girl said and shrugged her shoulder. 'A fresh start, I believe she said. Get away from the past, like. I'll get your order, sir.'

'Just a minute.' Joss's voice was urgent. The girl was looking at him strangely. 'Does anyone here know where she is? I — I need to get in touch with her on a . . . matter of business. It's very important,' he emphasized.

'I'll ask Fanny.' The girl drifted off to the kitchen.

Left. To get away from the past. Because I had broken her heart. Oh Rose, my only love.

'Here you are, sir.'

Joss jumped, he hadn't seen her coming back. All he could see was Rose's vivid face filling his mind, blotting out everything else. But the girl had put his pasty in front of him. 'Fanny don't rightly know, sir. Rose were going to write when she'd got somewhere to live, but she never did. She went somewhere down west, she do think, near to where she come from.'

Down west. Pretty vague, but he would go back again and ask around. Right away. Joss bolted his pasty and threw some coins on to the table. He would have gone to the ends of the earth to find Rose.

★ ★ ★

But Joss was prevented from beginning his search right away as he had intended, by an unexpected turn of events.

He was alone in the counthouse at Wheal Hope, having called to see Jack Trenerry in order to clear a few things up before he went. The other man had just departed for home and Joss, who had stayed behind to have a look at the account books, soon became aware that a storm was blowing up outside. He crossed the room to glance out of the window, wondering if he would get a soaking on the way home.

Towering plum-coloured clouds were marching in over the sea, pushed rapidly along by a freshening gale at their backs. The first drops of rain had already begun to splatter against the glass, and Joss swore under his breath. Would it be better to leave now and hope to race before the wind, or sit it out where he was, not knowing how long it might last?

As he debated the point, the decision was taken out of his hands by a terrific squall of wind and rain which suddenly hurled itself screaming at the window.

Joss decided that as he was marooned for the time being, he might as well have a further look at the figures to pass the time. He opened one of the great ledgers. The evidence was promising. As Jack had predicted, tin prices were booming, and that meant that they could sell as much ore as they raised. But the mine would be so much more productive once the new equipment was installed. Piles of timber and new iron ladders were at that moment at the pithead; the carpenters would start putting them in tomorrow.

He pulled another leather-cornered book towards him and studied the columns of neat copperplate handwriting. With a flip of excitement he discovered that they could now afford to install the much-needed pumping-engine he had set his heart on. But it had become so dark in the room that he could no longer see the figures. Joss took another look out of the window.

Below him the force of the wind combined with a high tide was flinging great breakers in to smash against the rocks, sending columns of flying spray thirty feet or more into the air. Such was the power of the elements that Joss felt the building shake as the earth seemed to tremble beneath him. The thought that the ground was riddled for miles with the labyrinthine workings of Wheal Hope was not a comforting one.

From the stable across the yard, Captain gave a whinny of fright as a sudden clap of thunder broke almost overhead. He would have to go over to him. Joss had his hand on the door-latch when he heard a different noise again. This a roaring, a splintering, a splitting, and the floor beneath him rocked in earnest now. An earthquake? Joss pulled open the door, and in the teeth of the gale which almost wrenched it out of his hand, he saw half the cliffside below him slowly detach itself from the rest. Joss slammed the door and leant upon it, gripping the handle as the wind sought to fling him over the edge.

For a second, the broken piece of land stayed upright and intact, like a slice of cake, before crumbling away almost in slow motion. It slid into the boiling water with a roar like a wild animal, breaking up into hundreds of tons of debris as it went.

Joss was too astonished to feel fear. Open-mouthed with awe, it was a few minutes before he realized that the wind had dropped and the storm was virtually over. Out at sea ragged streaks of pale sky were appearing as the clouds were swept away, and the rain was easing off.

Then over the pounding of the sea Joss could clearly hear the sound of a hooter. A fog-horn? But there wasn't any fog. A warning buoy for shipping? It came again and Joss's stomach lurched. He knew now with deadly certainty that it was the alarm signal from Wheal Hope.

11

As Joss, stormbound in the counthouse, had been gazing out to sea, down in the deepest level of Wheal Hope, sixteen fathoms beneath it, Martin Blewett and his pare were setting a charge in an outcrop of rock which was blocking the way to their lode.

One of the men tipped a little gunpowder into the newly bored hole, tamped it carefully down and lit the fuse. All three then scrambled well away to the end of the tunnel and sat down to wait for the blast. Nothing happened. Minutes passed.

'Something's up, Martin. Tamped it in good and proper, did you?'

''Course he did, I was watching. Been doing it years enough, haven't he?'

'Well, nothing's happening. Powder's damp, I reckon. I'm going back to see what's up.

'Better hang on a minute more, boy.' Martin Blewett was more cautious. 'Just to make sure, like.'

'Aw, come us on, Martin — can't sit here on our backsides all day, can us? My dear life, if you don't go, I will!'

The speaker jumped to his feet and turned

back, with Martin and the others following behind. Miners working on tribute, who knew they were on to a good lode, they begrudged any time wasted on a shift. The only sound in the tunnel as they trudged back to the pitch was that of their hobnailed boots ringing on stone, and the only light the dipping candles on their hats.

Suddenly there came a blinding flash of light which for a split second illuminated the whole working. But only for an instant. Then the tunnel was rent by a tremendous explosion, and with the grinding and splintering sound of stone parting from stone, great fissures appeared in the sides and roof as the solid rock began to move.

'Out!' cried a voice, 'run for your life!'

But his voice was abruptly cut off as the sea, no longer held at bay, burst into the level like a wild animal. It pursued its quarry down the maze of tunnels, roaring and clutching, carrying barrows, picks and shovels on its back as if they were matchsticks, and in a few seconds the entire level was completely flooded.

The greedy tongues of water licked ravenously through the narrow maze of passages, picking off those miners one by one who had been too far from the ladders to escape the slavering jaws. Some had hoped to survive by climbing the sides, by clutching at an overhang, by flattening themselves into crevices; all in vain. They were swallowed up in the maw of the monster as if they had never been.

And once their screams had been silenced, the only sound far underground was the hiss of seething water, and the grinding of stone upon stone like so many gigantic teeth, as the leviathan digested its meal.

★   ★   ★

Joss flung himself on to Captain's back and galloped the half-mile towards the shaft as fast as conditions allowed. The track was drenched and treacherous, slippery with mud and running with rivulets of storm-water draining away to the sea.

He arrived breathless to find a crowd of women gathered at the pithead in a bewildered huddle, crying children clutching at their skirts, babies snatched from the cradle in their arms. Joss sighted Jack Trenerry with a knot of other men and pushed his way towards them.

'What's happened?' he said tersely.

'There've been a fall — down in the bottom level. We do think the sea have broken in, boy.' He turned a grey and haggard face towards Joss. 'There's a group down there now, searching.'

A shout came suddenly from the mouth of the shaft and the grim face of a miner appeared, closely followed by two others. They dragged themselves wearily out, their naked torsos red-stained and glistening with sweat which was streaking through the dirt that caked their bodies. The first man sank on to an upturned barrow and removed his hard hat to wipe the back of a hand across his brow. The white cotton of the skullcap which he wore underneath gleamed incongruously against his grimy skin.

'It's bad,' he said shortly. 'Bottom level's awash. Shoring have all collapsed and the sea's broke in.' He covered his face with hands that shook. 'It's flooded to the roof and there's twenty-five men missing.'

'We're down there digging,' added the second man, 'but we can't do nothing really until it's pumped out. Bleddy old pump can't cope, see. It'll take days, maybe weeks, afore we can bring they up. All us can do is to try to get through to they what was further up nearer the ladders. But there's so much stuff come down, it's some job.'

'Give us some candles and more rope,' called out another of them. 'And planks — we shall need they for stretchers to get them to the shaft when we do start sending of them up. Come us on, Jim, let's get back down there.'

His companion was fixing a fresh candle to his hat with a bit of clay when Joss called out:

'Wait! I'm coming with you.'

He stripped off his shirt, grabbed a hard hat and followed the others. Jack Trenerry came up beside him.

'I've got about twenty of the surface workers waiting outside, ready to go down and help,' he said.

'We're working in relays,' replied the man called Jim. 'There isn't no room for all of us down there one time. Give us two or three and some more can relieve us in about an hour, say. All right, Jack?'

The mine captain nodded, and the men vanished one by one down the hatchway and out of sight. Knowing what they had to face, it was like watching them descend into hell.

★   ★   ★

It was nearly noon the next day before the rescuers acknowledged that there was no more that they could do. Of the twenty-five men, eight were still unaccounted for, presumed drowned. Fourteen had been brought up alive, some with mangled limbs,

311

some with head-injuries or internal damage from being crushed. Only time would tell whether these would recover.

Three bodies had been found beneath the fallen debris which had smothered them.

'George here was with them,' said one of the rescuers as he helped an injured man out of the great iron kibble normally used for hauling up the ore.

The miner had a bloodstained bandage around his head, but was able to take up the story. He sat down on the floor with his back to the wall, a dazed look on his face, as the crowd of women hung on to his every word.

'I was first to the ladder and started climbing fast as I could, so's the others could get a foothold on it too, see.' He paused and took a swig of the tea that had been thrust into his hand. 'I'd just reached over my head and grabbed at the second one, when I heard a scream from below. The bleddy old ladder had come away from the wall and pitched they two men to their death.'

He wiped a shaking hand across his dirt-streaked face and sobbed. 'I shall hear their screams until my dying day. Wasn't nothing I could do. I was hanging on just by my hands, with my feet kicking about trying to get a grip for myself before I went down after them. I managed to catch my heel on a stone in the wall and heave myself up. Then I didn't have no strength left. I just hung on there till they come for me.' He began to shake as shock set in, and was helped away to the miners 'dry' which was being used as a field hospital.

* * *

There was scarcely a family in the district which had not been affected either directly or indirectly by the accident. To Joss it was a body-blow all the more painful because of its timing.

In another few days the rotten ladders would have been replaced, a few weeks and the new pumping-engine would have been functioning. If only . . . Too late . . . All that money wasted. Money for which he had sacrificed his freedom and which had brought little more than tragedy in its wake. Firstly with Emma's condition and now this . . . Was nothing ever going right for him again? Joss punched a fist on his knee as thoughts like this numbed his brain and kept pace with the horse's hoofs as he made his way towards Camborne a few days later.

Equally hard to bear was the death of Martin Blewett, whom Joss had come to regard as a good friend. He had learnt a great deal from Martin in his early days as a miner.

Joss had attended his joint funeral with that of the other men from Wheal Hope, a harrowing experience and one he would never forget. Afterwards, Joss tried to remember the time when he had last been really happy. He could see only like a bright star shining far away, the day on the beach when he and Rose had made love for the first time.

Rose — he had been going to try and trace her before all this happened. And he still would — he must, but always something would keep coming up that he had to attend to first.

Today he had another duty. He was on his way to see how Nell Blewett was faring, although he would rather have been going almost anywhere else.

* * *

Alone in her squalid room Rose was in a desperate state. The scant few coins she had left would not last for many more days. By the end of the week she would be a pauper, no better off than the other wretches in this street of wretchedness. When she found that she had even lost her precious pawn tickets, it was the last straw. Rose buried her face in her hands and wept.

At the lowest ebb in her life, Rose leaned her elbows on the window-sill and gazed through the cracked pane at the clear evening sky. The horned tip of a graceful new moon was piercing a bank of low cloud and its beauty held her spellbound, deflecting her attention for a brief moment from her problems as she watched it metamorphose into a delicate golden crescent and sail into a patch of indigo sky.

Rose gave a trembling sigh and turned into the room again. She was now facing the looming spectre of the workhouse, which was becoming more real as the days went by. Her precious little baby would be born in the workhouse and brought up as a charity child.

No! Rose gave a silent scream and cradled the unborn infant to herself as if to protect it from this final humiliation. For there *was* still one other way. It was the last thing in the world that she wanted to do, but faced with such a stark choice she would have to do it.

Now even her pride was to be taken from her, for she was going to have to smother it and contact Joss Pencarrow. Not for herself, she told her conscience, but for this innocent soon to be born, which might, after all, be his own child. And even if it wasn't, it deserved a better start in life than it was facing now.

Before his bitter betrayal, Rose reasoned, they had been everything to each other, and even now she didn't want to come between him and his wife. All she would ask for would be Joss's temporary help just to tide her over the baby's birth and until she could get to her feet again.

Rose gritted her teeth, found a stub of pencil and wrote a simple message.

Joss. Please will you meet me on Thursday morning by the bridge over the red river. It is very important. I will wait until twelve o'clock.
Rose

One of her precious remaining coins would have to go on a postage stamp. Rose sighed and dragged her weary body down the street to send her letter.

★ ★ ★

Captain clattered down the narrow street of small grey cottages. Joss dismounted, tossing the reins to a grubby urchin who had appeared from nowhere with his hand held out.

Nell, self-controlled but so pale of face that her skin was almost translucent, opened the door, a clutch of solemn, round-eyed children at her side.

'Oh, Joss. Come in.' she said, closing the door quickly. A lace curtain across the street was twitched briefly by an unseen hand. 'There's no privacy round here. Martin always says — ' she clapped a hand over her mouth and her voice broke off abruptly.

'How are you, Nell?' asked Joss with concern. They were sitting in the kitchen in front of the range which was shining with new black-lead polish. Its brass knobs twinkled even more brightly.

Nell picked up a couple of dusters from the fender and tidied them away.

'I just been polishing,' she said. 'Got to keep busy. Don't have no time to think, then.'

'How ... how are you off, Nell? For money, I mean.' Joss spoke hesitantly, well aware of the fiercely independent nature of the Cornish people. 'You know you only have to ask ... '

Nell, sensing his embarrassment, leaned forward and squeezed his hand.

'Thanks Joss, 'twas kindly meant, but we'll be all right. I got the lodgers and the club money, and a little bit put by.' She stood up and pulled the kettle over the heat. 'I'll make a cup of tea.' She started rattling china.

'Martin was always careful, like,' Nell said

over her shoulder, reaching into a cupboard. 'He knew he was going downhill, see. His lungs was in some terrible state — he never ought to have been going underground, but you do know what he was like. And he thought he'd found a good sturt this time too . . . ' Her face began to crumple. Joss took out a handful of pence and passed them to the subdued children.

'Off you go,' he told them, 'and don't come back until you've spent it all.' Their faces transformed, they scampered off in glee, calling their thanks as they went. The front door slammed and Nell set the teapot on the table, wiping her eyes with a corner of her apron.

'How much will you get from the club, then?' Joss asked.

The 'club' consisted of those miners who chose to pay sixpence out of every thirty-shilling wage to a fund for the temporary support of those injured in accidents. A similar sum was paid in for the doctor, who was then bound to attend free of charge.

In addition to this, a shilling was deducted from each man to be given to the widow and family of a fellow miner who had died that month.

'It'll come to about ten pounds, they reckon.' Nell opened the fire door of the range and held out her hands to its warmth. 'Had a collection at the mine they did too — after the accident. They been very good to me, the men.'

'Martin was well-liked,' said Joss. 'He was a fine miner and will be greatly missed.'

'I was thinking just now,' she said, looking into the glowing coals, 'maybe it's better he went the way he did. Better than coughing his life away. He would have hated that, Joss.' Her shoulders heaved in a long sigh.

'That night — it was some queer. Like I knew he wasn't coming back. I waited all night at that there shaft. Mother came over to stay with the childer, and I knew . . . ' She shuddered and began to weep.

Joss let her cry, knowing it was the best thing for her, but he was relieved when the door was pushed open and Nell's mother came in.

He stood up to leave and placed a hand on Nell's shoulder.

'Let me know if there's anything I can do, any time.'

In a lower voice he said to the older woman: 'And if Nell is too proud to ask, I'm relying on you to do it for her.' She followed him to the door. 'I shall always remember Martin with affection, he was very good to me.'

'Thank you sir, for coming,' she replied and closed the door on their grief.

Joss retrieved his horse and swung himself heavily into the saddle. Just lately he had been feeling like an old man.

★ ★ ★

Joss's mood was not improved by the shock which was awaiting him at home. As he rounded the side of the house on his way to the stable, the door flew open and Anthony came running down the steps calling after him, a piece of paper flapping in his hand.

'Joss, Joss, a telegram came for you. Where on earth have you been? I expected you back ages ago.' He thrust the note under Joss's nose. 'Read this!'

Joss grabbed the yellow slip and scanned it. BAD NEWS OF EMMA. COME AT ONCE. MAUDE. he read. His face fell.

'*What* bad news?' he exclaimed. 'Why doesn't the stupid woman say what it is?' He crumpled the paper in fury and tossed it to the ground as he strode after his brother into the house. 'When did this come?'

'An hour ago,' Anthony replied.

His brother was already half-way up the stairs.

'I must just wash and change, and throw a

320

few things in a bag in case I have to stay. Then I'll go straight away,' Joss called back. 'Would you see that the groom has Captain ready for me? Thanks, Anthony, must dash.'

'There are a lot of other letters here for you, too,' his brother shouted, but Joss was out of hearing. Anthony shrugged and dropped the stack of envelopes back on to the hall table. Rose's letter was at the bottom of the pile.

★ ★ ★

Joss arrived at Bodmin by early evening. He went straight to St Lawrence's and up the stairs to Emma's quarters.

In an ante-room, Maude Robartes was sitting waiting for him, a ball of damp handkerchief in her hand. She rose to her feet as Joss was shown in and raised a chalk-white face to his as she clutched at his arm.

'What is it?' he said urgently. 'What's happened?'

'Oh, Joss,' she sniffed. 'Emma . . . '

'Ah — Mr Pencarrow.'

Joss turned as a male voice broke in.

'I'm Dr Harrison.' The newcomer smiled as he extended a hand and gripped Joss's firmly. Young, with a confident air about him that immediately inspired trust, he had a soft brown moustache and eyes of the same shade. Joss liked him immediately.

'How do you do,' he replied.

The doctor glanced at the sheaf of notes he was holding against his white coat and indicated that they should all sit down.

'Now, please tell me what this is all about,' said Joss, sitting on the edge of the seat and leaning forward with his hands on his knees. Beside him Maude smoothed down her skirt and sniffed again.

The doctor looked Joss squarely in the eye.

'As you know,' he said. 'Mrs Pencarrow is with child.'

Joss nodded in impatience. 'Yes, yes, go on.'

The doctor shuffled his feet and cleared his throat before continuing:

'I know how heartbreaking this must be for you all, but I have to tell you that some evidence has arisen which means that there is something you should know before she gives birth.'

'What?' Joss started and half-rose from the chair. 'What do you mean . . . ?'

The other man held up a hand and paused for a moment. He rustled his papers and cleared his throat again.

'In view of her mental condition we thought it necessary to do some research into past medical records of your wife's family.'

Dr Harrison's gaze was steady.

'I'm sorry to have to say that we discovered that there is a strain of insanity, going back some distance, on her father's side of the family,' he said.

Joss's eyes widened and his jaw dropped. He glanced at Maude, expecting their eyes to meet in mutual shock. But apart from being tearful, she seemed far less upset than he would have thought. Then the truth hit him like a thunderbolt and he rounded on her in fury.

'You . . . you *knew*, didn't you,' he snarled.

The woman recoiled, then nodded and gave a sigh.

'It . . . it was so far back . . . that I thought it would never happen again. I couldn't tell you, Joss — the . . . the shame of it . . . '

She sobbed defeatedly as Joss furiously thumped a fist on the arm of his chair, then rose to his feet and began to pace up and down in agitation.

'You knew all along that there was a chance of this happening, and you couldn't bring yourself just to mention it, because of your stupid *pride*?'

Maude bowed her head and snuffled into her handkerchief as Joss returned to perch on the edge of his chair.

'So of course,' the doctor went on, 'there is

the very real chance that the child could turn out to be a . . . congenital idiot . . . Forgive me, both of you,' he nodded politely to Maude's bent head, 'for speaking so plainly, but there is no way I can break news like this gently.'

Joss passed a hand across his face.

'I understand,' he said brokenly. Vanished and gone were his brief hopes of a normal family life. For ever. He mastered his agony and turned back to the doctor. 'And I appreciate your straight talking, I really do.' The man looked relieved.

Leaving Maude to her quiet sobbing, Dr Harrison drew Joss to one side.

'It happens like this sometimes in a small place like Cornwall,' he said in a low voice. 'Inbreeding among the limited group of landed families, you know. It never used to be mentioned, but in more progressive medical circles today it is recognized as an accepted fact.' He clapped Joss on the shoulder. 'I can't tell you how sorry I am, sir. A tragic case indeed.'

Joss, unable to speak, nodded as the doctor turned to leave.

'If I might suggest a cup of tea?' He indicated Maude's heaving shoulders.

'I'll see to it for you. Goodbye sir, until tomorrow.'

Joss grasped the extended hand as the doctor left the room.

'Goodbye, and thanks,' he managed.

★ ★ ★

Tossing and turning in his bed at Lanhydrock, all Joss's personal demons arose once more to haunt him. Was he never to be free of this infernal *guilt*? God knows, he had only tried to have some semblance of a normal married life — a man had to have some relief — and Emma had been willing to please him in every way. Now, Joss wept some bitter tears and thumped his hot pillow until the feathers flew. It *wasn't* his fault, any of it — but he could not rid himself of this self-loathing, despite what Anthony might have said. And as he drifted off to sleep at last Joss thought wistfully once more of the little family they might have been.

But Joss's troubles were far from over. Next morning he was summoned from the breakfast table by another telegram from St Lawrence's. 'Mrs Pencarrow admitted to Truro Infirmary' he read. 'Please come immediately.'

Joss jumped to his feet, threw down his napkin and was away in ten minutes. Surely he was still living in last night's nightmare? As the carriage bowled through the pleasant countryside Joss, forcing his weary brain to function, rubbed a hand across his burning eyes and saw none of its beauty.

He was met at the entrance to the wards by an unfamiliar doctor, who must have noticed Joss's haggard face as he put a sympathetic hand on his arm. 'I'm afraid I have some serious news for you, sir. Come through here and sit down.' He ushered Joss into a side room and indicated a chair.

Joss rasped a hand across his stubbled jaw — he had neglected to shave that morning and now was regretting it. 'Your wife was rushed in to us in the early hours of this morning, bleeding heavily, and has since miscarried the child she was expecting.' He paused and spread his hands. 'I'm so deeply sorry but there was nothing we could do as it all happened so quickly.'

Joss sunk his head in his hands as his mind reeled. He felt as if it might explode at any minute as a torrent of conflicting emotions flooded his brain. On the one hand there was relief — could this be for the best if the child were to be flawed as he had been told? There was grief — for might it not after all have been a normal child? Only God knew the answer to that one. And there was heartache in abundance. Joss could not prevent the tears from coming then and he wept, harsh racking sobs, for himself, for Emma and for what might have been.

The doctor had tactfully turned away until Joss recovered himself enough to ask him brokenly, 'How is Emma? Will she be all right?', when he nodded.

'Thank you,' Joss murmured, his eyes not leaving the other man's face. 'However,' the doctor added, 'she did lose a lot of blood and is very weak at the moment. You may sit with her if you wish, but she is not to be disturbed in any way, you understand.' Joss nodded. 'She's in a room of her own. If you'd like to follow me I'll show you the way.'

'One moment, doctor.' Joss laid a hand on his arm. 'The baby . . . would you tell me, what . . . ?'

'A boy,' he said briefly. 'I'm so sorry.' Ashen-faced, Joss followed him down the corridor to Emma's room.

In the high bed, propped on several pillows with her pale hair spread around her small white face, Emma could have been a china doll. Always slightly built, his wife seemed now to have physically shrunk, and Joss felt that if he touched her she would break apart.

He sat beside her for several minutes, lost in his own thoughts. Suddenly he became aware of a slight movement from the bed and looked up to see that Emma had opened her eyes and was looking straight at him.

Startled, and mindful of his instructions not to excite her, he whispered:

'Hello, Emma darling, how are you feeling?'

A smile hovered at the corners of her mouth.

'Pa — Papa.' Her voice was scarcely audible. Joss drew his chair nearer the bed, felt for her hand and squeezed it.

The small hand stayed resting in his and Joss lost all knowledge of time as his thoughts took him miles away again. Only when a cramp in his arm forced him into changing his position, he gently withdrew her hand from his and tucked it under the covers.

Leaving his wife to her dreams, Joss made his way slowly homewards to pick up the threads of his own life again, feeling as if he had lived through some kind of waking nightmare, the memory of which would haunt him for the rest of his life.

★ ★ ★

When Thursday came around, Rose gathered all her remaining strength for the uphill walk to the meeting place with Joss. With hindsight she wished it hadn't been so far, but she had thought at the time that it would be easier to talk to him on the familiar ground of their childhood, and would somehow make her request less humiliating.

It was a warm day and Rose felt heavy and listless. Too little food over a long period, coupled with the burden of her now enormous body, made the walk seem like double its distance. But she forced herself to climb the long hill to the top of Brea village where her former home was set in an isolated spot down a rutted track.

Tired as she was, Rose could not resist making a diversion down the lane to have a peep at it. She had not seen her father for over twelve years, since she had fled from his drunken wrath, and had heard nothing of him since. He could even have drunk himself to death by now for all she knew.

Every step of the way raised memories for Rose. This was the well where she had gone so many times to fill the heavy pitchers. Here was the turning to the hillside where she had gone to meet Joss for her lessons. Down there was the plank bridge where she was going to meet him today. Over the river where baby Sarah . . . but she didn't want to think about that now.

And here was the cottage. Rose was approaching it from the back and noticed that the yard where the scrawny chickens used to peck and squabble was full of nettles and brambles now. It was very quiet. She dragged herself down the lane to the front of the house. And could hardly contain her shock.

For the building was totally derelict. From this angle Rose could clearly see the boarded-up windows, the holes in the roof where slates had fallen and the leaning chimney stack. She stood for a moment to catch her breath, seized with a feeling of loss in spite of all her childhood privations, then turned away down the track to her meeting with Joss.

Rose sat on the grass in the appointed place for so long that after a while she lost all track of time. He wasn't coming. She'd been a fool to think that he would. After all, he had made it perfectly plain that he wanted no more to do with her, hadn't he? B — but, he had been her last hope. Rose leaned her head against a moss-covered boulder, covered her face with her hands and burst into bitter tears.

She must have sobbed herself to sleep, for when she came to the sun had shifted position and was shining right in her eyes. It was very hot on the exposed flank of the hill, and Rose was feeling dizzy and sick. She would go and sit in that patch of shade over there.

Clumsily she raised herself to her feet, but a spasm of red-hot pain suddenly seized her low down in the back and she screamed out in shock and agony. Another one soon followed, taking her breath away as Rose screamed once more, then everything went black as she fell senseless to the ground.

★   ★   ★

Joss was still in a state of despondency when he rode over to meet Jack Trenerry at the mine to survey the wreckage of all his hopes and dreams there as well as in his domestic life. Everything in fact, that he had originally defied his father for, and for which he had striven so hard ever since, seemed to have got him absolutely nowhere.

He had been away for three weeks and had neglected his business for so long that as soon as he had arrived home he had felt obliged to get over there without further delay. So he had left everything else — including his stack of unopened letters — to be dealt with later.

It had been a glorious summer and the sun was still shining from a sky of cerulean blue as Captain plodded along the narrow track to Wheal Hope, but Joss saw none of it.

True, he still had the money and the equipment he had been going to put into the mine. But faced with such tremendous damage, was it worth it? How much ore still lay buried down there? Had Jack been right about the new lode?

If so, where was it now? All these were unanswerable questions — perhaps the mine captain would have some constructive advice to offer.

The crunch of footsteps on gravel brought him back to the present. Jack was coming towards him now, across the yard.

To Joss's astonishment, the other man was looking positively cheerful, and was rubbing his hands together with what looked almost like glee.

'Joss, come in here and have a look at this,' he said without preamble, striding into the counthouse. Joss, intrigued, followed behind.

'What are you looking so cheerful about?' he asked. It was the first smile that had been seen on either of their faces since the tragedy.

Jack crossed the room to his desk and opened a drawer full of maps and plans of the workings. He took one and spread it out on the table top, anchoring the four corners with lumps of ore-samples which littered the room. He sucked reflectively on his pipe.

Consumed with curiosity, Joss remarked:

'Come on Jack, you're really looking far too smug for a man who could be about to lose his job. What are you up to?'

'Uh-hum,' came the absent reply. Jack frowned and traced a line on the plan before him with a gnarled forefinger. 'Ess.' He nodded to himself. 'Well, well, the Lord giveth and the Lord taketh away, like they do say.' He glanced up under his shaggy brows. 'I aren't no chapelgoer, Joss, but some things do make you wonder, sure enough.'

'You're talking in riddles, man,' said Joss, annoyed now. 'Are you going to tell me what this is all about, or not?'

'Sorry, Joss. But I had to be sure, see. Come round here and take a look at this.'

The mine captain leaned back in his chair, put another match to the tobacco in his pipe and sucked on it. When it was drawing nicely, he tossed the spent matchstick into the empty fireplace.

Joss pulled up a chair at his side and waited with more patience than he felt.

'You remember, don't you, how poor old Martin Blewett reckoned he was on to a good sturt, just before the accident, like?' He looked quizzically at Joss, who nodded.

'Well, he and his pare was working the bottom level, just where it do start running out under the sea. And,' he paused and met

Joss's eyes, 'in just the same spot where the landslip have taken away that chunk of cliff. Now, do you know what I'm getting at?'

Still bewildered, Joss shook his head.

'No, I don't. For goodness' sake man, get on with it.'

'Well, I just been down there to have a look. There isn't no proper path no more so I climbed down over the slip. Tide's out and I had a good look at the cliff from underneath. And,' he finished triumphantly, as a huge grin crossed his craggy face, 'if I'm not mistaken, there's a great copper lode there — just waiting to be picked out! From the *outside*, boy! What do you think of that, eh? No drainage problems, no going underground even. We can work it from the shore!'

Joss felt a mounting excitement to match that on the other man's face.

'Are you quite, quite, sure, Jack?' He hardly dared to hope. Could tragedy turn to triumph in such a short time? Joss felt as if he was on a seesaw. But that was mining, full of ups and downs. And Jack Trenerry had been in mining all his life — and his father and grandfather before him. He would trust his judgement absolutely.

'I'm sure,' Jack said with quiet certainty. 'I just wanted to see it on paper afore I opened my mouth. But here's the level, see, just where Blewett and his mates were to. And it do tie up exactly with where this lode do start. It's the same one all right. The one they was following the day they died. I got an idea they was blasting when the sea broke through. Come us on, I'll show you where it's to.' He began rolling up the map.

'I was here that day,' Joss remarked, 'during the storm. I saw that landslide, it was awesome.'

'I'm sure of it,' said Jack as they scrambled cautiously down the loose scree at the bottom of the cliff. 'Now, it's over there to the right.' He led the way to a massive cavern which had been hewn out of the end of what had been the old level. 'Don't touch nothing. All they rocks one side is loose. It'll take a fair amount of shoring to make it safe, but take a look at that, boy!'

Jack produced a candle and matches from a pocket and held the flame up high. By its flickering light Joss was able to see the tell-tale band of quartz which pointed the way to the lode contained within it, and he whistled softly.

Then he let out a whoop of delight and thumped the other man's shoulder with such force that the candle dropped into a pool of water where it guttered feebly and went out.

'You mean — we're *saved*, Jack? Wheal Hope — all the men's jobs, and with hardly any outlay to get the mine working again? I can't believe it.' Joss stared at the other man in wonderment. Such a reversal of fortunes in such a brief space of time had his brain spinning in circles.

'Bleddy miracle, I do call it,' said the mine captain, putting the whole thing neatly in a nutshell. He went straight down to the public to spread the good news among the miners. Joss rode home with his head held high and a smile on his face for the first time for weeks.

12

Now that the worst of his problems seemed to be over, or at least were being taken care of, Joss could at last turn his attention to the matter of tracing Rose.

Months had gone by without his realizing it, so preoccupied had he been with the dramatic events in his own life. But now the time had come to start living again. First of all, however, he had to deal with the mountain of letters which had accumulated in his absence.

Joss went through all the envelopes one by one, replying painstakingly to each personal letter and leaving the ones from business contacts for Anthony to deal with. He had almost reached the bottom of the pile when he sat back, stretched his weary shoulders and laid down his pen for a rest. He glanced idly at the remaining letters. Most of them looked like business and professional contacts. But this one? It was very unlike the others. He picked up a small, cheap-looking brown envelope, slit it open curiously, and scanned the short note which it held.

He started to his feet with an exclamation.

Rose! She had written to him! Joss looked apprehensively at the date and his heart sank. Three weeks ago! He put his head in his hands and groaned. And there was no address. He must go to her at once.

But where should he start? Redruth and Camborne, together with all the villages in between, covered a huge area. He could only suppose that Rose had fled back to her roots and hope that she was somewhere near where she had lived as a child. He left the house right away, with only a cursory explanation to Anthony, who looked after him in astonishment as he went galloping down the drive.

It was worse than looking for a needle in a haystack. He rode extensively in and around the village of Brea, among the mines and through the scattered crofts and cottages of the uplands around Carn Brea itself, asking and asking without success, growing more frustrated as the day went on. At last Joss slid from Captain's back, letting the horse browse at will while he sat with his back to a low stone wall and tried to think.

Put yourself in Rose's position, he told himself sternly. You leave the Red Lion, you want a complete change, a break from your present life. What will you need? A job and somewhere to live. Similar work to what you had been used to, perhaps. Hotel work? Yes!

Joss jumped to his feet and recaptured the horse, galloping back to the town in high hopes that he was on Rose's trail at last. The hopes were soon dashed. Nobody had heard of her at either of the two main hotels nor at the several smaller places where he also made enquiries. Fuming, Joss stayed for a meal at the last place he came to, and over a pie and a tankard of ale he suddenly had another inspiration.

Letters! Rose would have had her letters sent on to her. Her friends in Truro would be sure to keep in touch with her — as far as he knew they were the only friends she had — and as Rose had not left a forwarding address at the Red Lion, she must have been using the post restante and collecting them herself. He left the eating-house with a broad grin on his face and was at the post office inside ten minutes.

★   ★   ★

'Mrs Lanyon?' William Tippett the postmaster stroked his moustache, turned to the row of pigeon-holes behind him and pulled out an envelope. 'She was here a couple of times, and then she gave me an address to deliver to — it would save her a walk after her day's work, she said. But when I sent this letter

339

round there, the boy brought it back marked 'No longer at this address'.

'What was the address?' said Joss eagerly. 'I'm trying to trace Mrs Lanyon, you see.' He glanced eagerly at the envelope in the man's hand. *Care of Mrs Pascoe, Pendarves Road*, he read. 'Many thanks.' He was on his way again in under five minutes.

★ ★ ★

'Mrs Lanyon?' Joss stood at the top of Alice Pascoe's steps as the maid took his message through. She was back shortly followed by her mistress.

'Come inside Mr Pencarrow. That will be all, Gladys.' Alice Pascoe ushered him into a side room and indicated a seat.

'I'm trying to find Rose Lanyon,' Joss began without preamble. 'The postmaster tells me she doesn't live here any longer, but I'm hoping you can tell me where she went when she left here.' He cleared his throat. 'I'm an old friend of hers,' he added.

'Really?' Alice Pascoe looked him up and down, then drew in a breath. 'I'm afraid I can't help you, Mr Pencarrow. She left quite abruptly, with the minimum of notice, saying she'd found other accommodation. Quite secretive, she was. It surprised me rather,

340

because I'd been thinking what a nice young woman she was.' She sniffed and rose to her feet.

Then she crossed to the mantelpiece and took down some scraps of paper.

'As a matter of fact,' she said, 'she left these pawn tickets behind, and I've been expecting her to call back for them any day. She won't be able to redeem her possessions without them. But she never has.' She turned back to Joss. 'You may as well have them, they're of no use to me. If you ever do catch up with her you can hand them back.'

Pawn tickets? Was Rose short of money, then? But why? Joss's head was spinning.

'And now, if you'll excuse me, Mr Pencarrow . . . ' Alice was showing him to the door.

'Yes, yes of course. Thank you, you've been very helpful.'

Joss examined the tickets as soon as he was outside. They were all from the same place, at intervals of a few weeks, the oldest several months ago.

They told a heartrending story. A clock, a picture, two china ornaments, a woollen cloak. The last one was for — a gold wedding-band. So she had kept that until the last, symbol of her pride and respectability. Oh, my Rose. There were tears in Joss's eyes and he brushed them roughly away. So it seemed that the only thing he could do for her now was redeem her few precious belongings. He hurried down the street looking from side to side for the three golden balls.

So Joss returned home with a heavy heart and nothing to show for his exertions but the box of Rose's possessions, which he cradled carefully before him on the ride back to Great Place.

★   ★   ★

When Rose regained consciousness she found herself lying in bed. In a clean bed, looking up at the rafters of the roof above her. It was limewashed, like the walls. She raised her head from the pillow and looked about her. She was in a tiny, windowless cubicle not much bigger than a cupboard. Beside her was a cane table on which stood a jug of water covered with a beaded cloth, and a tumbler. There was also a copy of the Holy Bible and on the wall hung the painted text: *God be merciful to me, a sinner*. Rose flinched.

She could hear the sound of many voices in another part of the building, also the clatter of cutlery, as if they were having a meal. She glanced down at herself. She was wearing a white cotton nightgown. Someone had washed her, she could smell carbolic soap on her hands, and had tied her hair back with a piece of tape. Where on earth was this? A hospital? The workhouse? Not the workhouse — oh please, no! Rose gave a little whimper of horror and a woman put her head around the door and peeped in.

'Oh, you're awake — at last!' She was in her forties, Rose guessed, with a pleasant open face and was dressed in plain black with a spotless white apron.

'Where am I?' asked Rose, bewildered.

'This is the Christian Mission for Fallen and Destitute Women,' the woman replied. 'You were found collapsed this morning and were unconscious when they brought you in.'

In Rose's mind it all began clicking into place.

'Who found me?' she asked abruptly, as a small spark of hope lit up her face.

'A couple of farm workers. Apparently they heard you scream. How are you feeling now?'

So Joss had not come at all. Rose's mouth drooped.

'All right, I think, thank you,' she answered as from habit. Then she remembered. The baby! And the pain that had gripped her. She placed a hand on her stomach and felt a small movement. It was all right, then.

'You'd like something to eat, I expect?' The woman smiled.

'Oh, please.' Rose couldn't recall when she had last had a meal.

'I'm Jane Hobbs,' the woman said. 'What's your name?'

'Rose Lanyon. Mrs Lanyon,' she emphasized. 'I was recently widowed.'

'Oh, yes?' Jane Hobbs glanced at Rose's ringless finger.

'I had to pawn my ring,' Rose felt compelled to explain, 'when I fell upon hard times.'

'A lot of people here say that,' said the other woman, her hand on the doorknob. 'I'll go and get you some soup.'

'But it's true!' Rose called after her but the door had closed and Jane Hobbs was out of hearing. She doesn't believe me, Rose thought bitterly, and I've no means of proving otherwise. She thinks I'm a fallen woman.

The soup when it arrived was thick and nourishing with plenty of bread to go with it. It was followed by suet pudding and custard and a mug of strong tea. Rose cleared the lot and felt better than she had done for months.

But as she relaxed on to the pillows again she became aware of another pain low in her back similar to the one she had felt on the hill. This was soon followed by a second, so sharp that she cried out with it. Jane Hobbs, coming in for the empty dishes, took one look and went running for help.

* * *

Rose's son was born in the early hours of the following morning. In spite of the privations which his mother had suffered leading up to his birth, the baby was healthy and perfect in every way. He was placed beside her in an ancient crib which had served many others before him, snug in the little garments she had chosen for him and which she had never put into pawn, even in her darkest days. Some official had called at Gas Lane for her remaining belongings, and had paid the rent owing there.

Rose had never in her wildest dreams imagined how thankful she would be to accept charity. It had been a humbling experience, but with a touch of her old pride she vowed to repay her debt one day to the kind souls who ran such a refuge and had probably saved her life and that of her child.

She looked adoringly down at her sleeping son. No doubt as to his paternity now. It was umistakable, for he was the spit and image of his father.

'What are you going to call him, Rosie?' A voice broke in on her reverie. Jenny King, small, freckled and fifteen years old, had been saved from a life of prostitution and now worked here for her keep. Rose had learned that members of the mission regularly sent scouts out to the back streets and brothels, spreading a message of hope and rescuing the homeless wherever they could.

'Hello Jenny.' Rose was holding the sleeping baby close. He had just been fed and she was loath to put him down, loving the feel of his warm little body in her arms. He was all she had left now, this small person who was totally dependent upon her, and she would have laid down her life for him. 'His name's Jamie,' she said, and there was a faraway look in her eyes.

★　★　★

Rose gradually regained her health and strength with the plain, nourishing food provided by the refuge. With regular meals and the security of a warm, clean place to live, her face and figure filled out again and her hair regained its former lustre.

When she was up and about again she

discovered that she was expected to help out in the kitchen, or anywhere there was work to be done, in return for her keep. The Reverend Jasper Brown controlled the establishment, and there were about twenty girls and women, some with children like herself, who stayed until they were found other employment and accommodation by the mission. Rose got on well enough with them, they were mostly friendly and the child made a common topic of interest.

A store of clothing and boots given to the refuge by charitable bodies was kept ready for distribution to the needy who arrived there, and Rose was soon forced to take advantage of it. Her own clothes were so threadbare as to be past mending, and little Jamie was fast growing out of his first-size garments.

'Here you are, Rose, this looks about your size,' Jane Hobbs remarked as Rose entered the room where she was unpacking and sorting a pile of boxes and bags. She passed over a serviceable skirt. 'Oh, and here's another. There's still plenty of wear in those.'

'Thanks, Jane, I'll try them on.' Rose held out her hands and then stood stock still in amazement. She *recognized* that skirt — and this one as well. She clapped a hand to her mouth as the past came suddenly rushing back, threatening to overwhelm her with a host of emotions.

Kate! It had been just before she and Will had left for Australia. Rose could see it all in her mind's eye still. Kate had been sorting out her clothes . . . *those can go to one of Fanny's charities . . . she's involved in all sorts of things . . .* ' and she had tossed out a couple of skirts. These skirts!

If proof were needed, Rose knew that there would be a scorchmark on the blue one, just near the hem. An ember had fallen out of the fire one day when Kate had been putting coal on the range, and the skirt had been singed. Rose wrinkled her nose, smelling again the burning wool. She turned the skirt — yes, there it was. Rose clasped the garment to her and laid her cheek against the familiar fabric. What a coincidence that these things should have come to her. Rose felt cheered as she slipped on the blue skirt, and somehow less lonely.

It was time for the evening meal. Rose placed the other clothes in a box under her bed, checked that the baby was peacefully sleeping and joined the other women at the two long refectory tables in the dining-room. At the end of the room today another table had been placed for the Reverend Brown and his wife, who apparently had some visitors.

Half a dozen soberly clad men were talking earnestly together while the women on today's serving duty brought in the meal.

The minister stood to say grace and they all rose to their feet, A hush fell over the company as they bowed their heads and folded their hands.

'Today, ladies, grace will be said by our brother Joseph. One of our local members, whose group will be helping us with God's work for a week or two.' He nodded to the man at his side. Dressed in black, he was a slightly built person with a neatly trimmed sandy beard and moustache, and thinning hair.

'Brothers and sisters,' he began, 'as we give thanks to Almighty God for the blessing of this food before us, let us spare a thought for those who are starving still, and ask him to shine the light of his mercy upon this mission, that we may bring succour to those in need and the light of his word to those who know him not. For what we are about to receive may we be truly thankful. Amen.'

'Amen,' echoed the company and sat down to eat. Rose had been staring intently at the speaker during the prayer. He reminded her of someone. It had been the voice really, and all through the meal she could hardly take her eyes off the man. His mannerisms, a certain

349

way of holding his head to the side as he chatted to the others at his table, his profile, all combined to make her more certain. Rose felt her stomach lurch and she dropped her fork with a clatter. For 'Brother Joseph' was her own father.

The shambling, drunken father whom she hadn't seen for almost thirteen years. Not since he had flayed her flesh raw with his belt after his baby daughter had drowned. What had happened to turn him into this pious and respectable member of the church? And more — would he want anything to do with her — a reminder of those times?

Obviously he had not noticed her among the crowd of other women. Should she approach him? Or not? She would be an embarrassment, surely? His own daughter in a place like this. But Jamie was his grandson — although would he want to see him? Rose pushed her food around the plate as thoughts and questions tumbled through her mind until her head reeled.

But she had to decide quickly. And she had to get him on his own. She had no idea where the group were staying, and after her father left here she might never find him again. The meal was nearly over — once they had left the room they would probably be closeted away with the minister in his study. Rose took a deep breath. She would make herself known, and if her father disowned her — well — she had faced worse things in her life.

They were rising now, the group beginning to file out. But her father had dropped his napkin on the floor and was bending under the table to retrieve it. Now was her chance. Rose sped across the room. They were alone apart from a couple of women who were rattling dishes as they cleared the tables at the other end and chatted to each other.

'Excuse me,' Rose said as he straightened up. 'I believe you're Mr Vidney, aren't you?' Her throat was so dry that she could hardly form the words and her heart was thudding so loudly she was sure he must be able to hear it.

'Why, yes, I am.' He looked surprised. 'But wh . . . who . . . ?' They stared at each other for a long moment.

'Don't you know me, Pa?' said Rose softly.

Joe Vidney's jaw dropped and recognition slowly dawned in his eyes.

'R — Rose?' he stammered. Then, 'Rosie! My dear child, is it really you?'

He grasped both her hands and stared hungrily into her face.

'It is, it is. Well the Lord be praised, for he have answered my prayers at last!' With tears in his eyes he held out his arms and clasped his daughter to him in a long embrace.

'How you've changed,' Rose whispered into his shoulder. 'What happened?'

'I saw the light, child, and have repented of my evil ways. If you only knew how I've been searching for you ever since.'

'You have?' Rose drew away from him, her eyes wide with astonishment. She sank down on to a chair again, her legs trembling too much to support her. Joe sat down beside her and took her hand in his.

'Oh yes. We've got some lot to talk about, maid. What are you doing in this place, anyhow?'

'Oh, it's such a long story, Pa.' Rose's voice was weary. After all her apprehension, now that it was all right and he wasn't going to reject her, she suddenly felt exhausted. 'How long are you staying here?'

'Oh, only for today. I'm going home this evening.'

Rose recalled the derelict cottage that had been their former home.

'Where do you live?' she asked.

'I got a nice little place of my own, down to Brea village not far from where we lived when you was small. I do a bit of preaching here and there and travel a fair bit with the mission, saving souls. They do pay me enough to get by, and my clothes and boots do come out of the charity boxes. Life is good, maid, and now I've found you again, I haven't got no more worries in the world.'

His face clouded as a faraway look came into his eyes.

'I done you a terrible wrong, Rosie my handsome, when you was little. It was the demon drink in me what made me turn against you, child. And I've had that on my conscience ever since. Can you ever forgive me, maid?'

Rose looked at him. Her father had aged immensely since she had last seen him. Who knew how many years he had left? And she had almost died. What good would it do to harbour all the old pent-up bitterness of the past? Could she let go and start afresh? He was her only living relative, after all — bar one. Rose raised misty eyes to her father's face and smiled.

'I think so, Pa,' she said gently. 'And now there's someone I want you to meet.'

★　★　★

During the next few days Rose and her father spent as much time together as they could, catching up on the missing years. Joe doted on his grandson, so much so that he

353

remarked to Rose, one day: 'What are you going to do with yourself, maid? Can't stay in this here place for ever, can you?'

It was the question that Rose had been asking herself ever since she had recovered from Jamie's birth.

'I shall have to find work, Pa. I've no money, you see, and I'll have to get somewhere to live, too. I suppose the mission would advance me a loan to get started, and a reference. But it won't be easy with the baby.' They were in the communal sitting-room at the mission and Rose had been doing a pile of mending as part of her duties. Now her shoulders drooped as she laid down her needle and raised troubled eyes to Joe.

'That's what I been thinking,' he replied, then paused. Then, shuffling his feet on one of the rag-rugs which covered the wooden floor, he said: 'How about this, Rosie. How would it be if you and the tacker was to come and live with me. You could stay at my place as long as you want. 'Tidden very big, but I reckon us could manage. What do you think, maid. Like to, would you?' He cleared his throat and muttered something about: 'I could look after the little 'un perhaps . . . make it up to you a bit . . . for the past, like . . . '

A lump had come to Rose's throat and for

354

a moment she couldn't speak.

''Course, you don't have to,' Joe added hastily. 'If you want to live your own life . . . go your own way . . . '

'Oh, Pa. Thank you!' Rose's face was radiant. 'I'd love to.' It would be a respite, and would give her time to reflect before she made up her mind what to do with the rest of her life.

'With a roof over my head, I'm sure I could find work to do. I could take in sewing,' she placed a hand on the bundle of mending beside her, 'or work on a farm — harvesting or fruit-picking, that kind of thing — and take Jamie with me. I could manage. I don't want to be a burden to you, you understand?'

'You wouldn't never be no burden, my handsome,' he replied with feeling, 'and I shall see that dear cheeld growing up where he do belong.'

A week later Rose was settled in her father's tiny cottage, which he kept as clean and neat as a new pin. Rose never ceased to marvel at the change wrought in him by his 'conversion', and began to really get to know him as a person for the first time.

There was only one bedroom, which Joe had insisted that she must have for herself and Jamie, while he slept downstairs. Reluctantly Rose accepted, and made it up to him by taking over the cooking and some of the household chores.

In their new position of closeness, Rose took the opportunity to ask some of the questions to which she had always wanted answers, and which it had been impossible to voice when she was a child and Joe the drunken lout that he had been then.

'Pa,' she said one afternoon as Joe dandled his grandson on his lap and Rose sat sewing by the open window, 'tell me about my mother. I've always wanted to know who she was and what she was like. Aunt Winnie would never talk about her, and I was . . . afraid . . . to ask you.'

Joe grunted and looked uncomfortable, perfectly understanding her meaning. Jamie had begun to wail and as he passed the baby back to Rose his eyes studied his daughter's face. Then he said, simply:

'You do only have to look in the glass, my handsome, to know what she was like. You always did have a look of Hester,' he added, 'but now — my dear life, you're the very spit and image of her.'

He closed the Bible which had been on the arm of his chair and placed it on a side table as he rose and came to stand beside her. Then he stood looking dreamily out of the window with his hands clasped behind his back. Rose placed the baby in his cradle where he kicked and gurgled as she looked fondly down at him.

'How old are you now, Rosie?' Joe asked. 'I do lose track of the years — twenty-one or two, something like that, is it?'

'I'm twenty-three now, Pa.' But feel more like fifty, she could have added. Rose could not but keep asking herself, what next? After the wreck of her life so far, here she was, washed up with only an old man and a small baby for company, and still a young woman, with a young woman's needs and desires.

'You're the same age as Hester was when I first met her,' Joe was saying. 'Summertime. A lovely summer day it were. She came bowling down the lane where I was living to, in a pony trap. She had on a straw bonnet with real flowers what she'd stuck around the brim. Poppies they was, and cornflowers and suchlike. And a dress as green as grass.' He paused, miles away in another time. Rose waited patiently for him to continue.

'Anyhow,' Joe turned back from the window, 'there was this great stone down on the side of the road, what had fallen out of the hedge, see, and one of the wheels caught it and tipped the trap over. I was the only person around so I ran to it, caught hold of the traces and managed to calm the horse down so that he never bolted. I tied him to a tree and went to help her up.

'But she'd broken her ankle as she were tipped out, and she couldn't stand nohow. Well, I made her as comfortable as what I could, then ran for help.' He began to pace slowly up and down the room.

'Hester lived over to Illogan. Her husband were a wealthy man. One of the sort with a finger in every pie, you know?' Rose nodded. 'Owned property he did, and he were a pillar of the church and a magistrate and all. Lived in a great dark house like a prison they did, just the two of them.

Anyhow, she came back to thank me after she recovered, and we, well, we felt then . . . but she were married and I was only a struggling young miner. Never had no money — way out of her class, I was. We didn't have nothing in common really on the face of it. I used to see her around quite often after that — then it dawned on me that she were turning up in places where she knew I'd be. Like I'd be coming off core and she just happened to be passing. So we'd talk. We both knew by that time.'

Joe sighed and rasped a hand over his face. 'Then we took to meeting secretly when she could get away.'

Rose was thinking sadly of how her own

experiences had unknowingly echoed those of her mother.

'Her husband was a brute,' Joe said, his eyes darkening and his face grim. 'He used to beat her for . . . for his — um — well, you've been married Rosie, I can tell you straight. He ill-treated her to satisfy his own perverted desires. Know what I mean, do you?'

'Oh yes, Pa. I know.' Rose had learned a lot from the women she had mixed with in the mission.

'Well, Hester turned to me and left him. There was some great scandal of course, you do know what tongues are like in a village. Nobody wouldn't speak to us — they all looked down their noses and pointed their fingers, and whispered behind their hands. But they couldn't do nothing.

He couldn't do nothing either, more than turn her out, else he knew I'd tell the world what he was like. And she came gladly, my Hester, with nothing but the clothes she stood up in. She what were used to the best of everything. We loved each other that much, maid.' There were tears shining in his eyes now. 'And we was happy. Then when you was on the way we was happier still. Thrilled to bits, your ma were, to be having our baby.'

Joe came back to his seat facing Rose.

'She would liked we to have been married

proper and all,' he went on, 'but as we couldn't, it didn't make much odds. Then you was due to be born and that's when the trouble started. Two days in agony birthing you, she were. They never knew till too late that you was coming feet first. Time they found out, her strength was gone. Wore out she were, my poor little maid. She couldn't take no more.'

Tears were rolling down his cheeks in earnest now and Rose's face was sober. Sternly she told herself to be thankful for what she had. Her mother's sad history could so easily have been her own.

'So that's why I took to the drink, see. It was the only way I could forget. Just for an hour or two. And I got worse and worse. So Rosie, you do know the rest.'

Rose nodded.

'I would give anything to be able to go back and make it up to you an' Winnie,' Joe said wistfully. 'I were some trial to her, and her doing the best she could for us and all.'

'We all have to live with our mistakes, Pa,' said Rose softly. She was thinking of Matt and her own broken marriage, of her abortive liaison with Joss Pencarrow. Then she glanced down at her baby. Oh no, he was no mistake. Jamie was one of the best things that had ever come out of her life.

'Marrying Ellie was another mistake of mine.' Her father gave Rose a sideways glance. 'I was still a young man, Rose. I needed a woman. I thought she'd look after you and mind the house, but it never turned out like that. Then when our little Sarah drowned and she went demented, nearly, I took it all out on you, maid. Wasn't never your fault, none of it. You was too young to have had all that burden thrust on your shoulders.'

'It was all a long while ago, Pa. Time to bury the old memories now. For years I hated you for what you'd done to me, and for years I blamed myself for Sarah's death. But there comes a time when you have to let go and not let bad feeling poison the rest of your life. Don't you think so?'

'Of course I do, my handsome, and I'm some glad we got all that sorted out.'

Joe paused reflectively, then remarked: 'Talking about bad feeling, I never told you, maid, did I, how that cousin Reuben of yours tried blackmailing me once?'

'Blackmailing *you*?' Rose's head jerked up in surprise. 'No, you didn't. But he tried it on me too, ages ago now. Before Jamie was born. What did he say?'

' 'Twas one market day, over to Camborne, and we was singing hymns and trying to spread the word, like we do every week. Rattling the collection tin too, always in need of money for the Lord's work we are, as you do know.' He paused reflectively.

'Well?' Rose prompted.

'First time I'd set eyes on the boy since — well, since he left home and went out to work.'

'Since you and Ellie kicked him out, you mean,' Rose couldn't resist adding. Her father looked uncomfortable.

'Thass why I was glad to see him — wanted to make it up to him, like. Seemed that the Lord had delivered him to me just so's I could.' He carefully polished the lenses of his spectacles with a corner of his handkerchief. Rose waited with barely concealed impatience.

'But he wasn't having none of it, see. Refused the hand of friendship and said he only come over because he had some news fer me. Said he heard that I was looking fer you, and that he knew where you was to.'

'Me?' Rose frowned. 'Oh yes, he came to the Red Lion, delivering vegetables when I was working there — '

'Then by the time I got up there, you'd moved. Anyway, the great lout demanded *money* afore he would tell me, believe it, would you?' Joe's face was a picture of indignation. 'His own kin!'

'Oh yes, I believe it,' Rose said with feeling. 'He feels so hard done by that there's nothing he wouldn't do to us. I think sometimes he's possessed.'

'Well, we can only pray that one day the devil will let him go, and he'll see the light before it idden too late for him to change his evil ways,' remarked Joe with pious optimism.

He looked fondly down into the cradle and clicked his tongue at his grandson, whose face was beginning to pucker. The baby let out a resounding wail and Joe grinned.

'It do sound like teatime for he, and I got a few calls to make. So I'll see you later on, my bird.'

Rose put aside her sewing and attended to her son's needs. It was too good a day to sit indoors, she would catch up with the work this evening. At this moment she was going for a nostalgic stroll up Carn Brea hill.

13

With a feeling of history repeating itself, Rose tied Jamie into a comfortable sling over her shoulder with his weight resting on her hip, and set off. The summer sun was hot on her back and she could feel it striking her neck even through the cotton sun-bonnet she was wearing, but Rose revelled in it. The clear air was like wine and as she climbed higher, a small breeze off the sea fanned across the hill and cooled her flushed face.

There was an old disused quarry on this part of the carn, which had filled with water and could now have been a natural lake. Reeds and scrubby willow-bushes had colonized themselves around the edge and wild flowers grew on its grassy fringes. Today it drowsed in the sun, the breeze hardly rippling its glassy surface. Iridescent dragonflies of emerald-green and steel-blue swooped low and darted across the water, their gauzy wings shimmering, while pond-skaters danced on the surface.

Rose sat down on the grassy slope and untied the sling. She laid Jamie down on the blanket in the shade of a rock and fanned herself with her sun-bonnet. It was so peaceful. The rocky outcrop at her back made a natural wall and it was cool in its shadow. She leaned back and closed her eyes. It was bliss unimaginable to be here. She recalled the squalor in which she had briefly lived, and sighed. I have been so lucky, she whispered.

Try as she might to prevent their doing so, her thoughts began to drift towards Joss. She could not even now believe the way he had totally abandoned her and ignored her last desperate cry for help. Yes, he was a married man — and presumably with a family, for Emma must have had her baby by now — but even so, surely all they had been to each other must count for something? Wistfully Rose thought back to their last day on the beach together. *I have to get married* . . . he had said. His child would be a little older than Jamie now.

Rose glanced down at her son, peacefully asleep beside her. Try as she might to tell herself that Joss had no part of her life any more, a surge of raw and savage jealousy of his wife suddenly brought a sour taste to her mouth, and a vision of him and Emma in their marital bed raised a surge of fury so strong that it left her physically shaking.

★　★　★

Rose felt the dark shadow on her closed eyelids, looming over her and blotting out the sun, before she heard the familiar voice. When she did, her eyes snapped open and she leapt to her feet in sudden fear, flattening herself against the unyielding rock with palms spread wide. The sun was shining right in her eyes now. Reflected off the water it was piercingly bright as it pinned her to the wall.

'Well, well, what have us got here, then?' He chuckled. Rose squinted against the light and flinched as she caught a whiff of his breath. Reuben had obviously been drinking. 'If it isn't cousin Rosie and her little bastard.' He bared his teeth in a grin. 'Heard you had a brat and no ring ter yer finger. Soon got rid of that, didn't you? Like mother, like daughter, I said.'

Rose was slowly inching her way towards Jamie. Reuben Clemo, rocking on his heels with his hands in his pockets, leered down at her. Keeping her hands flat against the rock behind her, Rose moved as unobtrusively as possible, realizing that the baby was dangerously vulnerable.

Suddenly Reuben shot out an arm and grabbed one of Rose's breasts. With a savage pinch he pulled her towards him. She screamed as the pain knifed through her. She was still feeding Jamie herself and was swollen and tender. This was agony. He had seized the other one now and was pressing himself against her, while at her back the granite rock bit into her shoulder-blades. Rose flinched and screamed again.

'Reckon if you're so free with your favours 'tis about time I had my turn,' her cousin grunted, removing one hand to fumble with his belt. 'Who was it got me thrown in the clink, eh?' He leered. 'Now I'm going to get a bit of me awn back. Waited some long time fer this, I have. And yer goody-goody boyfriend idden around today to save yer, neither.'

Rose could see deep into his blank black eyes and wondered with a lurch of her stomach whether he was actually unhinged, or only very drunk. She bit her lip as little Jamie, awakened by her screams, began howling loudly with high-pitched, terrified cries. Fearfully Rose glanced towards him. The bulk of Reuben Clemo's body stood between her and her child, and she saw the vicious look he gave the baby. When he raised his heavy boot to kick at the downy head, she acted instinctively, like a wild animal protecting its young.

Rose brought her knee up between her tormentor's legs with all the force she could muster. As he roared and slackened his grip, with the strength born of desperation Rose pulled herself free. She snatched up the child and tried to run, but her body was aching all over and her legs were so weak with fear that she could only manage to stagger a few paces.

As she stumbled and just saved herself from falling, Reuben caught up with her. She could hardly have hurt him at all. And as Rose struggled to regain her balance, Reuben snatched the baby from her grasp and shook him like a rag-doll. Rose screamed again, panic-stricken now, as Reuben bellowed with laughter and began to stride towards the lake. 'Let's see if *this* little bugger can swim, shall us?' he yelled back over his shoulder. ''T'other one couldn't, could her?' And he gave a cackle of a laugh as he went.

Rose's shrieks echoed all over the carn. In her mind's eye she could see again the pathetic figure of drowned little Sarah floating in the river.

'*No!* Give him to me — don't hurt him — no-o. Help! Somebody — help me — please help!' Rose was ten years old again and Reuben had her by the hair. *Say, please Reuben. Say please and I'll let you go.*

'Please, Reuben!' she screamed. There. She'd said it. Now it would be all right. She repeated the magic words like a mantra as in a state of hysteria, her breath came in short, ragged gasps. His great boots were right on the edge now and he was talking to himself with the baby clamped under one arm. Rose began to sway. The scene had taken on an aura of unreality and had become the stuff of nightmares.

But all of a sudden she heard a shout. Above the screams of the baby, above Reuben's babbling, above her own sobs: the voice of a stranger. Rose watched transfixed as Reuben lumbered around to look over his shoulder. She bit on her thumb until it bled, as slowly, inch by inch he backed away from the water, his eyes on the person who was hidden from Rose by the rocks.

Rose recovered the use of her legs and flew towards her cousin, managing to snatch the hysterical baby from his grasp while his attention was diverted. Reuben only grunted like an animal as he released his hold and Rose darted out of reach. Then she put as much distance as she could between them before she sank down on to the grass, her legs no longer able to support her and tears streaming down her face to mingle with those of her baby. It had all been over in a few seconds, but to Rose it had seemed like hours.

And it wasn't quite all over yet. Down by the water, the stranger was haranguing

Reuben Clemo in language as colourful as any Rose had heard while she was living in Gas Lane. And as he did so he was driving the bully backwards, nearer and nearer to the edge of the water again. Then, as Reuben teetered on the brink, the other man shot out an arm, caught him a perfect right hook to the chin and sent him toppling in.

Rose dragged herself to her feet again to watch, one hand clapped to her mouth. At first her enemy sank like a stone, then, as she waited with baited breath to see if he would reappear, gradually he surfaced. Roaring, spluttering and thrashing his arms about, he was obviously unable to swim. Rose watched transfixed as her cousin grabbed at tree-roots and clumps of grass and eventually managed to drag himself out, covered with mud, bellowing abuse and shaking his fists impotently in the air.

Rose's tears turned to hysterical giggles and then tears again, recalling the first time her cousin had been sent packing after an assault on her. Then she dried her eyes and turned to face the stranger who was striding towards her. And her breath stopped in her throat, for of course it had to be him. She stood like a statue, one hand at her throat, the other clasping the baby close, as the

370

unmistakable figure of Joss Pencarrow drew nearer.

Joss stopped in his tracks like one stunned, and ran the last few yards to her side.

'Rose,' he cried, 'I had no idea it was you. What are you *doing* here? How are you? Is the baby all right? He didn't hurt either of you?' Joss laid a hand on her arm and looked closely into her face.

Rose regarded him over the top of Jamie's head and backed off a step or two. Nervously she plucked at her skirt of navy-blue and absently smoothed out the creases. Joss let his arm drop, but his eyes never left hers.

'Joss — I didn't realize it was you either,' she replied shakily. 'It was just like when we were children — all over again.' She shuddered. 'Thank you for what you did,' she added simply. 'Words aren't enough to describe what I was going through.'

'You'd think that Clemo would have given up by now. Did he attack you again?' Joss frowned under heavy brows and looked her up and down.

Rose nodded, her eyes huge in her strained face. Joss was appalled at how much she had changed. This latest ordeal had left her face pinched and colourless in spite of the summer sunshine. Her shoulders were still shaking under the thin cotton of her white blouse. How he longed to pick her up in his arms and just ride away — far away from all the troubles of the past, from the misunderstandings, and from real life which kept them tethered here by convention and the rules of polite society.

'I — I kicked him.' She bit her lip. 'Then he snatched Jamie — and I thought he really was going to . . . to throw him in . . . ' She swallowed hard and placed one hand across her mouth.

Joss's face was grim.

'I wish I'd pushed him under and kept him there,' he said savagely. 'Whatever possessed the man even to think of doing such a thing?'

'I think he *is* possessed.' Rose shivered. 'There was something about his eyes — and he'd been drinking, too. I've always known that he's a bad enemy — he never forgets a slight — ever.'

An awkward silence fell between them. There was so much Rose wanted to say, but she could voice none of it. Then, suddenly Jamie began to wail again and she pulled herself together.

'I must go,' she said. 'He needs changing.'

'I'll walk back with you. I left Captain over there. I'll catch you up.'

Joss returned, leading the horse, and they

strolled down the stony track towards the foot of the hill.

'Where are you living now, Rose?' he asked.

The sleeves of his white shirt were rolled up over his bronzed forearms and there was a bruise and a thread of dried blood on the knuckles of his right hand. The breeze was ruffling his hair in just the way she remembered, and Rose longed to smooth it back from his brow. To touch him. To have him touch her. Even now, after he had let her down so heartlessly. She clutched the baby tighter to keep her hand from reaching out to his, and reminded herself sternly that this was a married man, on his way home to his wife and child. The man who had ignored her desperate plea for help when she was at her lowest ebb. She could not bring herself to ask about them; her mouth would not frame the words. She tore her eyes away from his, and from the undisguised concern in their violet depths.

'With my father. He has a small cottage which I'm sharing for the time being.'

Joss rounded on her, looking quite dumbfounded.

'Your *father*, did you say? After the way he treated you in the past?'

'I know, but it *was* in the past. He's a changed man now, Joss, through religion, and we understand each other better.' Rose shrugged. 'It's a long story.'

'Rose, I tried so hard to find you, but I couldn't . . . ' He had one hand on the horse's reins, but Joss's eyes were far away, fixed on the distant sea.

Rose's heart missed a beat. She stopped and stared at the tall familiar figure by her side.

'What? You came to *look* for me?' she whispered.

Joss turned to her and nodded.

'After I had your letter. Oh, Rose, I'm so sorry, but I was away on — business — when you wrote, and when I got back it was too late to meet you as you asked. What was it you wanted to tell me?' His eyes were looking deeply into hers.

Rose lowered her head, unable to face his scrutiny. He sounded sincere. Oh, how she longed to believe that he was, but how could she be sure?

'It doesn't matter now,' she said brusquely. How it had mattered at the time, though! With a shudder she recalled the plight she had been in then, and how she had humbled herself to ask him for help. But now Rose raised her head and looked him in the face. She would give him the benefit of the doubt. Joss had not let her down deliberately — he had simply not received the note. And her spirits lifted a little.

'Oh, that reminds me,' Joss said, 'I've got some belongings of yours at home.'

'Of mine? I don't understand.' Rose raised her eyebrows. His free hand was so close to hers as they walked that she had to make an effort not to let it touch her own. For if they touched, she would have been lost.

'I found the pawn tickets you left behind, so I redeemed your things for you. It was all I could do,' Joss waved a hand in emphasis, 'as I wasn't able to find you in person.'

'My wedding-ring — the clock — all of them? You've got them? I thought the tickets had been stolen! Oh Joss, thank you. Thank you *so much*.' The obvious delight which lit up Rose's face at this news transformed her for a moment into her old self, and Joss grinned with pleasure.

Then Rose's smile faded and she lowered her eyes.

'Thank you, too, for looking for me. You'll never know what a pass I was in when I sent you that note. I was in dire straits, you see, with no money and no one to turn to. It was all because of this little one.' She dropped a kiss on top of the baby's head, then said defensively: 'I was managing all right before that. I was working and I was quite independent. And of course, everything's fine again now, thanks to Pa.'

She stopped for a moment to adjust the baby-sling.

'I shall be so glad to get those things back,' she went on. 'They're all I have left, you see, of the old life.' Her chin came up and she added with spirit: 'And I can pay you what I owe on them now.'

'I shouldn't dream of it,' came Joss's formal reply. 'And as for the — er — old life, you have that little bundle there to remind you of it, too. As long as you have Jamie, Matt will always be with you, won't he?' Joss's face was bleak. So she *had* loved the man.

'Forgive my asking, Rose, but how do you manage to keep yourself and the baby? If I can help you out in any way . . . '

She lifted her head and looked him straight in the eye.

'I take in sewing,' she replied, 'and in the autumn I shall help with the harvest and with fruit-picking and so on. I shall be able to take Jamie with me then. We'll be all right. But thank you all the same. I appreciate it.'

Rose stepped away from him, her hand on the latch of the gate. Deliberately turning the knife in the wound, she asked:

'What did your wife say about you hunting all over for me, or didn't you tell her?'

Joss looked blank. Jamie had started howling again and his reply was drowned by the child's cries.

'I must see to him,' Rose broke in. 'Goodbye, Joss, and thank you again, on both counts.'

'I'll call round with those things another day.' With a wave of his hand Joss mounted the horse and rode on his way.

Rose's father entered the house just as she finished changing the baby and settling him in his cradle. She was thinking ruefully that she had experienced none of the qualms of a first-time mother, but had handled Jamie with the skill born of long practice in her early life. Rose felt as if had always been a mother.

'I just passed Mr Pencarrow out in the lane,' Joe remarked, hanging up his hat on a peg in the passage. He followed Rose into the kitchen where she had gone to make a cup of tea. She badly needed a restorative after the drama of the last hour. 'He's looking some lot better these days. Poor young man — he's got a lot to cope with.'

Joe settled himself beside the unlit range, put his boots on the fender and unfolded a newspaper. 'He was looking fair worn out last time I seen him.'

'What do you mean, he's got a lot to cope with?' Rose turned to her father with raised eyebrows, the tea-caddy she was taking down from the cupboard poised in her hand.

'I'll have a cup of tea if you're making some, maid.' Joe looked up from the page. 'Mr Joss? Oh, I meant what with his wife going off her head like that — and so soon after they was married, too. Sad, weren't it?'

He jumped as the tea-caddy dropped with a clatter from Rose's outstretched hand. It fell out of the cupboard above the range, narrowly missing Joe's head, and spilt its contents all over the floor.

'Off her head?' Rose repeated, ignoring the tea. 'Do you mean Emma Pencarrow's mentally ill?' She stared ashen-faced at her father.

'Didn't you know that? Oh, it must have happened when you was away up to Truro. Yes, it would have been, come to think of it.' Joe nodded.

Rose locked her hands together to stop their trembling.

'How did it happen, Pa?' she said urgently. 'After she had the baby, was it?'

'Baby?' Her father looked puzzled. 'Weren't never no baby. 'Twas the influenza what left her with brain fever. Proper old plague of it, we had. Heaps of people round here died. You knowed the Hockings, did you, up to Troon? Four of them in one family was took, and then there was . . . '

Rose was no longer listening. She had clapped both hands to her face and her brain was reeling with unanswered questions. Why hadn't Joss said? Did he think she already knew? In that case, what must he think of her not to have mentioned it? She would go after him — now. She pulled at the strings of her apron before she realized that no, she couldn't, because of Jamie.

'You going to stand there dreaming all day are you, maid?' Joe's voice cut across her thoughts. 'Or are you going to brush up that there tea?'

Rose bent to the task, glad to hide her face in case it should betray her.

★　★　★

Joe was working on his sermon for the following Sunday, and was deep in books and papers which he had spread out all over the kitchen table. Rose had been fully prepared to do the week's baking when she discovered that the kitchen table had been already commandeered, and was not in the best of moods.

She was finding that living with her father was not easy. Although Rose would never cease to be grateful that he had brought her back to Cornwall and given her a roof over her head, as time went on she found living in such a small space increasingly restrictive.

'Are you going to be long, Pa? At the table, I mean,' she said to him, 'only I wanted to do the baking while Jamie's asleep.'

'Mmm?' Joe looked up absently and chewed the end of his pencil. 'Couldn't really say, maid. The Lord's work can't be hurried. You can do it later on, can't you?' He picked up his Bible and began thumbing through it. 'I think for my text next Sunday I'll take, 'Blessed are the meek', Where is it again? Ah, here we are. Matthew, chapter five . . . 'for they shall inherit the earth'.'

Rose tossed her head to the ceiling in frustration. All the meekness in the world wouldn't put food in their mouths. Since Rose had been living with her father she had noticed that he was increasingly taking it for granted that she would put meals on the table, do the housework and washing, and generally look after him. In Joe's eyes this was woman's work and the natural order of things. The fact that his daughter had a small child and also work of her own to do never entered his head.

At first Rose had been glad to do things around the house as a token of her gratitude to him, but now that she was expected to do so, it was different. After all, he had managed long enough without her when he lived on his own. Now he never lifted a finger to help.

She had recently also become very aware of Joe's irritating little habits, like his tuneless whistling between his teeth as he sat reading the paper, or the Bible. And once aware, it grated on her nerves more than ever, until eventually she began to resent his very presence in the same room.

If she was getting the baby off to sleep, he would be bound to come in and bang the door, or call up the stairs, or noisily shovel coal into the range. His overt displays of religious fervour Rose found sickening, although she tried to tolerate it all. This was his house, she was the interloper, and if it were not for this very religion which she found so distasteful she knew she would be living in the workhouse. But still the praying, the twice-daily Bible-readings aloud, the all-pervasive self-righteousness of the man which bordered, Rose felt, on smugness, stretched her patience to its limits.

Sternly Rose told herself yet again, as her heart sank at the state of the kitchen, that she was lucky to be here, but her soul cried out for the freedom of a home of her own, as it had been crying all her life. Lately she had been feeling like some kind of refugee.

Wearily she hung up the clean apron she had just taken out for the baking session and left the room.

★ ★ ★

Rose wondered every day after their meeting when Joss would call round with her possessions, and expected as she answered each knock at the door to find him standing on the doorstep. Days went by however with no sign of him, and when the days turned into weeks she hid her bitter disappointment in the best way she knew, that of hard work. She would wash the windows outside, they were dusty from the long hot spell, she would scrub the doorstep, pull up the weeds from the path, she would do everything she could think of to keep her mind from dwelling on the fact that he had abandoned her once more.

True, the first time had not been his fault, Rose accepted that. But now! Why, for goodness' sake, he'd had long enough just to call round and deliver a box to the door. So she took out her fury on the doormat, beating it against the wall of the house in a frenzy, as if she wished it was Joss Pencarrow himself she was belabouring, and plunged into an orgy of housework.

Four weeks later he came. Rose was pegging out washing on the line at the side of the house with her back to him and neither saw nor heard him approaching. When his voice at her elbow made her jump and whirl around, she kicked over the basket full of clean towels into a muddy patch, accidentally stepped on them and promptly burst into tears.

'Now look what you've made me do!' she yelled, 'it's all *your* fault!'

Your fault that I upset the washing, your fault that I've been waiting all this time for you, your fault that we can never be together, everything's *your fault*.

Joss flinched. That remark had struck home, coming on the heels of the hell he had been through over the last few months, and he saw red. He put down the box and gripped Rose's upper arms hard, bringing her round to face him. She kicked out at him in temper but he neatly side-stepped and retained his hold until she suddenly went limp, all the fight draining out of her on a long sigh.

Rose twisted out of his grasp. And because she was so overjoyed to see him and because there was no way she could tell him so, instead she scowled darkly at Joss and laid into him with the sharp edge of her tongue.

'You took your time,' she snapped, as she

flounced away and began to grab the spoiled washing. 'I expected to see you long ago.'

'And what *you* want must always come first, of course,' Joss retorted, moving the cardboard box of her belongings out of the way and dumping it on the doorstep. 'Rose Lanyon, we have a lot of talking to do, and there are too many curious eyes and ears in this street. So get your hat and come with me. Now.'

Rose wiped her face with a mud-spattered tea-towel, glowered at him over the top of it as she thought of refusing point blank to be ordered around, then thought better of it and did as she was told.

'Father's out. I'll have to bring Jamie as well. He's in his bassinet over there.' Rose went round the corner where her son was asleep in the shade of a great sycamore tree which overhung the cottage.

'I'll bring Captain round and tether him to that tree until I come back,' Joss said.

They walked away from the village and down to where the red river flowed under the bridge near where they used to meet as children. To passers-by we must look like a perfect small family, Rose thought with a pang, strolling along together and enjoying the summer day. If only . . .

'Rose, you've obviously not heard the

news, so I'd better tell you right away.' Joss's profile was stony. 'Emma died three weeks ago.'

'*What?*' Rose dragged the perambulator to a sudden halt. 'She *died?*' she whispered, struggling to take it in. 'But how . . . what . . . ?' She could not take her eyes from Joss's haggard face. She hadn't noticed until now how ill he was looking, so wrapped up in her own concerns had she been.

'She died of a haemorrhage brought on by a miscarriage,' he replied tonelessly. 'I've been up at Lanhydrock since then . . . the arrangements and so on . . . ' He passed a hand over his face and looked her in the eyes. 'I was called away urgently one night. She died the next morning.'

'Oh Joss, I'm so *sorry!*' Rose laid a hand on his arm. 'Can you ever forgive me?' She looked up at the tall figure beside her and he nodded grimly. 'What a selfish fool I've been,' she whispered. 'You were so right. I *am* always thinking only of myself.'

But, her soul cried out in anguish, it's only because I've always had to do so. There's never been anyone to look out for me, for me to turn to. For support, for guidance. Only once in my life, for the few brief months I shared with Matt . . .

She snapped back to the present.

'Joss, there's something I have to say to you,' Rose began. He turned his head enquiringly and laid one hand on the handle of the baby-carriage to help her over a rough patch in the road. 'The other day, when we met again for the first time, you must have thought it strange that I didn't mention Emma's name then, or . . . ' she lowered her eyes and nibbled at her bottom lip, 'or her — mental condition.' Rose raised her eyes and found Joss looking down at her with such an expression of tenderness that her stomach clenched.

They had come to a wide grassy verge at a point where four roads crossed, and as if he had recognized her feelings, Joss gave her a long look.

'Shall we sit down for a minute and have a rest?' he suggested.

The grass was cool and very green in the shade of the hawthorn hedge. Rose took off her straw hat and fanned herself with it. They had walked further than she had realized.

'I didn't know, Joss. Can you believe it? I didn't know that Emma had been taken ill. I was so completely out of touch for all those months — '

'And you had enough of your own problems, goodness knows. Of course I believe you, Rose. We've each been fighting our private battles, haven't we?' Joss fell silent, chewing on a stem of grass, preoccupied with his private thoughts.

'There's something else as well.' Rose persevered, determined that there should be no more misunderstandings between them. She twisted the ribbons of the hat which lay in her lap as she went on; 'That day on the beach . . . when you told me that you had to get married. I thought — I took it to mean . . . that Emma was pregnant,' she blurted. 'I was wrong, wasn't I? She turned her face to his. 'What *did* you mean, Joss?'

'Oh, my poor little Rose,' he said gently, taking her hand in his. 'It's such a long story, my love, it will take a different time and place to go into it all. But know this — I never once stopped loving and wanting you.'

He squeezed her hand and moved away, pacing the grass as he went on: 'I thought about you all the time, but I was helpless, trapped in this web of circumstances which I mentioned. Also,' and he pointed a finger, 'I thought you were still married to Matt, remember. It wasn't until long after the accident — when I'd recovered enough to think straight and was married myself — that I found out that he'd died.'

He turned to face her and Rose could see the pain in his eyes as he spread his hands wide and continued: 'How do you think I felt in my marriage, knowing that I was in love with another man's wife?' Joss resumed his restless pacing up and down. 'Dammit, I went through hell, Rose. I was tormented with such guilt, you cannot imagine. Because of you, because of Emma . . . I thought there would never be an end to it.'

Joss returned to his place beside Rose and fell silent for a moment, his eyes fixed on some distant point. Then he turned towards her and his face was haggard.

'And now there *has* come an end to it — my wife and unborn son are both dead,' he said. 'Oh Rose,' his eyes met hers and they were dark with anguish, 'it would have been a little boy — and I wanted a son so much . . .' Tears stood on his eyelashes and Rose reached out to him for comfort.

Joss's face softened and he bent to take both her hands in his and raise her to her feet.

'Oh, my Rose,' Joss said with a catch in his voice, 'now that we're both free, do you think there might be a future for us together? If so, I promise that I'll never, ever leave you again.'

Rose's bones turned to jelly and all her heart was in her eyes as she held on tight to his hands to keep herself upright. 'B . . . but,' she nodded towards the baby-carriage, 'how do you feel about Jamie?'

Joss followed her glance.

'My darling, I'll care for him as if he were my own son. The son I always wanted,' he added softly. Joss paused and looked down into her eyes. 'It's the least I can do for Matt,' he added, 'after . . . after . . . ' He swallowed hard and his face was grim. Fiercely he clasped her to him and buried his face in her hair. 'Just tell me you'll be my wife and that's all we need say for the moment.'

'Oh Joss, yes and yes!' she cried, and the feel of his arms around her gave Rose strength to tackle the last remaining obstacle between them.

'That's not quite true,' she began, lifting her head and looking into his face. Joss raised his eyebrows in surprise.

'What do you mean?' he asked, releasing her but keeping one arm still loosely clasped about her shoulders.

'I mean there's something else I need to say now,' Rose replied.

She jumped to her feet and went over to the bassinet. Jamie was awake now and waving his chubby fists in the air. She lifted him out and came back to sit beside Joss again. 'It's about this little one.'

'Your baby?' Joss looked completely mystified and his face hardened. 'I've told you I'm willing to raise him as if he were my own. What more can I say?'

'Look at him, Joss. Really look. And think. See those deep-blue eyes? See that tuft of hair which grows just that way, and the smile? Who does he remind you of? Not Matt, nor me. Neither of us had blue eyes.'

Joss looked blankly back at her, then at the child. Then he suddenly sprang to his feet, shaking his head.

'Oh, no Rose — you can't be implying what you seem to be.' He snorted and backed away, his face transformed. 'You certainly take some beating, don't you! Do you seriously think that you can suddenly present me with an infant that's all of what — three or four months old? Expect me to believe that it's mine, and that you haven't even bothered to find me before this and just *mention* it?'

He strode away a few paces, then back as he pointed a finger. 'That *is* what you mean, isn't it?' He glowered at Rose, who was clasping the baby close as if for comfort. All the colour had fled from her stricken face as she listened to him. Each word came crashing like a hammer-blow through her head.

'Joss, *stop* it!' Rose shouted at him as he thrust both fists in his pockets and began to stride away, his shoulders hunched over like those of an old man.

She dropped the baby back into the bassinet and flew after him, tugging at his arm, forcing him to listen.

'It was that last day — on the beach,' she panted. 'You can't have forgotten, Joss. I know you haven't!'

She felt rather than saw the flicker of interest that crossed his face, although his voice still rasped savagely as he said:

'Why now — after all these weeks that you've been back — why wait until now before telling me?'

'I've just told you — I thought you were still married to Emma and that you had a child of your own!' Rose's face was blazing now with indignation. 'I was thinking of you and your position.'

Joss had turned back for a second look at the baby. Rose picked up her skirts and ran after him. Suspicion was still written all over his face as he peered down at little Jamie, but Rose sensed a softening in the line of his jaw, even a hint of dawning tenderness around the eyes, that made her heart leap with hope.

Suddenly as Rose held her breath and waited, Joss reached out a finger to the baby and gently touched his cheek. A chubby hand immediately grasped the finger and tried to propel it into its mouth. The tenderness then in Joss's face made Rose want to laugh and cry at the same time. He turned to look at her in wonderment.

'And you mean that this — this is *my son?*'

Rose nodded, for a moment incapable of speech. Then she swallowed and said simply:

'Why do you think I called him James if not after your middle name?'

Joss gently disengaged the tiny hand and turned towards her with his soul in his eyes. He clasped her hands between his own.

'Oh Rose,' he said, 'forgive me for all those things I said. I'm so sorry — it was just such a shock. I had no idea at all, you see . . . ' They stood for a moment regarding one another, locked in the tide of bitter-sweet memories which washed over both of them.

Then, 'This makes up for everything,' Joss said simply, as he folded her closely to him. 'Oh Rose, my only love. Can we at last put the past behind us and really start our lives together? Now, from this day, from this very minute?'

She nodded and laid her head on his chest, feeling his heart beating under her cheek, steady, reliable, safe. Rose had come home at last.

Simply she replied: 'It's what I've always wanted, Joss.'

They walked slowly back the way they had

come, their arms around each other's waists, pushing their son's baby-carriage between them. And like a benison, a shaft of brilliant sunshine suddenly pierced a grey cloud and wrapped them in its radiance.

THE END

We do hope that you have enjoyed reading this large print book.

Did you know that all of our titles are available for purchase?

We publish a wide range of high quality large print books including:
Romances, Mysteries, Classics
General Fiction
Non Fiction and Westerns

Special interest titles available in large print are:
The Little Oxford Dictionary
Music Book
Song Book
Hymn Book
Service Book

Also available from us courtesy of Oxford University Press:
Young Readers' Dictionary
(large print edition)
Young Readers' Thesaurus
(large print edition)

For further information or a free brochure, please contact us at:
Ulverscroft Large Print Books Ltd.,
The Green, Bradgate Road, Anstey,
Leicester, LE7 7FU, England.
Tel: (00 44) **0116 236 4325**
Fax: (00 44) **0116 234 0205**